THE

LAST SURF

A Tale of Waves, Resilience and Renewal

Robert James Waller

Copyright © Robert James Waller 2024
This book is sold subject to the condition that it shall not, by way of trade or otherwise, be lent, resold, hired out, or otherwise circulated without the publisher's prior consent in any form of binding or cover other than that in which it is published and without a similar condition including this condition being imposed on the subsequent publisher.
The moral right of Robert James Waller has been asserted.
ISBN: 9798338502341

This is a work of fiction. Names, characters, businesses, organisations, places, events and incidents either are the product of the author's imagination or are used fictitiously. Any resemblance to actual persons, living or dead, events, or locales is entirely coincidental.

To My Father

My father, John Michael Waller, was a constant source of support and encouragement. He believed in me unconditionally, even when I had little confidence in myself. His battle with prostate cancer was a testament to his strength and resilience. Though he passed away in December 2023, his legacy lives on in the values he instilled in me. This book is dedicated to him, in the hope that he would be proud of what I have achieved.

I am grateful for the experiences and challenges that have shaped me. My struggles with dyslexia, my discovery of rugby, and my career in fitness have all contributed to my deep desire to help others. Whether through specialised rehabilitation or energetic group classes, my goal is to make a positive impact on people's lives. And above all, I strive to honour my father's memory by continuing to grow and succeed in all that I do.

CONTENTS

PROLOGUE 1
CHAPTER 1 *Dreams* 4
CHAPTER 2 *Surfing* 14
CHAPTER 3 *Rob Martin, Robbie's Coffee* 25
CHAPTER 4 *Jamie Forrunner* 34
CHAPTER 5 *Aurora Winters* 43
CHAPTER 6 *Joanna and Michael Florence* 52
CHAPTER 7 *Love at First Sight? Bullshit* 64
CHAPTER 8 *Sponsor Deal* 74
CHAPTER 9 *Physical Attraction, Chemical Reaction* 83
CHAPTER 10 *Can You Mend the Broken?* 96
CHAPTER 11 *Worthy Love* 113
CHAPTER 12 *Fighting Back* 124
CHAPTER 13 *Desire* 137
CHAPTER 14 *Healed Scars* 151
CHAPTER 15 *Brave New World* 168
CHAPTER 16 *The Ties That Bind* 176
CHAPTER 17 *A Tangled Web* 190
CHAPTER 18 *The Fan Dance* 206
CHAPTER 19 *Home and Away* 224
CHAPTER 20 *Tragedy* 243
CHAPTER 21 *One Year Later* 258
CHAPTER 22 *Over the Hills and Far Away* 265
ABOUT THE AUTHOR 270

Thank you for all the support:

Sharron, Joanna, Lesley, Tom, Leanne, Amy, Lauren, Andy, Hayley, Paul, Gary Johnston Smith, Jonathan.

PROLOGUE

The coastal town where Bonnie lived was a place where the ocean's whispers told tales of both triumph and tragedy. The waves that kissed its golden shores carried the echoes of surfers who sought solace and salvation in the embrace of the sea. Bonnie Florence was a woman whose life had been intertwined with the rise and fall of those very waves.

Bonnie had grown up with the salty breeze in her hair and the rhythmic pulse of the ocean in her veins. A revered surfer, her father had taught her everything she knew about the sea's unpredictable temperament. His lessons were not just about riding waves but about life itself – how to balance, how to fall and rise again, and how to face the inevitable storms with unwavering resolve.

But life, like the ocean, was capricious. The death of her father had left a void in Bonnie's heart, a hollow space where hope once thrived. She retreated from the competitive surfing scene that had once been her sanctuary, her father's absence casting a long shadow over her passion. The waves that had once been a source of joy now reminded her of loss and longing.

Yet, the sea never truly releases those it claims. Bonnie found herself drawn back to the shore, the call of the ocean too powerful to resist. She began to teach the next generation, the local surf school owner's son Henry among them, finding in their innocent enthusiasm a reminder of her own youthful dreams. Each lesson she gave was a step towards healing, each child's laughter a balm for her soul.

This small town was not just home to Bonnie's memories but to a close-knit community that rallied around its own. Friends like Jamie, a steadfast companion with a heart as vast as the ocean; Shannon and Sally, whose vibrant personalities could light up the darkest of days; and Madge, the ever-supportive elder whose wisdom was matched only by her cheesecake-making prowess.

Each person in Bonnie's life was a thread in the tapestry of her journey, each one essential to the unfolding story.

The town itself seemed to breathe with life, its festivals and traditions a testament to its resilience. From the local food festivals where families gathered to the surf competitions that drew in crowds from far and wide, this small town was a place where past, present, and future collided in a beautiful dance of continuity and change.

Bonnie's path was not linear. It was a winding road of self-discovery marked by moments of doubt and flashes of clarity. Her story was one of finding strength in vulnerability, of embracing the lessons imparted by her father while forging her own way. It was a tale of rekindling a love for the waves that had once defined her, and of learning that sometimes, the greatest triumphs come from within.

As the sun rose over the local surf school, casting its golden light on the tranquil waters, a new chapter began. Bonnie stood at the water's edge, surfboard by her side, ready to face the waves once more. In the distance, she could see the silhouettes of her friends and family, their support a beacon of hope. With a deep breath, she stepped into the surf, the journey ahead as limitless as the horizon.

This is a story of love and loss, of courage and community, of falling and rising again. It is the story of Bonnie Florence and the waves that carried her forward – over the hills and far away.

CHAPTER 1

Dreams

Bonnie woke from a dream of summer and travels, including the recent tour competition, the Rip Curl Pro Bells Beach. This had taken her to places she had never been and was as intense as it gets. She placed 8th overall. New sponsors were looming for this sexy surf lady.

Still fresh from her dream, the smell of the sea breeze as the wind gently pushed waves towards where she had been standing mingled with the sensation of being relaxed from head to toe. The warmth that travels up from your toes when you wake soon left her, like it wanted to travel up her legs and out through her fingers. A touch around her waist from a figure she didn't recognise. The touch then turned into a tight squeeze. That feeling and memory of the dream was starting to fade.

Bonnie stretched out in bed, the soft morning light filtering through the curtains. She sighed with a mix of satisfaction and longing. Placing 8th at the Rip Curl Pro was a significant achievement, especially after the year she'd had. Yet, she couldn't shake the feeling that there was more out there for her. More waves to ride, more places to explore, more adventures waiting just beyond the horizon.

She sat up, running a hand through her tousled hair. The memory of the dream was still vivid, the touch around her waist lingering like a phantom sensation. She couldn't help but smile, wondering who the mysterious figure in her dream was.

Perhaps it was a sign of things to come, a new beginning.

Bonnie got out of bed and padded over to the window, looking out at the ocean. The waves were calling to her, as they always did. She felt a surge of excitement at the prospect of new sponsors. With them, she could travel even more, pushing her limits and exploring new surf spots around the world.

She turned away from the window and grabbed her phone, scrolling through the notifications. There were messages from friends, updates on the competition, and a few inquiries from potential sponsors. But one message caught her eye – a message from Aurora:

'Congrats on the Rip Curl Pro! 8th place is amazing but not good enough but I'm still proud of you. See you soon, dickhead.'

Bonnie smiled. It was just like Aurora to say that.

'Thanks! It was a tough competition but I loved every moment. Would love to catch up. Let's plan something soon, maybe meet at Robbie's coffee shop.'

She hit send and put the phone down, her mind already

buzzing with possibilities. The dream, the competition, the new sponsors – it all felt like the start of something new. Something big. She felt alive, ready to embrace whatever came next.

Bonnie got back into bed, the summer sun shining through the blinds casting a warm glow over her. She pulled the duvet off, feeling the warmth from the sun spread over her legs and body. The touch from the unknown figure in her dream lingered, making her feel both powerful and relaxed. The soft fabric of her nightwear against her skin heightened her awareness of her body. Bonnie enjoyed the feeling of her hand moving up her leg, the pressure intensifying as her fingers travelled up toward her inner thigh. She savoured the sensation, the touch, her fingers gently entering her. Pushing her hips back into the bed, her head tilting back as if someone was pulling her hair. Lifting her chest, her breasts felt the warmth from the early morning sun, making her want to push her fingers further inside. She began to climax as her fingers pressed deep. Feeling warm throughout her body, she knew this was a great start to a sunny Saturday morning. The warmth from the sun and the memory of her dream blended into a perfect moment.

Bonnie always liked to shower before heading downstairs in the morning. There was something invigorating about the warm water flowing over her body first thing. Her heart still racing, she stepped under the rainfall of water, letting it wash over her. With one hand against the wall she bent her knees slightly, lifted her chest, and let the water and her touch take her to another climax. She felt powerful and alive, enjoying the connection with her body.

Bonnie grabbed her surfboard and headed out the door, the early morning sun casting a golden glow over the beach. As she made her way to the water, she felt that familiar thrill. The waves were waiting, and so was she. With a determined smile, Bonnie paddled out, the dream fading but the feeling of possibility lingering. She was ready for whatever the ocean, and life, had in store for her.

Saturday morning would normally be a busy time as Bonnie would do her CrossFit exercise class after her early morning surf. She would see her mum Joanna and dad Michael followed by coffee and cake with friends, then delivering a late surf lesson.

Bonnie lived south of Sydney, in a busy city full of life. Wollongong is a coastal city along the Grand Pacific Drive. Surfing beaches and rack pools line the coastline. Trails encircle the forests and rocky cliffs of Mt Keira in the Illawarra Mountain Range. This is a magical place to live.

Bonnie had grown up surfing on weekends and was now in the World Surf League River Pro. With the dream and the stranger still in her mind, the touch and power Bonnie experienced had been overwhelming. She didn't know what this meant but felt confident, and her body felt powerful and strong, sexy. The start of a beautiful adventure.

Bonnie's CrossFit session was harder than normal today; the air was filled with warmth from the summer sun and as most CrossFit gyms go, air-con isn't something they think about. This makes for a very hot and sweaty environment. Bonnie wasn't scared of a little hard work and today's goal was to work up to a max clean and jerk. This is something taken from weightlifting.

On these days, the gym came alive with competition

and testosterone as the packed class worked to their max. Often new members would attend these sessions; today was no different. One particular male caught Bonnie's eye from a distance. She couldn't quite make him out as the workout was intense, and as the sweat began to drip fatigue set in and heads dropped. Bonnie remained aware of his presence. As shirts were taken off from the sweat and heat, her eyes were drawn to this figure of a man. His chest and arms started to fill from the pump of the workout. She could also see sweat running down from his chest onto his shorts. Bonnie had never had these thoughts while in a class, well, as far back as she could remember. Her workouts had been so driven and focused on becoming the best surfer she could that she didn't have time for anything else. Her priority had been her work and how far she could push herself; she hadn't made time for these distractions, especially while working out. This was different and her eyes couldn't hide the fact that she was feeling something warm inside her. Bonnie smiled to herself. Could this just be the adrenaline of the workout taking her heart rate higher, or was this something else that she couldn't describe? It felt good.

Bonnie missed her last lift. This wasn't normal for someone renowned for mental resilience under pressure. She had trained for so long, and having competed many times as a pro surfer, it shouldn't have happened. A dark thought crept into her mind like a storm cloud slowly passing overhead, pushing down on her. This had happened a few times since Bonnie's surf incident late one Sunday evening around six months ago.

She replayed that evening in the moment of her failed clean and jerk.

The light was fading and rain had started to fall, creating perfect conditions for a training session. She had been surfing with confidence when something hit her board. A powerful wave took her under and she gasped for breath, swallowing saltwater. She felt like she was being pushed down, unable to regain herself. This was a moment all surfers went through, but something unexplained happened. It felt like someone had pulled her up by her underarms and gently placed her on the sand. Coughing and spluttering, unable to catch her breath, she saw a dark figure moving away in the distance.

"Bonnie, snap out of it," she said to herself as the barbell hit the floor.

The workout was over, and when she turned her head to catch a glimpse of the unknown man who had caught her attention earlier, he was gone. She wondered who this strong, muscular figure was. A smile formed at the side of her mouth for a moment and then disappeared as her friend Sally playfully pushed her in the back.

"You were shit today," Sally teased.

Bonnie chuckled, replying, "Well, not as shit as you, Sally. See you in the shower."

The rest of the day unfolded with a mix of activities. Bonnie joined her parents for lunch, enjoying the warmth of family and delicious homemade food. The sun continued to grace the coastal city, casting a golden glow on everything it touched.

Later, Bonnie met up with some of the surf school staff. Old hand Madge was present and in fine form. Madge wasn't too keen on Aurora and did say she hoped she wouldn't be in attendance. After all, she didn't work at the surf school and she was just so damn arrogant. The coffee and cake were great. Laughter and shared stories filled the air as they enjoyed their time together. Bonnie couldn't help but be distracted by the memory of the mysterious man from the gym. It was a feeling she couldn't shake, and she found herself lost in thought as her friends chatted around her.

The late afternoon brought Bonnie to the ocean, her true sanctuary. As a professional surfer, the waves held a special place in her heart. The rhythmic sound crashing against the shore and the salty breeze in the air brought her a sense of peace.

Bonnie paddled out into the ocean, feeling the cool water against her skin. The sun was beginning to set, casting a warm and vibrant display of colours across the sky. The horizon painted in hues of orange and pink mirrored the warmth she felt inside.

As she waited for the perfect wave, Bonnie reflected on the day. The encounter at the gym, the unexpected distraction, and the memories of her near-drowning incident all swirled in her mind. The ocean became a therapeutic space for her thoughts, a place to find clarity and connection.

Bonnie caught a wave, riding it with skill and grace. The rush of adrenaline and the connection with the ocean washed away lingering thoughts. In that moment, she felt alive, powerful, and free.

As night fell, Bonnie returned home, tired yet content. The warmth of the day, the physical exertion, and the connection with the ocean had left her in a reflective mood.

She settled into bed, the memory of the mysterious touch from her dream and the encounter at the gym still lingering.

Moonlight filtered through her window, casting a gentle glow as she drifted off to sleep. The events of the day had sparked something within her – a sense of adventure, a newfound awareness of desire, and the realisation that life's journey was full of unexpected twists and turns.

As Bonnie drifted off, the echoes of the day's events played in her mind like a soothing melody. The mysterious man at the gym, the supportive presence of her family and friends, and the powerful connection she felt with the ocean all intertwined, creating a sense of anticipation for what lay ahead.

*

The next morning, Bonnie woke up feeling refreshed and more determined than ever. The memory of the near-drowning incident still lingered, but she had come to see it as a turning point, a reminder of her resilience and strength. She decided it was time to take charge of her journey and embrace the unknown with open arms.

After her morning routine, Bonnie headed back to the gym for another session. The intense energy of the previous day still hung in the air, but she was determined to stay focused this time. As she pushed through her workout, she couldn't help but scan the room for the mysterious man who had caught her eye. To her disappointment, he was nowhere to be seen.

Bonnie shrugged it off and immersed herself in her training, competitive spirit driving her to give it her all. By the end of the session, she was drenched in sweat and feeling accomplished.

Sally caught up with her as she made her way to the showers. "You were on fire today, Bonnie!" she said, giving her a playful nudge.

"Thanks, Sally. I needed that," Bonnie replied, smiling.

They chatted and laughed as they cleaned up, the camaraderie between them helping to shake off any stubborn doubts. As they left the gym, Bonnie's thoughts returned to the ocean. She had a surf lesson to teach later that afternoon, and she couldn't wait to get back in the water.

The surf lesson with little Henry was always a highlight of her week. His infectious enthusiasm and boundless energy reminded her of why she fell in love with surfing in the first place. As they paddled out together, Bonnie was entirely content. She was exactly where she needed to be.

"You're doing great, Henry!" she called out as he caught a wave and rode it with surprising skill for his age.

"Thanks, Bonnie! I want to be just like you when I grow up," Henry replied, his eyes shining with admiration.

Bonnie's heart swelled with pride. "You keep practising, and you'll be even better than me one day."

As the lesson came to an end, she and Henry sat on their boards watching the sunset. The sky was ablaze with vibrant colours, and the rhythmic sound of the waves created a soothing backdrop.

"Bonnie, do you ever get scared out here?" Henry asked, his voice filled with curiosity.

She thought for a moment before answering.

"Sometimes, Henry. But I've learned that fear is just a part of the journey. It's what you do with that fear that matters. You face it, learn from it, and keep moving forward."

Henry nodded thoughtfully, absorbing her words. "I think I understand. Thanks, Bonnie."

They paddled back to shore, and as Bonnie watched Henry run off to his parents she felt a renewed sense of purpose. The challenges she had faced, the fears she had overcome – they had all shaped her into the person she was today.

As she made her way home, her thoughts turned to the future. The new sponsors, the upcoming competitions, the possibility of new adventures – they all held promise and excitement. She was ready to embrace whatever came next, knowing that she had the strength and support to face any challenge.

That evening, she received a message from Aurora.

'Heard about your killer workout today. Proud of you, dickhead. Let's catch up soon.'

Bonnie smiled, feeling a surge of gratitude for her friends and the journey that lay ahead.

'Thanks, Aurora. Let's do it. Coffee at Robbie's?'

As she hit send, she settled into bed, the gentle hum of the ocean outside her window lulling her into a peaceful sleep. The future was still unwritten, but with the love and support of those around her, she felt ready for whatever came her way.

The adventure was just beginning.

CHAPTER 2

Surfing

The next morning, Bonnie woke to the sound of her phone buzzing on the nightstand. It was a message from her CrossFit coach reminding her about the new training schedule. This should complement her surfing training. Still groggy, she stretched and reached for her phone, squinting at the screen. As she read the message, the memory of the previous day's workouts and the mysterious man flashed in her mind.

Determined not to let her thoughts distract her, Bonnie decided to focus on her surfing. She had a big competition coming up and needed to be at her best. After a quick breakfast, she grabbed her surfboard and headed to her favourite beach. The waves were perfect this morning, crisp and clear, just how she liked them.

As she paddled out into the water, Bonnie felt the familiar rush of adrenaline and excitement. The ocean was her sanctuary, and nothing else mattered when she was riding the waves. She caught a few good ones, her body in sync with the rhythm of the sea. Each wave brought her closer to the clarity she sought, washing away thoughts of her dreams and gym distractions.

After an exhilarating session, Bonnie lay on her board, basking in the sun. The rhythmic rise and fall of the ocean lulled her into a meditative state. She closed her eyes, letting the warmth of the sun and the gentle rocking of the waves soothe her.

A sudden splash nearby startled her. She looked up to see a familiar face from the surf school. Ronnie, little Henry's mum and wife of the surf school owner, was paddling towards her, a friendly smile on her face. "Hey there, didn't expect to see you here," she called out, her voice carrying over the sound of the waves.

Bonnie smiled back. "Yeah, you know this is my favourite spot."

"That's funny. Same here. You know that anyway." She extended a hand as she balanced on her board.

They spent the next hour surfing together, exchanging stories of the morning. As they took a break, sitting on their boards and watching the horizon, they continued to chat, enjoying the peacefulness of the ocean. There was an easy camaraderie between the two; their shared love for surfing had created a strong bond.

"So, how's Henry doing with his surfing?" Bonnie asked, genuinely curious.

"He's improving a lot," Ronnie replied with a proud smile. "Thanks to your lessons. He talks about you all the time, you know. He even wrote a little story about you, called it 'The Last Surf'."

Bonnie chuckled with a warm sense of pride. "That's sweet. He's a good kid with a lot of potential."

Ronnie nodded, her expression turning thoughtful. "You know, Bonnie, I think he looks up to you more than you realise. You're a role model for him."

The words struck a chord. Bonnie often got so caught up in her own goals and challenges that she forgot about the impact she had on others, especially the younger surfers who admired her.

"That means a lot. I'll make sure to keep that in mind," she said, her tone sincere.

As the sun climbed higher in the sky, they decided to head back to shore. Walking up the beach, Bonnie's renewed sense of purpose intensified. She was determined to not only excel in her competitions but also continue inspiring the next generation of surfers.

Back at her apartment, she reviewed her new training schedule. It was intense, but she knew it was necessary to push herself to the next level. She spent the afternoon balancing her CrossFit regimen with her surfing training; her body grew stronger and more resilient with each session.

In the evenings, Bonnie found herself thinking about the mysterious man from the gym. She couldn't shake the feeling that there was something significant about him, something that kept pulling her thoughts back to that moment. But she also knew that distractions could be dangerous, especially with upcoming competitions. She resolved to focus on what she could control – her training, her surfing, and her mental fortitude.

As the days passed, she fell into a comfortable routine. Early mornings at the beach, pushing her limits with her surfboard, followed by intense CrossFit sessions that left her exhausted but satisfied. She made time for her friends and family, enjoying the moments of connection and support they provided.

One evening, after a particularly gruelling workout, Bonnie received a message from Aurora. It was a simple note, but it carried a weight she couldn't ignore.

'Hey, I heard about the new training schedule. Proud of you for sticking with it. Remember, you're not alone in this.'

Bonnie felt a surge of gratitude. She had always been fiercely independent, but moments like these reminded her of the importance of her support network.

'Thanks, Aurora. Your support means a lot. Let's catch up soon.'

As she settled into bed that night, Bonnie felt a sense of peace. The challenges ahead were daunting, but she was ready to face them head-on. With her father's spirit guiding her, the love of her family and friends surrounding her, and a renewed sense of purpose, she knew she could conquer whatever came her way.

The next morning, Bonnie woke with a sense of determination. Today was a new day, and she was ready to embrace it. As she headed out of the door with her surfboard, she couldn't help but smile, feeling the warmth of the sun on her face and the promise of the ocean ahead.

She was ready for whatever the waves, and life, had in store for her.

Bonnie had always been athletic. At five foot three she was average height for a woman, and her trademark dark hair reached down below her chest. She was ranked in the top 25 hottest female surfers in the world right now, and having started at the age of 13 on her father's board, at 28 she was currently 9th in the world.

Bonnie was a little curvy for a professional surfer, which gained her much attention, and her stunning looks earned her a large following. She was one of the most fearless female surfers in the world, had won many awards, and was known for being a fierce competitor. Also known for her incredible style and grace, she was brave and had a certain level of confidence that gave her the ability to catch waves. Clothing brands such as Passenger and Roxy were happy to have her as an ambassador.

Unlike some women who chose to hang back on the beach and watch their friends, she was always eager. This gave Bonnie an edge that excited most men and women; you could even say that just watching her got people hot and bothered. Bonnie was one of those athletes who knew how to make a spectator feel like they were right there with her on the waves.

Surfing had brought Bonnie so much joy, but being in the limelight had its drawbacks. There had been much unwanted attention from both male and female fans. One male fan even managed to assault her on the beach; pictures were all over the internet as he had managed to pull her top off for the world to see.

Bonnie wasn't ashamed of her body as it went along

with the job to wear very little. Not much was left to the imagination. Sex appeal had brought much attention to the sport, along with the big-money sponsors. With this, there was also pressure to look a certain way. Everything is currently driven by sex and what you can get. Nothing seems real. Social platforms such as Instagram portray the reality that everyone looks a certain way, life is some sort of extended holiday, and we crave this attention in the form of likes and views on what we post. A certain expectation people have is that you can get what you want from a swipe left or right and the choice is endless. People don't seem willing to put the work in. Surfing wasn't like that. It wasn't perfect, you had to work hard, stay focused on what mattered, and get better at what pro surfers did.

Showering at the CrossFit box was a different experience than, say, your normal leisure club, where you have individual cubicles, towels, and several free beauty products. The CrossFit box felt like she was back at high school. Open shower room, benches to get changed on; there was no room for hiding any insecurities. It was so open, that from time to time the odd male had walked in and positioned himself for a shower. The steam was unbelievable at times; it felt like a sauna and to be fair, you could probably get away with anything if you really wanted to. Bonnie had experienced a sexual encounter at high school with one of the rugby players. The steam from the shower brought back memories of this day when the player in question happened to walk into the wrong shower room to find Bonnie rubbing herself down with a soapy sponge – the type filled with scented, moisturising glycerine soap. The air was fresh and ambient. Before Bonnie could do anything the young man in question had grabbed her by the back of her neck, bent her over, and instantaneously buried his thick cock inside her. She was so wet from her bum to her upper legs. This encounter was filled with pure adrenaline; it was fast and hard due to the nervous energy. They could have been caught or heard at any time.

The slapping of bum cheek against upper leg and belly. Bonnie could hardly breathe as her head was pushed down and her legs were wide. She could feel him deep inside her. This didn't last long; as quickly as it started, it ended. Lucky for Bonnie, the young man was her boyfriend, and this wasn't the first time.

The workouts from the days before were good but today's had been even better. The shower felt good and left Bonnie feeling fresh and a little excited for the rest of the day. This was a good thing, as she had arranged some surfing lessons later. As well as being a pro, she did a little coaching as this was something she always enjoyed. Helping others.

Pines Surfing Academy Wollongong was a great place; the staff were friendly and professional, it was great value for money, and the banter was next level. Bonnie had been described as 'the best instructor ever! A patient, lovely person that motivates you with her attitude and love for surfing! Amazing!! Killalea Beach (The Farm). Just amazing.'

The surfing beaches of this pristine coastline feature stunning views in all directions. Killalea Beach is famous among surfers throughout the region.

The coaching session was a blast. Bonnie found this grounded her and she was able to remember her routes; the simple things that if done correctly are the pillars of anything you do. Without these, you will never find your true potential.

Teaching this to the children was a great way for them to relax, be themselves, be brave, and let go of any insecurities they may be holding on to. Bonnie felt this every time she coached. She felt privileged that she was able to give back to the sport that had given her so much.

Her next stop was a little coffee shop she frequented for more reasons than just a good coffee. Known as Robbie's, it was a quaint little place with a warm and inviting atmosphere. It was a familiar spot for Bonnie, a place she could unwind, enjoy a cup of coffee, and soak in the comforting ambiance.

As Bonnie entered Robbie's, the rich aroma of freshly brewed coffee enveloped her. The barista behind the counter greeted her with a friendly smile, already aware of her usual order. Bonnie appreciated the small-town feel, a welcome contrast to bustling city life.

She chose a corner seat by the window, allowing the soft sunlight to filter through as she gazed out at the world passing by. The sound of steaming milk and the hum of conversations provided a soothing backdrop.

Bonnie's thoughts drifted to the events of the day – the invigorating workout, the surfing lessons, and the joy of coaching eager learners. She cherished these moments of connection with others who shared her passion for the ocean.

Sipping her coffee, Bonnie scrolled through her phone, checking messages and social media. The digital world was a double-edged sword for her – the platform for showcasing her surfing skills and connecting with fans, but also a space where unwanted attention and expectations thrived.

As Bonnie continued to scroll through her phone, a message from her manager caught her eye.

'Hey Bonnie, just a reminder about the photoshoot with Roxy tomorrow. It's at 10 AM on Bondi Beach. Be there a bit early if you can. Also, there's been some buzz around your latest video. Looks like you're trending again!'

'Got it, I'll be there. Thanks for the heads-up!'

She set her phone down, a mix of excitement and nerves bubbling up. The constant balancing act of her career – between the thrill of surfing, the demands of sponsors, and the attention from fans – was both exhilarating and exhausting. But she knew this was all part of the package, and was grateful for the opportunities that came her way.

Finishing her coffee, she left Robbie's and headed to Pines Surfing Academy for her scheduled lessons. The drive to Killalea Beach was scenic, the road winding along the coastline with breathtaking views of the ocean. The sun was shining brightly, promising another beautiful day on the waves.

At the academy, the staff greeted her warmly. Bonnie quickly changed into her wetsuit and gathered her group of eager learners, a mix of children and adults, all excited to hit the waves. She enjoyed these sessions, finding joy in sharing her knowledge and watching her students improve.

"All right, everyone," she called out. "Let's start with some warm-up exercises on the beach. Remember, surfing is not just about riding the waves; it's about being in tune with the ocean and understanding its rhythm."

The group followed her lead, stretching and practising their paddling techniques on the sand. Bonnie moved among them, offering tips and encouragement. The kids especially looked up to her, their eyes wide with admiration.

Once they were in the water, Bonnie felt at ease. Teaching allowed her to revisit the basics and appreciate the simplicity of surfing. Watching her students catching their first waves was deeply satisfying. This was what it was all about – passing on the love for the sport and helping others find their own joy in the ocean.

After the lesson, Bonnie headed back to the academy to rinse off and pack up with a sense of fulfilment and peace, the morning's surf session having rejuvenated her. She knew there was a busy schedule ahead, but these moments of connection and teaching grounded her.

Bonnie decided to take a walk along the beach before heading home. The sand was warm beneath her feet, and the sound of the waves was soothing. She reflected on her journey – from a young girl learning to surf on her father's board, to becoming one of the top surfers in the world. It hadn't been easy, but every challenge had shaped her into the person she was today.

As she walked, she spotted a familiar figure in the distance. It was Sid, sitting on the sand, watching the waves. He waved her over and she joined him, grateful for the company.

"Hey, Sid," she said, sitting down beside him. "Didn't expect to see you here."

"I figured I'd stick around after our chat at Robbie's," he replied with a grin. "Couldn't resist the waves."

They sat in comfortable silence for a while, watching the surfers in the water. Sid turned to her, a thoughtful expression on his face. "You know, Bonnie, you've accomplished so much, but don't forget to take time for yourself. It's easy to get lost in the demands of this life."

Bonnie nodded, appreciating his words. "Thanks, Sid. I need to remind myself of that sometimes."

As the sun began to set, casting a golden glow over the beach, Bonnie's sense of purpose had been recharged. She was ready to face the challenges ahead, knowing that she had the support of friends like Sid and the calming presence of the ocean to keep her steady.

Heading home, Bonnie felt a wave of contentment wash over her. She was living her dream, navigating the highs and lows with grace and determination. And as long as she had the waves, she could handle anything that came her way.

CHAPTER 3

Rob Martin, Robbie's Coffee

Straight from lessons, Bonnie's first stop with the other coaches and lifeguards of the surf school was back at Robbie's Coffee.

Just off the main road and not far from the beach, it was a popular hangout spot. More than just a coffee shop, it was also a licensed bar, where many Saturday nights after coaching or training were spent. Sometimes, the lifeguards and surf coaches would stay late, or on occasion, not go home at all. Where they stayed, Bonnie didn't really care. She always had a bed above the shop.

Rob Martin, known to everyone as Robbie, had only been the owner for two years. Rob was a handsome man with a serious demeanour, which surprised many customers who expected his personality to match his beautiful face. At only 5'10", he was a little short for Bonnie, but he would do for now.

Bonnie had been there from the first day he opened the coffee shop and bar. She found his seriousness intriguing. Rob liked the arts and was creative in a different way than Bonnie. He wasn't interested in surfing, which she appreciated. He never asked her about the surf community or her life as a pro. This suited her just fine; she didn't want to talk about her job or life story. Bonnie wanted no emotional intimacy, just someone to talk to about everyday life and the occasional hook-up. Her encounters with Rob were varied and exciting, a blend of intensity and desire, a secret part of her life that remained unspoken yet vividly real. There were times when the place was almost empty, and Bonnie found herself behind the bar with Rob discreetly putting his hand down the back of her shorts. She would position herself in such a way that no one could tell he was deep inside her with his fingers. She would feel his hand all the way up inside her and his knuckles pressing against her. These moments left Bonnie wanting more.

When the last customer left, she would pull Rob from behind the bar, push him down onto a stool, and showcase her deep-throat skills.

When the opportunity arose, Bonnie would take control, her eyes filled with a mischievous spark. Kneeling before him, she would start at the top, taking the tip of his penis onto her tongue. Slowly, she would take the fully erect penis down, as deep as she could. Bonnie's lack of gag reflex allowed her to go as deep as she wanted, holding him there, savouring the sensation.

Rob loved to keep her pressed against him, feeling the warmth and tightness of her mouth until he could no longer hold back. When he finally released, Bonnie welcomed the sensation, loving the feeling of him ejecting his load and swallowing as much as she could. It was an unspoken dance between them, a blend of pleasure and intimacy that both enjoyed without the complications of deeper emotional ties.

These encounters were purely physical, an escape from the pressures of their daily lives. For Bonnie, it was a way to release tension and feel a different kind of connection, one that didn't require words or promises. It was a perfect arrangement, allowing her to maintain focus on her surfing career without the distractions of a traditional relationship. Bonnie and Rob had many erotic encounters over the last two years. This was all it was – no emotion, and that's how she liked it. She didn't see herself settling down because her career was so important. She had seen many friends meet someone and then never fulfil their ambitions.

Although, most of her friends who had kids and great partners seemed to have found something entirely different; maybe Bonnie was just fearful of the unknown. This scared her the most. The idea of settling down, of trading her independence and career for a conventional life, was something she couldn't reconcile with her ambitions. The ocean was her true love, the waves her constant companion, and the thrill of the surf her greatest joy.

Bonnie was dedicated to her sport, understanding the sacrifices required to stay at the top. Relationships, with their potential for drama and emotional entanglement, were risks she wasn't willing to take. She valued her freedom too much to let anything come between her and her dreams. For now, the arrangement with Rob was perfect – an outlet for physical needs without the complications of deeper emotional ties.

In the quiet moments, though, there was a nagging doubt. She couldn't help but wonder if she was missing out on something more profound, something lasting. The fear of the unknown, of what a different path might bring, was always there. Yet, for Bonnie, the waves were calling, and she knew that as long as she could surf, she was exactly where she was meant to be.

The coffee bar wasn't overly busy on this Saturday evening. As she walked in, the heat of the lattes radiated into the air. Bonnie always sat in a corner booth, sometimes alone, other times with her friend Sally. Sally had long blonde hair and was slender, but appeared to slouch sometimes as she was always tired. Back in the day Sally was considered a top-quality girl. She was also loads of fun and when she was out for a drink, she really would be out, letting her hair down, as they say, away from the busy life of being a mother and partner. Everyone needs a little time to themselves.

She could hear Rob talking to the other baristas. Bonnie's stomach dropped and she wanted to disappear. Some of the local lifeguards had walked in. She wanted to submerge herself in the hot liquid, leaving this coffee shop without drawing attention to herself. Two of the older lifeguard team, who knew Bonnie's father, always seemed to interrupt her time to herself. Bonnie needed this as working with kids could be so tiring.

Adrian and Sid were a great laugh and the banter these two would come out with was borderline bullying. They both came from a rugby background, where it was kind of accepted that taking the piss out of everyone all the time was normal. Some of the stories from the rugby days seemed a little farfetched, as we all know that when old boys retell past events, they seem a little over the top. Bonnie remembered that every new player, after their first team debut would be made to strip naked and kicked off the coach to run a mile back to the club house. On arriving they would have to neck a beer at the bar no matter how busy it was. You just wouldn't get away with this now.

There are hundreds of stories, to name another where a player jumped into a big bath, which all players would use, to be bent over, and someone tried to put soap up his bum. Bonnie didn't know what was worse, the fact that everyone shared a bath or that grown men played with soap.

Adrian was a little man with short legs and a bald head. Well, he had been going bald from the age of 18, apparently. What he lacked on his head, he certainly made up for elsewhere – he was very hairy. He was known as Rod or Big Rod to the ladies. Bonnie hated it when he sat near her as his trousers would ride up a little and go tighter, showing off his girth, and she could see his bulge. It was like a car crash. You didn't want to look, but you did.

Sid, on the other hand, was a little scrawny and could only be described as a bit lanky and a bit awkward. Still, he was known as the silver fox for his full head of hair. He was also full of life, without a care in the world. He was the type of lifeguard who would have one leg propped up on the side while sitting in his short shorts with this thing dangling down. This was to the amusement of everyone and he came to be known as Long Schlong Man.

No matter how annoying these two could be at times, they always ended up making her laugh. For now, at least, they made Bonnie happy. She wondered if she flirted with them a little, they might buy the drinks for the rest of the night.

The clock on the wall read 11:00 p.m. Bonnie knew she'd have to leave soon, as she was meeting up with her parents and her friend Aurora early in the morning.

Aurora had done a little surfing but opted for a more practical job as a mechanic. She worked in Bonnie's father's garage and was known as the goddess of the dawn. Bonnie and the guys were still drinking, though Sally had left about an hour ago.

As midnight neared, Rob looked over from the bar and made eye contact with Bonnie. He didn't hold it long, glancing down at her lips and then back to her eyes. A little drunk, she felt the familiar pull of his gaze and stood up, maintaining eye contact. There was a door just by the restroom that led up to Rob's apartment. Bonnie paused at this door for a second, then looked back at Rob and gave him a smile, lifting her eyebrows slightly. She placed a hand on her bum and lifted her short skirt just a little, making sure Rob noticed before she entered the ladies' restroom.

The coffee bar was almost empty, so all Rob had to do was make his way to the door to his apartment and then slip into the ladies' restroom without anyone noticing. On entering, he saw Bonnie with one leg up on the long granite sink, her skirt pulled up. One hand was on the hard surface, and the other was touching her bum, inviting Rob to get closer to her. This was risky business, and he didn't want to get caught. Not that their relationship was a secret, but as the owner, this wasn't professional. But this was exactly what Bonnie liked. Rob thought, *Let's get into it.*

He moved closer, pushing Bonnie's bum cheeks apart so

he could place his tongue as deep as he could. He liked to trace his tongue up towards her rounded, peachy buttocks, a sensation that made Bonnie shudder. Alternating between placing his fingers inside her and then moving to her arse, Rob gave her the kind of foreplay she enjoyed. They stopped and Rob left the ladies' room, leaving Bonnie wanting more. He made his way to his apartment, and Bonnie followed.

As soon as they entered, Rob shut the door behind them with a deliberate click, the sound echoing ominously in the stillness. He grabbed Bonnie by the wrist, pulling her close, their breath mingling as their faces almost touched. The look in his eyes was predatory, and Bonnie felt a shiver of anticipation run down her spine.

Without a word, he shoved her against the wall, his hands roughly exploring her body. Bonnie gasped as he tore at her clothes, the fabric ripping under his impatient fingers. Her blouse and bra fell away, exposing her breasts to the cool air. Rob's mouth descended on her, biting and sucking with a ferocity that made her moan.

Bonnie's hands fumbled with his belt, her fingers trembling with urgency. She managed to undo it, yanking his pants down enough to free his erection. Rob's hand slipped between her thighs, his fingers finding her wet and ready. He didn't tease her this time, plunging two fingers deep inside her, his thumb rubbing her clit in rough circles.

"You're so fucking wet," he growled against her neck, his teeth grazing her skin.

Bonnie's only response was a breathless moan, her hips bucking against his hand. She needed more, and she needed it now. She reached down, wrapping her hand around his cock, stroking him slowly at first, then faster as he matched her rhythm with his fingers.

"Turn around," Rob commanded, his voice low and dangerous.

Bonnie obeyed, pressing her palms against the wall, her ass pushed out towards him. Rob grabbed her hips, positioning himself at her entrance. He teased her for a moment, running the tip of his cock along her wet folds, before thrusting into her with one hard stroke. Bonnie cried out, a mix of pleasure and pain as he filled her completely.

Rob set a punishing pace, his hips slamming against her with each thrust. Bonnie's nails scratched at the wall, her moans echoing in the small apartment. She could feel him hitting deep inside her, each thrust sending waves of pleasure through her body. Rob's hand reached around to rub her clit, his fingers moving in time with his thrusts.

Bonnie's orgasm built quickly, the intensity almost too much to bear. She felt herself tightening around him, her body trembling as she came with a loud, guttural moan. Rob didn't slow down, continuing to fuck her through her orgasm, his movements becoming more erratic.

With a final, powerful thrust, he came inside her, his growl of release vibrating against her skin. They stayed like that for a moment, his cock still buried deep inside her, both of them breathing heavily.

Rob finally pulled out, his cum dripping down her thighs. He turned her around, kissing her hard, his hand tangling in her hair. Bonnie kissed him back with equal fervour, her body still tingling from the intensity of their encounter.

"Let's take this to the bedroom," Rob said, his voice rough.

She nodded, following him to the bed, her body already aching for more. Tonight, there would be no limits, no holding back. Just raw, unbridled desire. And that was exactly what Bonnie wanted.

CHAPTER 4

Jamie Forrunner

Bonnie woke with Rob beside her, his arm draped across her waist, and his erect penis pressing against her bum cheeks. She could feel the subtle movements of his body, a clear indication that he was eager for round two. However, it was 6:00 a.m., and as always, a familiar feeling of regret washed over her. The physical connection they shared was intense, but Bonnie couldn't muster the emotional intimacy she yearned for. She needed to leave.

She carefully slid out from under Rob's arm, trying not to wake him. Her body felt drained from the rigorous training and coaching sessions the day before. As much as she wanted to escape the awkward morning after, she also craved the comforting routine of a free coffee from Rob's bar. Making her excuses, she whispered, "I need to get going, Rob. Busy day ahead."

Rob stirred, opening his eyes slightly. "You can shower and take your time," he mumbled, his voice thick with sleep. "I'll meet you downstairs in the coffee bar once you're finished."

Bonnie appreciated his decency. Despite their lack of emotional connection, Rob was always courteous, never pressing her to stay longer than she wanted. She grabbed her clothes, heading to the bathroom to freshen up. The hot water cascaded over her, washing away the remnants of the night before. She tried to focus on the day ahead, pushing aside any lingering regret.

After showering and dressing, Bonnie made her way downstairs. The bar was quiet at this early hour, the familiar aroma of freshly brewed coffee greeting her as she entered.

Bonnie loved it first thing in the morning as they opened. The scent was warm and cozy, a comforting blanket of familiarity that wrapped around her the moment she stepped inside. She always found the aroma of a fresh pot of brewing coffee arguably more delightful than the coffee itself. It was a scent that stimulated her salivary glands and invigorated her senses. It was simply delicious. Bonnie always thought it stimulated her brain, waking her up more effectively than the caffeine ever could.

She breathed in deeply, savouring the rich fragrance that promised a day filled with possibility. This ritual had become a cornerstone of her mornings, a small indulgence that helped her gear up for the challenges ahead. As she waited for her order, she let her mind wander, thinking about the day's plans and the people she would meet.

Rob was already behind the counter, his movements efficient and practised. He had just finished making her favourite latte and slid the steaming cup across the counter to her.

"Morning," he greeted her with a familiar smile.

"Morning," Bonnie replied, taking the coffee gratefully. "Thanks, Rob. I really need this today."

Rob nodded, his eyes lingering on her for a moment longer than usual. "You sure you're okay?"

Bonnie forced a smile, trying to shake off the fog of regret from the night before. "Yeah, just a bit tired. Got a busy day ahead with my parents and my friend Aurora."

"All right," Rob said, not pressing further. He understood her well enough to know when to leave things alone.

Bonnie took her coffee to her usual corner booth, the heat radiating through the cup and into her hands. She took a sip, letting the warmth seep into her, and tried to focus on the present. The coffee bar was still quiet, the hum of the espresso machine the only sound breaking the early morning silence.

As she sat there, savouring her latte, the bell above the door chimed. The door opened with some force, and Bonnie was taken aback. She was just about to say something to the person behind the door when her eyes caught a glimpse of who it was. *It couldn't be,* Bonnie thought to herself. Was it the man from the CrossFit session the day before? Surely not! The man also seemed a little startled. They made unwavering eye contact, and Bonnie felt warm inside and began to blush.

He was just as she remembered – muscular and around 6'1". His curves were visible through his clothing, with muscles straining against the fabric at his forearms, biceps, and chest. They both said, "HI," at the same time and then laughed.

Bonnie, slightly flustered, said, "Didn't I see you at the CrossFit session yesterday morning?"

The man replied, "Sorry, what do you mean? I was there. Were you the girl who missed the last clean and jerk?" He didn't know why he said that – what was he thinking, criticising this beautiful lady?

Bonnie was a little taken aback by this. Before she had time to react, Rob called out her name. Her heart sank into her chest. What was he going to say? She hoped it was nothing about the night before. Rob simply walked over and handed her a coffee, then walked off.

The stranger then asked, "Are you not staying?"

Bonnie replied as she looked up over her coffee, "Sure, I can stay for a while, even though you just insulted me about my lifting."

The stranger replied, "I'm Jamie, by the way. Nice to meet you, Bonnie."

She made her way to the outdoor seating. The outdoor area was like a haven for fresh air, with no walls obstructing it. This was needed as Bonnie had consumed way too much alcohol the night before. She was trying to hide the fact that she was tired and hungover with her sunglasses and cap. The smell of the coffee was most powerful this morning, sending a signal to her brain. In that moment, she felt she had a better understanding of the world – or was it this stunning man sitting beside her?

Jamie apologised for his earlier remark. Bonnie couldn't make out his accent so asked where he was from. She guessed it was somewhere in the United Kingdom, possibly Scotland, but she wasn't sure.

Jamie replied, "Well, I've lived in a few places. If you've heard of a place called York in England, I grew up there before joining the military. I ended up in Edinburgh, Scotland, before my travels. I've been on the road for a while now." He didn't give too much away and didn't want to say he was in the Paras from the age of 18. Although he had been all the things that the military gave him, he didn't want to admit it. Jamie was a natural-born leader and was able to navigate most social situations with ease. This was different with Bonnie; he felt like he was stuttering and didn't really know what to say. In fact, he just wanted to stare at her and say nothing. Jamie was also fiercely loyal, which is why the military suited him. He would protect his family and loved ones at all costs, even if it meant making sacrifices for himself. Jamie didn't want to talk about this kind of stuff. He just wanted Bonnie to warm to him, as most people did due to his self-confidence and charisma.

Bonnie asked if Jamie knew who she was, as this was a surfing area and she was a bit of a big deal in these parts. She asked this due to previous meetings with men who had been a little dishonest, as they did in fact know who she was and wanted to get a quick story. Bonnie found it hard to trust people sometimes, as they always seemed to want something from her.

Jamie didn't really know much about Bonnie other than she liked CrossFit and looked like a surfer type of girl. He liked this. He told her about his sister, who was into CrossFit and rugby. She kept saying he needed to find someone who had that smile that would light up his day and keep him on his toes. Jamie said, "You know, like when lightning strikes, you know."

Bonnie had that smile. She replied, "I think I know what you mean." She didn't say anything, but her father had said something similar when he met her mother. She gave a half-smile and couldn't help but look Jamie in the eyes.

The conversation must have only been 10-15 minutes, but this was enough for both. Bonnie said she had to go as she was meeting someone, and Jamie was also on his way to start a new job.

They stood up together awkwardly and made their way out of the café. Jamie and Bonnie smiled at each other, and Jamie said, "I like you so much and would very much like to have another coffee."

Bonnie was a little taken aback by this and didn't know where to look, at the same time holding back a smile from the side of her face. She replied, "I would very much like that."

A voice called out Bonnie's name. As she turned, her friend Aurora arrived on her jet-black motorcycle.

Jamie said, "Well, until we meet again, perhaps we have that second cup of coffee, get to know each other some more, then maybe go for lunch. And if that goes well, we could talk more over dinner, and after that, we can see what happens." As they both walked off, Jamie and Bonnie turned to look back but missed each other. Bonnie looked back one last time before she turned a corner to meet

Aurora. She lingered for a moment, bit her lip, then smiled and walked on.

Jamie had turned just as Bonnie disappeared. He looked down and smiled, thinking about the second cup of coffee. He stood still, frozen, not knowing what to do. A horn beeped, and it was like he awoke from a dream. He realised he was standing in the middle of the road. Jamie thought to himself, *That was the girl I helped from the water one night. Why didn't I tell her about it?* He walked off with a slight smile on his face, thinking about the mysterious and captivating surfer he had just met.

Bonnie and Aurora sped off on the motorcycle, the wind whipping past them. Bonnie's thoughts were a whirlwind. Aurora glanced over her shoulder, noticing her friend's contemplative expression. "What's got you so dreamy-eyed?" she called over the roar of the engine.

"I met someone interesting," Bonnie replied, barely audible over the noise.

As they arrived at their destination, Aurora parked the bike, and they dismounted. "Interesting how?" she probed.

Bonnie hesitated for a moment, then shared, "I met this guy, Jamie, at the café. We connected, and there's something about him. I can't quite put my finger on it."

Aurora smirked. "Sounds like someone has a little crush."

Bonnie rolled her eyes but couldn't hide her smile. "Maybe. But it's more than that. I feel like I've met him before. Like there's some unspoken connection."

Aurora raised an eyebrow. "Well, don't let him slip away then. Go for that second cup of coffee."

Bonnie nodded, determination in her eyes. "I will. I'm not going to let this one pass by."

Meanwhile, Jamie walked through the streets, replaying their encounter in his mind. The way Bonnie smiled, her laugh, the spark in her eyes – it all felt so familiar. He found himself drawn to her, not just physically but emotionally, too.

As he made his way to his new job, he couldn't shake the feeling that fate had a hand in their meeting. He decided he would find her again, have that second cup of coffee, and see where it led. The thought brought a smile to his face as he stepped into his new workplace, ready to face the day with a newfound sense of excitement and possibility.

Jamie arrived at a sleek and modern gym that specialised in high-intensity training and CrossFit. The gym buzzed with energy as people pushed themselves to their limits. Jamie felt right at home in this environment, a stark contrast to the calm, focused feeling he had when thinking about Bonnie.

He greeted his new colleagues and began his day, leading a few training sessions and assisting clients with their routines. Despite the busyness, his thoughts frequently drifted back to Bonnie. He replayed their conversation, the way her eyes sparkled when she laughed, and how easy it was to talk to her. During his lunch break, Jamie pulled out his phone and checked his social media, hoping to catch a glimpse of her or maybe find a way to connect. He remembered Bonnie mentioning that she was a bit of a big deal in the surfing community, so he started by searching for local surfing events and prominent surfers in the area.

Luck was on his side. He found Bonnie's profile, filled with stunning photos of her riding waves and interacting with the local surf scene. He hesitated for a moment, debating whether to send her a message. He didn't want to come off too strong or seem like he had been stalking her online. But his curiosity and desire to see her again didn't win out; he didn't send her a message.

CHAPTER 5

Aurora Winters

Little did Bonnie know that this unexpected encounter with Jamie would open a new chapter in her life, intertwining the thrill of the waves with the enigmatic charm of a stranger who seemed to hold the key to unlocking something more profound.

Aurora, pulling up her Yamaha R6, was magnificent. The way she dismounted was like something out of a martial arts movie, effortlessly kicking her leg over in a swift, controlled manoeuvre. Bonnie always thought it looked like slow motion, a graceful yet powerful display that somewhat annoyed her because it just looked so sexy. Seeing Aurora in her black leathers, exuding confidence and power, was always a sight to behold.

As Aurora removed her helmet, her short dark hair, shaved up the sides, came into view. The style suited her perfectly, giving her an edgy yet feminine look. Her black hair contrasted with her bright eyes and perfect smile, which could light up any room. At 33, Aurora was very much like Bonnie – single, independent, and looking for someone who could be both an equal and a good friend. She was a timeless beauty, curvy like a wave that just wouldn't quit, and she loved the reactions she got from guys when she wore her yoga pants.

Bonnie walked over slowly, and they exchanged greetings. Aurora was the first to speak. "You haven't been with that twat again, have you? Rob! I told you it wouldn't lead to anything good. The three-time rule, remember? You've well and truly broken that one!"

Bonnie sighed, knowing Aurora was right. She didn't like Rob; she always had a gut feeling that something wasn't quite right about him. And Aurora's gut feelings were usually spot on.

"Anyway," Aurora said, breaking the tension, "get back on my bike. We're off for a ride. It'll clear your head, and we'll have some fun."

Bonnie hopped onto the back of Aurora's motorbike with a mix of excitement and curiosity. She shared more details about her encounter with Jamie, emphasising his charm and the instant connection they seemed to have. Aurora listened with a knowing smile, her confidence and sense of adventure contagious.

As they sped down the highway, Bonnie held on tight. The acceleration was almost overwhelming, a rush of speed and adrenaline that was both exhilarating and liberating. Riding a motorcycle, like surfing, was a combination of exhilaration, fear, relaxation, and pleasure that changed you forever.

Aurora craved the physical and emotional pleasure of these rides, with a layer of anxiety and adrenaline that mirrored her sexual desires. Bonnie knew all about this, having heard the stories of Aurora's kinks and her love for the adrenaline rush. There was no denying the thrill that came from a motorcycle ride.

The girls rode along the coast, the salty sea air whipping past them. Bonnie felt the familiar rush of acceleration, her body adapting to the high speed. She couldn't help but feel alive, the ride clearing her mind and giving her a sense of clarity she hadn't felt in a while.

Aurora finally pulled over at a scenic overlook, the ocean stretching out before them. They took off their helmets, their hair tousled by the wind.

"You're smiling," Aurora said, nudging Bonnie playfully. "Feeling better?"

Bonnie nodded. "Yeah, I am. Thanks for this."

Aurora leaned against her bike, her eyes thoughtful. "So, about Jamie... He sounds like he might be worth a shot."

Bonnie smiled, thinking about the mysterious man who had made such an impression on her. "Yeah, he does. I think I'll go for that second cup of coffee."

Aurora grinned. "Good. Now, let's enjoy this view and just be in the moment."

They stood there together, looking out at the ocean, feeling the wind on their faces. In that moment, Bonnie felt a sense of peace and possibility, ready to embrace whatever the future held.

As the bike revved up again, ready to set off once more,

Bonnie held on tightly, bracing herself for the thrilling ride ahead. Another rush of adrenaline surged through her veins, heightening her senses as the engines roared to life. With her expertise, Aurora knew just how to push the limits, igniting the intense thrill of the ride.

With a powerful burst of acceleration, the bike shot forward, tearing through the streets with electrifying speed. The wind whipped past them, carrying with it the essence of freedom and liberation. Bonnie's heart pounded in sync with the thunderous roar of the engines and Aurora's mastery of the bike was evident as they weaved through traffic, their movements fluid and precise. The sheer exhilaration was intoxicating, sending waves of pleasure coursing through Bonnie's body.

The bike came to a stop, and Aurora looked over at another biker who gave her a nod. Bonnie held on tight, knowing what was coming. From a standing start, the two bikes started to rev up. The thrill, the exhilaration, the release of dopamine was enough to make Aurora feel a rush of pleasure. The acceleration reminded her of the intensity she felt when someone choked her while deep inside her. She opened the throttle, and both Bonnie and Aurora felt the rear tyre grip the pavement. They were off.

The race ended with a nod as both riders went their separate ways. They pulled up just before Bonnie's father's garage. There was a little burger bar out front with a few tables and seats. The girls talked over some fries and hotdogs. Bonnie shared a bit about Jamie, the mysterious man she had met, though she held back from saying too much, not wanting to be judged. For all her bravado and confidence, Aurora was still a girl who longed for someone special.

Bonnie and Aurora liked nothing more than a chick flick; some of their favourite films to watch together were 'Notting Hill' with Julia Roberts, or 'About a Boy'. One film that always got Bonnie was 'Meet Joe Black', or maybe it was Brad Pitt! Aurora was more of a Ryan Reynolds fan and definitely liked 'The Proposal'. They also enjoyed reading, though their tastes were different. They both loved a good erotic thriller.

The conversation turned to a bike race called the Isle of Man TT. The Isle of Man is a self-governing British crown dependency in the Irish Sea between England and Ireland. It's known for its rugged coastline, medieval castles, and rural landscape rising to a mountainous centre. The Isle of Man TT is a major annual cross-country motorcycle race around the island. Aurora wanted to go and even take part in what is widely regarded as the most dangerous motorsport event on the planet. This was an adventure both girls wanted to do together, but due to the pressures of surfing and little time, neither had committed to a vacation in the UK. Aurora would probably meet an Englishman, as she really liked the British and had met a few on her travels.

She shared a story Bonnie had heard many times, but she didn't mind. Aurora had met this older man; she thought he was around 40. He knew what he wanted, and he definitely got it.

Bonnie gagged a little on her hotdog as Aurora shoved it into her mouth unexpectedly. She laughed and said, "Pay attention, Bonnie, girl. That night," she began, her voice lowering to a sultry tone, "I had that strong desire for something, especially sex. I got straight to it, wanting to feel that throat spasm that makes swallowing or breathing difficult. As I took the man's pulsating manhood into my mouth, that's exactly what I got. My eyes watered as I clawed at his hands, struggling to take a breath. He quickly turned me and performed what I could only describe as rear-entry bondage. He bent me over and tied my wrists to my ankles. My legs spread, which made it easy for him to pull my hair, spank me, and penetrate me, then perform oral sex. I felt exceptionally gorgeous, my every curve taunting gravity and mocking time. Every joint and shadowed hollow begging to be tongued."

Bonnie felt sexy hearing this, and the way Aurora told the story with a wicked sense of humour, imagination, and confidence. She also wanted a little more emotional intimacy. The story had left both girls a little wet and turned on, especially after the bike race.

Bonnie listened, her mind drifting back to Jamie and the connection she felt with him. She wondered if he could be the one to break through her walls, to offer something more than the casual encounters she had with Rob. As Aurora's story came to an end, Bonnie smiled, feeling a sense of hope and excitement for what the future might hold.

"Maybe we should plan that trip to the Isle of Man," she suggested, her eyes gleaming with excitement.

Aurora grinned. "Absolutely. Let's make it happen. It's time for a new adventure."

It was time to come back to reality. Aurora was due at work and Bonnie was meeting her parents. Mick's garage was not more than 100 yards away.

The girls walked in, and as always, Aurora was a little

late. She said her goodbyes to Bonnie and proceeded to give the guys at work some banter. They then headed to Mick's office.

Bonnie's parents exchanged a warm hug as they met her there. There was an unspoken understanding between them, a shared bond that didn't always require words. Together, they made their way to the family camper van parked outside.

Mick looked over at Bonnie with a smile. "Ready for another adventure, kiddo?"

Bonnie grinned. "Always, Dad. Where are we headed today?"

Joanna chimed in. "We thought we'd take a drive along the coast, maybe stop by that little seafood place you like, or we could just head home."

Bonnie's face lit up. "Sounds perfect. I could use some fresh air and good food."

As they settled into the camper van, the familiar hum of the engine brought a sense of comfort. They pulled out of the garage and headed towards the coastline, the wind carrying the salty scent of the ocean. The drive was filled with easy conversation, stories from the past, and plans for the future. Bonnie was at ease, a stark contrast to the whirlwind of emotions she had experienced earlier that day.

Back at the garage, Aurora was in her element. She joked with the guys, teasing them about their work and keeping the atmosphere light. Her presence was a mixture of strength and playfulness, a dynamic that kept everyone on their toes.

One of the guys, Luke, nudged her with a grin. "You

seem in a good mood today, Aurora. Got a hot date or something?"

Aurora smirked. "Something like that. Just had a great ride with Bonnie this morning. Nothing beats starting the day with some speed."

Luke raised an eyebrow. "And maybe something more?"

Aurora's eyes twinkled mischievously. "Maybe. A girl's gotta keep some secrets, right?"

Aurora was hard at work, her mind half-focused on the task at hand and half-drifting back to the morning's ride and Bonnie's intriguing encounter. The guys in the garage were used to her playful banter, but today, they sensed an extra edge to her energy.

During a break, she gathered with the guys in the corner, wiping grease from her hands. Luke, always the instigator, leaned in with a smirk. "All right, Aurora, you've got that look. Spill it. Got any wild stories to share?"

Aurora grinned, her eyes glinting with mischief. "You boys really want to hear one of my stories?"

A chorus of eager nods and chuckles urged her on. Aurora settled back, adopting a mock-serious tone. "All right, gather around. This one's a doozy." She took a deep breath, leaning forward. "So, I was out at this biker rally a few months back. Met this guy – huge, rugged, the kind that looks like he's carved out of stone. Name was Jake. We hit it off right away, and after a few drinks, we decided to head back to his place."

The guys leaned in closer, their eyes wide with anticipation.

Aurora continued, her voice dropping to a husky whisper. "When we got there, things heated up fast. But let me tell you, I was not prepared for what Jake was packing. The man was... well, let's just say he was blessed. So big, I nearly couldn't take it."

The guys exchanged glances, clearly impressed and a little envious.

Aurora's smile turned wicked. "He pushed me to my limits. There was this moment, right when he was about to enter me, that I thought, 'No way is this going to fit.' But he was patient, took his time. I could feel every inch stretching me, filling me up. It was intense, almost too much, but I loved every second of it."

One of the younger mechanics, eyes wide, asked, "Did it hurt?"

Aurora nodded. "Oh, it did. But in that good way, you know? That mix of pain and pleasure that drives you wild. Jake knew exactly what he was doing, how to push just enough without breaking me. By the time we were done, I was spent. Every muscle ached, but it was worth it."

The guys let out a collective breath, a mix of awe and respect in their expressions. Aurora leaned back, smirking. "And that, boys, is why you should always be up for a challenge. You never know what kind of unforgettable experiences you'll have."

Luke chuckled, shaking his head. "Damn, Aurora, you sure know how to live. Makes our lives seem pretty dull in comparison."

She laughed, the sound rich and full of life. "Just remember, it's all about pushing boundaries and embracing the thrill. Life's too short for anything less."

CHAPTER 6
Joanna and Michael Florence

The drive back to the family home was a quiet one. No one said much, but the silence was comforting, punctuated only by the hum of the engine and the occasional sound of passing cars. Bonnie's mother, Joanna, a renowned relationship therapist and author, sensed her daughter was in a bit of emotional turmoil. She resisted the urge to pry, knowing that any attempt to ask questions would probably come off as intrusive. Despite her professional expertise in relationships and infidelity, she knew that giving advice to her own daughter was fraught with complexities.

Before Joanna could break the silence, Bonnie's father, Michael – better known as Mick – jumped in with one of his trademark dad jokes. "Bonnie, why did the coffee file a police report? It got mugged." The joke was predictably terrible, but it never failed to make Bonnie smile.

She laughed. "Dad, your jokes are the worst. But I love them."

Mick grinned, following up with a more serious note. "Remember, Bonnie, never love something that can't love you back. Don't be a material girl." He glanced at her in the rear-view mirror, a knowing look in his eyes. "You know what Aurora is like with her bikes. Don't let that happen to you."

Bonnie chuckled. "Don't worry, Dad. Aurora and I are just fine. She's like a sister to me."

Mick nodded, satisfied, and she leaned forward, throwing her arms around him from the back seat. "I love you, Dad," she said, squeezing him tightly despite the awkward angle.

Joanna watched them, a soft smile on her face. "You seem a different sort of happy today, Bonnie," she observed gently.

Bonnie blushed, feeling the warmth and support from her parents. Her family had always been a rock for her, especially during the ups and downs of her professional surfing career. Their home was a haven of security, care, and open communication, where every member felt valued and respected.

As the camper van pulled into the family driveway, Bonnie noticed the surf school owner, his wife Ronnie, and their son Henry, waiting for them. The families often had lunch together, and today was no exception.

As soon as Bonnie stepped out, Henry, a lively eight-year-old, ran towards her and jumped into her arms, giving her the biggest hug he could muster. Bonnie adored

Henry. She had been helping him with his education, especially since he, like her, had dyslexia.

"Hey, buddy!" Bonnie greeted, spinning him around. "How's my favourite master builder today?"

Henry beamed. "I built a new Star Wars set! It's the Millennium Falcon this time."

Bonnie's eyes lit up. "That's awesome, Henry! You have to show it to me later."

He nodded enthusiastically. Bonnie had always related to Henry's struggles. Growing up, she often felt isolated and bullied due to her dyslexia, and she was determined to help Henry avoid the same fate. Surfing had been her escape and saviour, and she hoped to find something similar for Henry.

Ronnie and David approached, smiling warmly. "Thanks for coming over," Ronnie said, clapping Mick on the shoulder.

"Wouldn't miss it for the world," Mick replied, returning the smile.

As they headed towards the house, Henry tugged on Bonnie's sleeve. "Can we build something later, Bonnie? Maybe something even cooler than the Death Star?"

Bonnie laughed. "You got it, buddy. We'll build the most epic thing ever."

She felt the adrenaline from the ride with Aurora wearing off as she waved back to Shannon from across the road. Shannon, who had benefitted greatly from Joanna's expertise with her daughter in the past, had invited the Florence family over for leftover BBQ food, cheesecake, and a few beers from her party the other day.

Shannon and her husband Hugh Jackman (not the actor, though he fancied himself just as charismatic) were younger than Joanna and Mick. Shannon had just turned 50, and Hugh was a store owner who was obsessed with his home gym. Despite the fact that he had invested an obscene amount of money into his gym equipment, he wasn't exactly the Wolverine. Nonetheless, he was kind-hearted and always welcomed his neighbours warmly.

As they made their way to the Jackmans' massive backyard, Bonnie marvelled at the setup. It featured a swimming pool and an impressive outdoor kitchen area that resembled a small island. It had everything needed for a BBQ, including a grill and ample counter space. Shannon's daughter was there with her three kids. Daniella, three years older than Bonnie, had surfed alongside her during their childhood and had always been a bit of an enigma, especially regarding her romantic preferences.

Daniella's children were running around wildly. Just as Bonnie turned to say hello to Bella, the middle child, little Jack, the youngest, bit her on the leg. Bella grabbed little Jack by the scruff of his neck and pulled him away, causing him to hit his head on the grass. Amidst the chaos, Daniella shouted at Bella, and both children burst into tears. Bonnie, still in pain from the bite, angrily exclaimed, "Get your feral child under control, Daniella!"

This caused an uproar. Toby, the eldest at 11, began crying as well. Everyone turned to Bonnie, scolding her for being mean. Ronnie burst out laughing and told everyone to get a grip, reminding them that kids did this all the time. She then teased Bonnie. "I bet you wouldn't mind if that

Rob bloke bit you somewhere!" Everyone laughed, but Daniella started crying too, having driven her car into the driveway wall earlier.

David stood in disbelief and remarked, "Just another normal day then. Now, where's the food? I'm hungry."

Ronnie and David's unconventional relationship was always a topic of amusement. They had met at the surf school, where Ronnie, a younger lifeguard, had caught David's eye after a breakup. Despite the age difference, they made a great couple. Bonnie had witnessed their first meeting, which was still recounted with much laughter.

The story involved a low-key charity photo shoot for a local calendar that could have easily been mistaken for soft porn. David and Byron, another local lifeguard, had posed naked, with Byron hugging David from behind as if he were pregnant. The photos were taken in black and white, adding to the absurdity of the situation. Despite – or perhaps because of – this strange introduction, Ronnie had been attracted to David's confidence and charm.

As everyone gathered around the BBQ, Shannon handed out beers and plates of leftover food. Bonnie watched as the chaos of the children and the laughter of the adults filled the air. It was a perfect distraction from her own worries. Hugh was manning the grill, showing off his culinary skills and sharing workout tips that no one really asked for.

Having finished her banter with the guys at the garage and arriving fashionably late, Aurora joined them, bringing her infectious energy. She noticed Bonnie's slight discomfort and nudged her. "Hey, you okay?"

Bonnie smiled weakly. "Yeah, just got bitten by a little hyena."

Aurora laughed. "Kids, right? They're like tiny, adorable psychopaths."

The evening continued with food, laughter, and shared stories. At one point, Aurora captivated everyone with another one of her darkly humorous sex stories. "So, there was this guy," she began, leaning in conspiratorially. "He was so big, I almost couldn't take it. I mean, it was like trying to swallow a telephone pole."

Everyone laughed nervously, a mix of fascination and discomfort on their faces.

Aurora continued, her tone darkening slightly. "He bent me over, tied my wrists to my ankles, and... Well, let's just say it was an experience. By the end, my throat was sore, my eyes were watering, and I was left gasping for breath. But damn, it was exhilarating."

Shannon was stunned into silence for a moment before Ronnie, trying to lighten the mood, quipped, "You sure know how to pick 'em, Aurora."

She grinned wickedly. "You know it. Life's too short for anything boring."

Bonnie shook her head, smiling. Aurora's tales were always a bit too much for her, but she admired her friend's confidence and openness. As the night wore on, Bonnie felt the warmth of her family and friends envelop her, grounding her amidst a whirlwind of emotions. Despite the day's chaos and unexpected bite, she knew she was home.

She always thought Byron would meet a nice girl; the only problem was that he was a little useless when it came to talking to them. He had a great body, sculpted by years of swimming, and was also a popular group fitness instructor. People loved him teaching Les Mills Body Pump. *Maybe he should get with Daniella*, Bonnie thought, smiling to herself.

The afternoon and evening had been a great distraction, just what Bonnie needed. There had been loads of banter and old stories. The food was fantastic. As the evening wound down, everyone began to leave, and Bonnie found herself wandering back to her parents' house. She had decided to stay the night.

*

A couple of nights had passed. Bonnie was still at her parents' house. There was something special about staying in her old room. Good home cooking from her mum. The food just seemed to taste better. A simple omelette was better for no other reason than her mum had made it. The fridge was always full and like every child visiting a parent's house, the first thing she always did was raid the fridge for food. Staying over was brilliant as she didn't have to do anything. Even though Joanna was retired, she was always working from her office. Mick was always helping around the house. Bonnie loved the time she spent with her dad; he was such a loving man. You could say trust, respect and love, intimacy, involve more than being loyal. Unconditional love. No matter how badly Bonnie messed up, he would be there. She had messed up many a time.

They had gone for an early morning jog, which was something they liked to do together. They had done so for years as it was a good way to chat with one another. Bonnie found it helped with her dyslexia. For some reason, exercise really helped her focus; normally her mind was a little like a tornado, spinning round and round. Talking to her dad while running just seemed natural. There was even a little competition now and again. Mick's legs couldn't really keep up with Bonnie nowadays, but he also liked the challenge.

They were going at it a little hard today as Bonnie was thinking about Jamie; she couldn't get him out of her mind. Mick pulled up just as they turned the last corner before reaching home. He was out of breath and looked a little pale. He complained about being lightheaded and suddenly dizzy, unusually fatigued. They waited a few minutes before entering the house. She had never seen her dad like this before and was a little worried. It passed and Mick assured her he was okay, and that it must have been because they hadn't had breakfast or much water before running. Bonnie didn't think any more of this as her dad had always been really fit and would tell her if anything was wrong.

As Bonnie set off in her dad's camper van she oscillated between thoughts of the upcoming sponsor meetings and Jamie. She was eager for both professional success and the chance to see Jamie again, their initial encounter having left a strong impression on her.

Meanwhile, back at the family home, Mick grappled with the lingering discomfort in his chest. The pressure and tightness he had felt earlier had subsided somewhat, but a lingering unease persisted. He decided not to worry Joanna or Bonnie with his symptoms, attributing them to the exertion of their morning jog and hoping that rest would alleviate it.

Throughout the day, Joanna noticed that he seemed off,

though she couldn't pinpoint exactly what was wrong. She gently suggested that he take it easy, but Mick, not wanting to alarm her, downplayed his discomfort and assured her that he just needed some rest.

By the time Bonnie arrived home, she had received a call from Joanna, who mentioned Mick's earlier episode of discomfort. Bonnie's concern heightened, and she insisted on speaking directly to her dad. Sensing her worry, Mick reassured her that he was feeling better now and chalked it up to fatigue from their jog.

Relieved to hear her dad's voice and reassurances, Bonnie reluctantly accepted his explanation but made him promise to keep her updated. She couldn't shake off a nagging worry and made a mental note to check in with him regularly.

Mick sat in his favourite chair that evening; the discomfort in his chest continued to nag at him. He knew he couldn't ignore it any longer. As much as he wanted to believe it was just fatigue or a passing ache, the persistence of the tightness weighed heavily on his mind.

Joanna, sensing his unease despite his attempts to downplay it, quietly observed him from across the room. She had spent years working with couples, helping them navigate through issues of health, trust, and vulnerability. The same principles she applied in her work were now playing out in her own home, with her husband.

"Maybe you should see a doctor, Mick," Joanna suggested softly, breaking the silence that hung between them. Her tone was gentle yet firm, conveying both concern and conviction.

He hesitated, conflicted by his desire to not worry Joanna further and his growing realisation that he couldn't ignore this any longer. "I'll be fine, Jo," he replied, his voice betraying a hint of uncertainty.

"You know I'm always here for you," Joanna said, her voice steady and reassuring. "But sometimes we have to take care of ourselves too."

Mick nodded slowly, knowing she was right. He had always been the pillar of strength for his family, the one who offered support and reassurance. Now, faced with his own vulnerability, he felt a twinge of fear.

Later that night, after Bonnie had settled into her room, she couldn't shake off the worry about her dad. She scrolled through her phone, considering calling him again, but decided to wait until morning. She knew he needed rest and didn't want to disturb him.

In her room, surrounded by familiar sights and sounds, Bonnie reflected on the day's events. The excitement of the upcoming sponsor meetings was overshadowed by concern for her dad. She knew he was strong and resilient, but she also understood the importance of addressing health concerns promptly.

The next morning, Mick woke up early, the discomfort in his chest still present but not as intense as the day before. He knew he couldn't put it off any longer. With Joanna's encouragement echoing in his mind, he made an appointment with his doctor for later that day.

Meanwhile, Bonnie prepared for her day of meetings, her mind divided between professional obligations and thoughts of her dad. She hoped his doctor's appointment would provide some answers and put her own worries to rest.

As Mick drove to the doctor's office later that morning, he felt a mix of apprehension and relief. Apprehension about what the doctor might find, but relief that he was finally taking action. He glanced at his phone, noticing a text from Bonnie wishing him good luck. It brought a small smile to his face, knowing his daughter was thinking of him.

At the doctor's office, Mick underwent a series of tests and examinations. The doctor listened attentively as Mick described his symptoms and medical history. After what felt like an eternity of waiting, the doctor delivered the news.

"We'll need to do some more tests, Mick," the doctor said gently. "There are a few things we need to rule out."

Mick nodded, his heart pounding with a mix of fear and determination. He knew this was just the beginning of a journey toward understanding his health better.

Back at home, Joanna awaited Mick's return anxiously, her mind filled with worry and hope. She knew Mick's strength, but she also knew the unpredictability of health.

As Bonnie wrapped up her meetings that day, she checked her phone incessantly, waiting for news from her dad. When he finally called, his voice was calm yet serious as he updated her on the doctor's appointment.

"They're going to run more tests," Mick explained, his words measured. "But I'm okay, Bonnie. Don't worry too much."

Bonnie nodded, her relief mingled with concern. "Keep me posted, Dad," she urged softly. "I love you."

"I love you too, sweetheart," Mick replied, his voice warm with affection. "I'll let you know how it goes."

And as Bonnie hung up, she couldn't help but feel grateful for the bond she shared with her dad, and the strength and love that held their family together, no matter what challenges they faced.

CHAPTER 7

Love at First Sight? Bullshit

Working at one of the biggest clubs in the area, Jamie found himself immersed in the vibrant nightlife scene. His military background had prepared him well for security work, and he took his responsibilities seriously. Depending on the club, the age restrictions varied between 18+ and 21+, each with its own set of rules and regulations. For the 18+ clubs, Jamie was familiar with the systems in place to verify patrons' ages, ensuring compliance with UK laws regarding alcohol consumption. He encountered a diverse range of people, from fresh-faced youngsters experiencing nightlife for the first time, to seasoned partygoers.

Regardless of the age group, Jamie approached his job with professionalism and vigilance, keeping a watchful eye on the crowd to maintain order and safety within the club. His military training instilled in him a strong sense of discipline and dedication, qualities that served him well in his role as a security guard.

Jamie loved a specific smell inside clubs: maybe perfume and sweat. He even enjoyed the scent of empty bottles and cups left on tables that surrounded the dance floor. Usually, these were plastic cups, so they wouldn't break. For some reason, though, he remembered beer bottles being allowed. As he was security, or you could say a bouncer, the odds were that he would ID people coming in, and he loved this. Drunk women were usually just as friendly as the stereotype, from his personal experience. Jamie did have a few encounters in the ladies' bathrooms where they got very friendly. He remembered one time in particular.

Jamie had just finished his rounds when he noticed a woman stumbling towards the restroom. He recognised the signs of someone who'd had a bit too much to drink: the unsteady walk, the glazed eyes, and the slight slur in her speech as she asked him where the ladies' room was. Jamie nodded and pointed her in the right direction, watching as she made her way through the crowded club.

A few minutes later, he decided to check on the restrooms. It was part of his job to ensure everything was in order, but he also knew from experience that drunk patrons often needed a bit of assistance. As he approached the ladies' room, he heard a faint voice calling for help. Pushing open the door slightly, he saw the woman he had directed earlier struggling with the lock on one of the stalls.

"Everything okay in there?" Jamie called out, keeping his tone professional.

"No, I can't get this door to lock!" she replied, sounding frustrated and a bit helpless.

Jamie stepped inside, making sure the restroom was empty except for the two of them. "Let me take a look," he offered, approaching her stall.

The woman stepped aside, allowing him to inspect the lock. It was indeed broken, and Jamie knew there was little chance of fixing it on the spot. "Yeah, this one's busted. You'll have to hold it shut if you need to use it."

She sighed and leaned against the wall, her balance wavering. "I just need a minute. Can you stay here? Just in case?"

Jamie nodded. "Sure thing."

As she stepped into the stall, he turned his back to give her some privacy, but the door didn't close entirely. He could hear her shuffling around, and then the soft sound of her sitting down. Moments later, she called out again. "Jamie? Can you help me? The door keeps swinging open."

He glanced over his shoulder and saw her struggling to keep the door closed while trying to maintain her balance. He walked over, pushing it shut firmly. She reached up and grabbed his arm, using it to steady herself as she finished up.

"Thanks," she murmured, meeting his gaze. There was a look in her eyes that Jamie recognised – a mix of vulnerability and flirtation that he'd seen many times before.

"No problem," Jamie replied, his voice low. He tried to maintain his professionalism, but her grip on his arm tightened, and she pulled him a little closer.

"You're really sweet, you know that?" she said, her voice a bit husky. "Not many guys would help out like this."

Jamie smiled, feeling a familiar rush of adrenaline. "Just doing my job."

She bit her lip, her gaze lingering on his. "Is this part of your job too?" she asked, leaning forward and brushing her lips against his.

Jamie hesitated for a moment, then responded to her kiss. It was brief but charged with a heady mix of alcohol and desire. When they pulled apart, she was breathing heavily, her eyes dark with need.

"Can you help me with one more thing?" she whispered, her hand trailing down his arm.

Jamie swallowed hard, knowing where this was heading. "What do you need?"

She didn't answer with words but instead pulled him into the stall, the door swinging shut behind them. Jamie pressed her against the door, his hands roaming her body as she moaned softly. The lock might have been broken, but at that moment, it didn't matter.

With one hand, Jamie held the door closed, and with the other he explored her curves, his touch eliciting gasps and sighs from her. She wrapped her legs around his waist to pull him closer, their movements growing more frantic as the sounds of the club faded into the background.

In the dim light of the restroom, they lost themselves in the moment, driven by a mix of lust and the intoxicating thrill of doing something forbidden. Jamie knew it wasn't the most appropriate place or time, but the heat between them was undeniable, and for that brief interlude, nothing else mattered.

*

The place was super busy this Thursday night. You couldn't move without bumping into someone. There were tables, but you had to be lucky to snag one if you were in a group; it wasn't a guarantee. The people sitting at the bar had others pressing in behind them to try to get the bartender's attention.

Jamie had to keep an eye on these people as they tried to order a drink. Most would go up to the bar or catch one of the waitresses walking around. There was a menu with the place's specials (all video-game-themed), but there was also the assumption that if it was a 'normal' drink, you could order it. So, they wouldn't have 'gin and tonic' on the menu, but they could still make it. Getting the bartender's attention took a while sometimes because it was so pushy. Most were friendly, even though it was super busy.

Jamie liked to keep his drinks simple at clubs. Whiskey Coke or rum and Coke. Or just beer.

It was loud; you would have to lean over and speak up to hear each other, but it wasn't deafening.

Jamie was aware of one thing most people aren't: if you're going to a bar, never lose sight of your drink. Date-rape drugs, or roofies, are something women especially need to be vigilant for. So, if you leave the table, watch your drink. If you're mingling, you're holding your drink with you. If someone buys you a drink, and you're okay with that, then you go to the bar with them and watch the bartender make it.

Jamie noticed an attractive and mysterious girl dancing;

there wasn't anything special playing. She danced with the air; her movements seemed to flow like water. With a wave of the arm or a toss of the head, she seemed in control of her body. Jamie was aiming to lock eyes with the dancing girl as he thought he recognised her. She turned as the music changed and scanned the bar and dancefloor as if looking for someone. Jamie just happened to meet her gaze as he stood not far from the bar. He wasn't sure what happened, and he hadn't intended on it. The attractive girl slowly walked over. He felt a little uneasy, which was unusual for him. As she approached, Jamie recognised that smile. It was Bonnie, whom he had met the Sunday just gone. Hoping he would meet her again, Jamie had been to the CrossFit box three times this week already but hadn't seen Bonnie. He wondered why she would be out clubbing.

Bonnie walked straight over and got a little closer; the wordless chemistry between them was obvious. She told Jamie that she hadn't planned to go out clubbing that night. As the music was loud, she had to get in close and touched him flirtatiously. Jamie couldn't believe it; Bonnie looked so good, and all she was wearing was jeans and a T-shirt.

"I'm glad I decided to go out tonight. I don't usually drink, though. I'm here to dance, and I'm the type of person who hates driving downtown but will stay sober to drive home at the end of the night in case something happens. Or to just stay sober as Aurora can get a little drunk sometimes. Plus, drinks at clubs are way overpriced. I also almost never bring a jacket or purse or anything into the club with me, even if it's the middle of winter. I leave the purse at home and the jacket in the car. I wear jeans with pockets, so my cash, credit card, and ID are in there. Phone, too. That's it. Or tall boots where those things can be stashed in the leg."

Jamie could see she was a little drunk tonight, though, and didn't expect this. At this point, Aurora came straight from the bar and got a little too close to Jamie. She gave him a slap on the bum and turned to Bonnie.

"What are you two talking about? That guy over there thinks you're sexy. Come on, we have drinks waiting."

Aurora pulled her away from Jamie. Bonnie tried to wrap her arm around his waist but was pulled away. She looked over her shoulder and smiled at him. Jamie didn't really know what had just happened, and as he was working he had to focus on what he was doing. There had been reports of a few dealers on the premises tonight. Bonnie wasn't the only person he had to keep safe. The bartender, who wasn't far from Jamie's side, called him over.

"Do you know her? You do realise that's Bonnie Florence. She's currently the 9th ranked female surfer in the world. I hear she just got a big sponsorship deal with Nike for the next five years."

The bartender whipped out his phone and showed him Bonnie's Instagram post from today. Jamie wasn't a big social media person. He didn't have time to follow idiots who post everything just for likes nowadays. Life just wasn't like that.

Jamie lost sight of Bonnie. He paused to draw breath, his face hiding his disappointment but also the relief and luck of finding her again. He had this strange feeling inside. Was this anxiety over when he would see her again? What would he say?

Just be yourself; don't try to be something you're not;

she'll see through it, he thought. Jamie told himself to relax as he had a job to do.

The night was going well for a Thursday. Normally there were more younger students clubbing, which always meant trouble as they just couldn't handle their drink as well as, say, people in their 30s or 40s. Or was it the fact that it was so expensive the younger generation would drink before going out, so they were already well and truly drunk before they hit the first bar?

Whichever it was, it wasn't good to see. As a sober person, it could really put you off going out. Seeing people get in such a mess wasn't attractive. The younger women seemed to be worse than the men.

An old-school classic came on. Jamie remembered this from a festival in the UK. Inspired by Hoppípolla from Sigur Rós came Chicane's Poppiholla. Jamie loved this kind of trance music. He found it very relaxing in a strange way. It was one of those songs he wished could go on for hours, not just a few minutes and he found it so uplifting. Jamie just happened to get a glimpse of Bonnie on the dancefloor, swaying to the music with her hands up over her head, turning her body with the flow, hips moving provocatively; it seemed like she was trying to excite someone. It seemed, to Jamie's eyes, that Bonnie's body didn't belong to her, but rather belonged to others.

As Jamie stepped onto the dancefloor he looked closer and noticed she was confused and had some difficulty walking. There had been a sudden change in her behaviour. Younger men had made their way over to Bonnie and Aurora with their cell phones pointed at the girls. They were filming Bonnie. One of them tried to put his arm around Bonnie and pull her close. She stumbled a little and fell into his other arm. Jamie could see the confusion in her eyes. The young man put his hand down the back of her jeans.

Panicking, she tried to pull away, but had no control over her limbs. In the confusion, she lost her balance and fell onto the dance floor, hitting her head.

Bonnie vomited.

Seeing what had just happened sent Aurora into a fit of rage. She pushed the young man and then proceeded to kick him. Her coordination wasn't what it should be, as she was very drunk. This wasn't the best idea she'd ever had. Jamie, along with another member of the security team, stopped Aurora in her tracks. Removing her from the situation immediately calmed the young men's nerves. Jamie left the team to deal with what had just happened, as Bonnie was still on the floor. Seeing that she was clearly shaken, Jamie picked her up.

Slurring her speech, she tried to say something; he didn't know what it was.

Another team member who recognised Bonnie said, "Get Florence out of here. She shouldn't be seen like this. Go, do what you must do."

Jamie scooped Bonnie into his arms, her grip around his neck tight. He knew it wasn't the ideal action – Bonnie might need medical attention – but before he could decide, he was ushered out through a discreet side entrance. He needed to get her somewhere safe.

Unexpectedly, Aurora was also escorted out with a female staff member. Now somewhat sober, she recognised Jamie from Robbie's coffee shop and demanded he take them both home. Jamie felt he had no choice but to comply.

This girl is rude, he thought, ensuring Bonnie was secure before helping Aurora into the car. As he drove, he hoped neither of them would be sick.

Jamie glanced at Bonnie, her head resting against the window, eyes closed. Aurora, sitting in the front, was silent, seemingly lost in thought. Jamie's mind raced, wondering what to do next. The night had taken an unexpected turn and he had to figure out how to handle the situation responsibly.

CHAPTER 8

Sponsor Deal

The previous day, Wednesday, Bonnie's attention had shifted to her crucial meetings. "Bonnie, you're running late," she muttered to herself, anxiously glancing at the clock. "This is the biggest deal you're ever going to get. What are you playing at?" She had been home in good time after her run, and the camper van was running like a dream. She loved that vehicle so much. Determined to be prepared, Bonnie decided to get her surfing gear ready and pop some supplies in the van, just in case she had a late evening.

As Bonnie busied herself, she failed to notice the presence of someone else in her house until she saw the bike. "Aurora?" she cried, opening the door to a scene that resembled a porn movie. Aurora, completely engrossed with Byron, was riding him, and not just on their bikes.

Aurora's hand pressed against Byron's chest, holding

him down as she took him inside her. Her hips moved rhythmically, matching his thrusts. Aurora's eyes gleamed in the semi-darkness, visibly enjoying herself. Her breaths were shallow and rapid, a soft moan escaping her lips with each movement. Byron's hands gripped her thighs, their bodies moving in perfect sync. The air was thick with the scent of sweat and lust.

Aurora's back arched as she quickened her pace, her fingers digging into Byron's chest. The sound of their bodies colliding filled the room, a rhythmic, almost hypnotic beat. "Aurora, what the fuck?" Bonnie stormed in, eyes wide. "What the hell, you two? Please, stop!" She closed her eyes, turned away, and went upstairs to get ready.

When she got out of the shower, they were still at it. Aurora's moans had grown louder, more desperate, mingling with Byron's groans of pleasure. Bonnie, now more frustrated than ever, fumed, "I'm so late now. You two better be finished when I come down."

"I'm sorry, Bonnie," Aurora panted, her voice heavy with desire. "We were that close; we couldn't stop." She gasped, riding Byron harder, her body trembling with the effort. "I'll make it up to you. First, we need to get you to your meeting. Hop on the bike; I'll get you there, and we'll talk afterward about what just happened. Are we good, Bonnie?"

"Whatever, Aurora. You better make it up to me. I really don't want to see that again. I don't know what's worse: hearing you or seeing you." Bonnie shook her head, trying to erase the image from her mind.

Leaving the camper behind, Bonnie allowed Aurora to drop her off. She arrived just as her agent was about to call her. This was a massive deal and if she wasn't careful, she was going to lose it. It's not every day that Nike wants to sponsor you. "Good luck, Bonnie. See you later to celebrate or maybe tomorrow night," her agent said.

The meeting was little more than formalities. Nike wanted an athlete who could create a love mark for customers, and Bonnie was it. She had a story full of emotion, family values, and conflict, but above everything, was someone who had achieved more than they could have imagined through hard work. Bonnie embodied Nike's core values and the belief that 'every athlete in the world' deserves to be represented. She wasn't the world number one or even in the top ten, but she had something people would buy into and follow.

*

Meanwhile, Mick continued to experience intermittent chest discomfort. He decided to keep it to himself, not wanting to distract Bonnie during her crucial meetings. Joanna, however, grew increasingly uneasy about his condition.

By the time Bonnie wrapped up her meetings, Joanna, unable to contain her worry any longer, shared Mick's symptoms with her. Concerned, Bonnie insisted they take Mick to the hospital for a check-up.

Aurora had no idea what had happened. "Bonnie, girl, I told you." She was waiting outside with the van. Bonnie ran towards her and jumped into her arms. "I'm still mad at you for this morning. You need to make it up to me."

"No worries, my sexy lady. I've got you a wild night out planned," Aurora replied.

Bonnie's agent planned to release a statement and post something on her social media in a few hours. "You did well today, Bonnie. Remember, your story isn't over yet. This is the start of something special."

Bonnie understood that with such a high-level sponsor would come crossover work, and her profile would reach millions more. Aurora urged her to get in the van quickly as she was starting to attract attention already. Luckily, the van had blacked-out windows in the back. Bonnie quickly got in. "Hold on, girl." Aurora suddenly drove off.

"Beach now, Aurora. I don't care what you thought you had planned; I'm surfing."

Bonnie received a call from the hospital. The medical staff had conducted various tests to determine the cause of Mick's discomfort. The results revealed a heart condition that required immediate attention. The news was shocking for the Florence family, especially Bonnie, who felt a mixture of guilt for not being there earlier and concern for her father's well-being.

Mick, always the strong and supportive figure in Bonnie's life, now found himself facing a health challenge. Bonnie placed her Bose earbuds in, looked through Apple Music, and said, "What's this? Best of Blink 182 and Green Day. Why not?"

Aurora tried to talk to Bonnie the whole drive, but Bonnie didn't say a word to her. She had forgiven Aurora and wasn't in the slightest bit bothered about catching her and Byron having sex. Bonnie thought to herself that Aurora should really work on her legs and bum as they weren't that toned. They even looked a little wobbly and disappointing.

Aurora was getting annoyed that Bonnie was ignoring

her. In typical fashion, she did her best to get her attention by throwing things into the back or trying to lean back and give her a little slap.

The beach was just ahead and as the road began to narrow, Aurora had to slow down as there were plenty of people on either side of the road, some women with barely covered bottoms. Aurora smiled, even admiring a good-looking female body. Bonnie wanted to spend the afternoon catching waves, feeling that intense rush of adrenaline and excitement. She wanted that perfect wave to come.

Looking out onto the beach, she said to Aurora, "I can't believe it. Look down there." A crowd had gathered, about 30 or so young people. They could hear laughter, chatter, and the waves crashing against the shore. There was something in the area that Bonnie didn't like today. Within the gathering, some were engaging in volleyball, their energetic shouts providing the soundtrack of the sea breeze.

"What do you mean? Let's get amongst it," said Aurora. She had already stripped off, just wearing a little T-shirt and thong bikini.

"You need to work on that bum of yours. Remember, I've seen that wobbling today." Bonnie laughed, proceeding to give Aurora's bum a big slap. "Definitely disappointing, that bum of yours, Aurora."

"What the hell? You've left a mark, Bonnie."

"I thought you liked being marked. Get over it."

Both girls continued down to the beach, exchanging harmless banter. Aurora turned to Bonnie. "Sorry about this morning. It wasn't the best idea I've had, especially as it was your big day. So, am I going to get some leftover stash when you get your first order from Nike?" she asked.

"No, you don't fit the brand. I'm not having you make me look bad wearing the same stuff as me." Bonnie knew that having such a big sponsor would mean building lasting relationships with everyone she met. She was on board with Nike's purpose to unite the world through sport, creating a healthy planet, active communities, and maximising people's potential. More importantly, improving lives through sports and creating a better future for all.

They could smell the rich, sweet smoke of barbecue in the air. A shout from the crowd: "Florence, what the fuck?" Bonnie recognised that annoying voice. The girls turned to each other, saying, "Addison."

Addison wasn't Aurora's biggest fan, probably due to both of them having slept with Byron. She always had to outdo everyone.

Bonnie knew Addison from high school but more recently as Daniella's two youngest kids went to the childcare centre she worked at. From time to time, Bonnie picked up the little hyena, Jack.

At one time Bonnie thought Daniella and Addison even had a little sexual thing going on.

Addison's first words to the girls were, "Do you want some sausage? Come on, I know how much you love a big sausage," laughing as she proceeded to deep-throat the meat. "Well, it's contagious… It makes you want to have it."

Comments like this made both Bonnie and Aurora roll their eyes. "Why is it that every other word has to be some sort of innuendo bingo with you, Addison?" Bonnie shook her head.

Addison just smiled, then licked her lips and said, "Come on, girls. Join us."

There were a few younger surfers trying to catch some waves. Bonnie could see they were lacking a little etiquette. Some were paddling around to get into the inside position, and a few were dropping in. Dropping in means that the surfer who is up and riding inside to the peak of the wave (the part that breaks into white water first) has priority on that wave. The person who dropped in should immediately get off. Bonnie noticed this and said she would have a word with the young guys when she was out there.

Aurora sat with a beer as Bonnie entered the water. At this point, the crowd noticed, and someone said, "Isn't that Bonnie Florence?" Aurora smiled, kept quiet, and enjoyed the show.

Bonnie paddled out, and the sea cleared as if to say, "It's your time now." She was the only one out there. Sat on her board, she looked out to sea and said, "What a feeling." A calm took over her body as she controlled her breathing and closed her eyes. The crowd was in amazement. Bonnie was fantastic; she looked at peace, as if she belonged in the water.

Bonnie felt the rush of the waves beneath her as she paddled out, the sea becoming her sanctuary. The crowd on the beach didn't faze her; she was in her element. Surfing was not just a sport for her; it was a connection to something deeper, an escape from the chaos of everyday life.

The beachgoers, now aware that they were witnessing a performance by the renowned surfer Bonnie Florence, were in awe. Aurora sat on the shore, nursing her beer, her eyes fixed on Bonnie with admiration. The atmosphere held a mix of excitement and reverence for the surfing legend.

Meanwhile, Addison, the provocateur of the group, continued with her suggestive banter, trying to lure Bonnie and Aurora into her playful antics. Her innuendos and double entendres were met with eye rolls and amused sighs from the two friends. Addison's persistent attempts to get a reaction only fuelled Bonnie's determination to focus on the waves.

As she paddled into position, she noticed the group of younger surfers who seemed unfamiliar with proper etiquette. Dropping in on waves and not respecting the priority rules, they disrupted the rhythm of the lineup. Bonnie made a mental note to address this after her session.

In the water, Bonnie embraced the rhythm of the ocean, catching waves with grace and precision. The crowd watched in awe as she navigated the waves effortlessly. Her surfing was a symphony, each move a carefully choreographed dance with the sea.

Back on the beach, Aurora finished her beer and approached Addison. The tension between them was palpable, fuelled by past conflicts and shared romantic entanglements. The dynamic between Bonnie, Aurora, and Addison added an intriguing layer to the beach scene.

As Bonnie emerged from the water, she was greeted with cheers from the onlookers. The younger surfers who had been disrupting the lineup were now attentive, perhaps realising the privilege of sharing the waves with a surfing icon. Bonnie, though focused on her craft, decided it was a teachable moment.

Approaching the group, she offered some friendly advice on surfing etiquette and the importance of respecting the lineup. The younger surfers, a bit starstruck and chastened, listened attentively to Bonnie's guidance. Observing from a distance, Aurora and Addison shared a glance that hinted at a begrudging respect for Bonnie's authority in the water.

The sun began to set, casting a warm glow on the beach. Bonnie, having shared her wisdom with the next generation of surfers, returned to the others. The three women, each with their unique energy, stood together facing the sea. The tension from the earlier encounter had dissipated, replaced by a shared moment of appreciation for the beauty of the ocean and the bonds forged through surfing.

As the day drew to a close, the trio, with their complicated history and unspoken connections, embraced the magic of the beach, leaving behind the marks of laughter, rivalry, and the enduring love for the sea. The sun dipped below the horizon, casting long shadows on the sand, and the beach became a tranquil haven bathed in the echoes of a day well spent.

CHAPTER 9

Physical Attraction, Chemical Reaction

Aurora, now sitting in the back with Bonnie, seemed to be in a playful mood. Despite the chaos at the club, she started to tease Jamie, making suggestive remarks and touching his shoulder. Jamie was trying to focus on the road and keep the atmosphere calm, but Aurora's behaviour was making it challenging.

Bonnie, still recovering from the incident at the club, was slouched in the back seat, occasionally muttering something unintelligible. Jamie wasn't sure if she was aware of what was happening around her. Aurora, on the other hand, seemed determined to make the car ride more interesting.

As they approached Jamie's place, he contemplated how to handle the situation. He wanted to ensure Bonnie's safety and well-being but dealing with a drunk and flirtatious Aurora added an unexpected layer of complexity.

Upon reaching their destination, Jamie helped Bonnie out of the car and walked her to the door. Still in a mischievous mood, Aurora wanted to continue with a nightcap. Jamie hesitated, considering the circumstances. Undeterred, she leaned in and whispered something to Bonnie, who responded with a faint smile. Jamie couldn't quite catch the conversation so took a deep breath, processing the events that had unfolded. He decided it was best to maintain a professional distance from Aurora and focus on ensuring Bonnie's safety. However, the unexpected twists of the night left him with a lingering sense of curiosity and a newfound awareness of the unpredictable nature of life.

Jamie had felt a little nervous with two very drunk girls in his car. It was now into the early hours of Friday morning. Bonnie had more or less passed out in the back; Aurora, on the other hand, was demanding pizza.

"Look, we are not going back out. If you want to go out, I don't care about you." Jamie was getting a little irritated with the attitude now. After all, he was trying to help. Maybe he should have called a cab. What was he thinking?

Somehow he managed to get both girls into his flat. He left Aurora to it; she found a place at one end of his sofa and within minutes Jamie could hear snoring. She was fast asleep. Bonnie, on the other hand, needed a little more help. Jamie managed to get her into his bedroom and luckily, she had started to sober up.

She remembered that face. "Thanks for looking after

me. Maybe we can go for that next cup of coffee now. Did you think I didn't remember? I saw you at the club looking over at me... I think I'm going to be sick."

Jamie managed to get Bonnie to the toilet. She needed a shower now as she'd been sick everywhere. Poor Jamie. Lucky for him, Bonnie was able to get herself undressed. He didn't want to look, but he did.

Stumbling into the shower, Bonnie quickly pulled the door closed behind her so as not to get any water on the floor. She also didn't want Jamie to see her like this. She stood up, took her bra off, and put her head under the warm water.

Jamie placed his shirt down on the floor and begin to take off his pants and underwear. As he rolled them off, his legs got colder. He noticed they had sick on them so grabbed a cloth and used it to clean himself up as best as he could.

"Are you okay in there?" Jamie stood outside the shower with towels, and some of his best joggers and a T-shirt for her to wear.

"Thanks, I won't be a minute. I'm feeling much better now. I'm sorry. I didn't want to meet you again like this." Bonnie was a little embarrassed. *There's no way he'll like me after tonight*, she thought.

With relief, as Jamie had left the room, Bonnie noticed the towels and clothes left out for her. She quickly dressed and had already decided she couldn't go home. Luckily, Aurora would be there to protect her if Jamie turned out to be the ultimate weirdo. The streets were dangerous and there were too many weirdos around nowadays. Or maybe

Jamie would think they were the weird ones, staying at a stranger's flat. Aurora wasn't going to be much help, though; she was laid with her head back, mouth open, snoring.

Bonnie made her way into Jamie's room. The floor was a little cold and this travelled up into her legs. All she wanted to do was curl up under the covers "Hey. Thank you for this." Bonnie climbed into bed and pulled the covers up just under her chin.

Jamie sat next to her on the edge of the bed, placing a glass of water on the bedside table. "I don't know. It's fine, Bonnie, you don't have to thank me. I wanted to help you."

Her eyes began to close. "Thanks, Jamie. I really hope we can go for that second coffee tomorrow. I do really like you, even though I don't know you. You make me feel safe."

Bonnie's voice was lowering, and Jamie could barely make out what she was saying. "I feel the same and you fall asleep before I get to say I like you." Jamie looked at her, smiled, and then pulled a blanket from the bottom of the bed up to her shoulders. As Aurora was at one end of the sofa Jamie positioned himself at the other end, knowing he wouldn't get much sleep. Jamie didn't care.

*

Bonnie woke. The bed was comfy and Aurora was lying next to her. As she looked around, she thought this was strange. She'd had way too much to drink and her head was hurting. It felt very similar to the crash after drinking too much caffeine. The behind-the-eyes headache, the nauseous feeling, the sensitivity to light. It basically felt like she'd been hit by a bus.

"Bonnie, how did I get in here? The last thing I remember, I was sat at the end of the sofa in the other room."

Bonnie heard footsteps. Her breathing began to change. Her chest felt tight.

Jamie walked in with two cups of coffee. "I thought you both would need this after last night, and thanks for smashing into every wall when you decided to get up from the sofa."

Aurora looked at Bonnie and thought, *Oh well, the wall shouldn't have been there.*

"I'll leave you both to get changed or showered. If you both want to borrow some stuff, that's fine."

Bonnie was a little embarrassed and replied in a low pitch, "Thank you. That would be great."

Jamie thought to himself, *Bacon, eggs, toast. Don't ask them, just get on with cooking.*

Aurora turned to Bonnie. "What was that! Oh my god, that was sooooo sexy of you. Come on, I know you like him. Wasn't he the one from the other day? If you don't, I will."

"Stop it. I feel like shit and probably don't look much better."

"Bacon, eggs." Bonnie could smell the cooking. It brought back memories of her mum cooking breakfast. It was like pyjamas and a fresh paper. It smelled like little white grease bubbles in the crispy black frying pan. *Awesome.*

If there was one way into Bonnie's heart, it was through food. For her, this was the most habitual meal of the day, a routine so key to her inner well-being you could call it a psychic anchor. "Four bloody Marys then for me, a half-pound of either sausage, bacon, or corned-beef hash with diced chillis, plus quite a few other things," shouted Aurora.

"Aurora, stop messing around and let the man cook." Bonnie was happy with a simple breakfast and the coffee.

Everything was neatly laid out; Jamie had placed Bonnie and Aurora's plates at the other side of the kitchen island. The coffee machine was warming up again.

Aurora was simply dressed in her outfit from the night before. Bonnie, on the other hand, was in Jamie's grey joggers and T-shirt. He thought she looked cute wearing his sweatpants; it was out of the ordinary. Aurora had already made a call and one of the guys from Bonnie's father's garage was on his way to pick up both girls.

"It's Jamie, isn't it? I'm really sorry, but we need to get off. Thanks for the hospitality. I'm sure Bonnie will give you her number and make it up to you. Right, Bonnie?"

She didn't reply, busy eating her bacon and eggs, instead just thought, *I wish Aurora would give it a rest. She'll scare him off.*

Jamie thought he would try to change the topic as he noticed Bonnie had started to go red in the face. About 20 minutes passed and no one said much; it wasn't an uncomfortable silence as Aurora was sitting on the sofa playing on her phone. Bonnie and Jamie were not sitting that far apart, mirroring both breathing patterns and hand and body movements. Both would make eye contact and then look away. Bonnie wanted to ask, 'So you're married, or you have a girlfriend? How can a man so attractive be alone in this world? I'm lucky to have met you.'

Jamie assumed she must be married or otherwise have someone. *How can a woman so attractive be alone in this world? I'm lucky to have met you.*

Aurora's phone went off. "Yep, we'll be down in a few minutes. Bonnie, we need to go."

"I'll walk you down. After all, you need to give me your number so I can get my clothes back and return yours." Jamie followed Bonnie all the way to the car waiting for them.

Turning to Jamie before getting into the car, "So, tell me, am I lucky to have met you? Don't answer yet, I left my number for you in your flat," Bonnie gave him a kiss on the cheek.

As they drove off Jamie couldn't help wondering when he would see her again. He wanted to message her straight away and why not? He liked her and didn't want to play games. More often than not, nowadays all people say is, 'Don't message them straight away and definitely don't reply to a message straight away; you need to play hard to get.' This was different. Jamie felt the hairs stand on the back of his neck when he thought about Bonnie.

Bonnie spent the whole drive back to Mick's garage wondering when Jamie would message. "I should have got his number, Aurora." She immediately regretted saying that as Aurora would now just take the mickey.

"Please tell me you haven't told him you like him. If you have, shall we turn back so you can both get a room? You disappoint me, Bonnie. I thought you were made of stronger stuff. I bet you're getting wet thinking about him now, aren't you?" Aurora couldn't help herself. She tried to keep a straight face but couldn't contain herself anymore and burst out laughing.

*

Jamie had made himself a coffee and stood staring at Bonnie's number, thinking, *Close your eyes and be brave. You were in the military.* The parachute regiment was famed the world over for their ability to overcome physical and mental challenges so why was this girl making Jamie go weak at the knees? The attention and interest from Bonnie, was this lust or falling in love? It seemed irrational but that's what typically happens when boy meets girl and intentions are honest. Or could it be that between the knees, or rather the legs, are the genitals, full of nerves? When those are triggered an inward motion occurs, which can make it seem as though the problem originated in the knees.

Jamie laughed at himself. *Sod it. Message her. What's the worst that could happen?*

*

Bonnie's phoned pinged. Her heart jumped a few beats. Before she could read the message Aurora had taken her phone, read the message, and replied. "You can thank me later. I've just broken the ice for you so you don't spend three days arranging a date."

Bonnie was mortified.

The reply to Jamie was simply: 'I'm wet and I want you inside me.'

The correct response should have been: 'Yes, let go for that second cup of coffee.'

Jamie didn't expect the response he got, as all he had

sent was: 'Hey, let's meet for that second coffee. I'm free tomorrow at 10:00 if this is good for you?'

*

Stood outside the office of the garage, Mick didn't look happy.

"You're late. The lads are waiting for you, Aurora. You need to make it up to them."

Bonnie could tell her dad wasn't in the best mood as he didn't say anything to her, it was just a look. She followed him into his office.

"Mum, what are you doing here! You trying to seduce Dad in the office with your sexy ways?"

"It wouldn't take much now, would it, Bonnie? I am, after all, a renowned therapist." Joanna quickly changed her tone, opened up her Instagram and showed Bonnie. "Take a look. This girl is the spitting image of you. Please tell me it's not as bad as it looks." And there it was. Someone had filmed her, extremely drunk, just before she fell.

Bonnie's face turned white. She had that feeling of impending doom spreading over her body.

She sat next to her dad on the sofa where she had cuddled up to him so many times before, and felt safe. "Look, the problem now is that everything we do, people have access to. You are unable to hide. I'm sure it will be fine and won't affect the sponsor deal."

Mick turned from being disappointed to wanting to protect his daughter. He knew a little thing like this would really affect her confidence.

Mum, on the other hand, wanted to know who the very

handsome man who helped her up and carried her off was. This hadn't gone unnoticed.

Joanna brought coffee over, and got straight to the point. "Bonnie, so you and Aurora were... Did you stay last night, then? Don't answer that yet. Have you both been silly? We all know what Aurora is like with men." Joanna could tell the girls had stayed at this stranger's place but wasn't sure. She just wanted to know they were both safe. "I'm just asking this as I'm still your mum and want the best for you. You're here now so drink your coffee and we can drive you home. You can tell me all about this, should I say, stranger."

Bonnie's colour came back instantly and felt herself going a little red. Forget about the Instagram post, she felt more embarrassed about telling her mum what had happened. Bonnie knew she was about to get a lecture about how irresponsible she was. Adding fuel to the fire, her phone pinged with a message from Jamie. She hesitated to open it in front of her parents but decided to take a quick glance. The message read: 'Coffee tomorrow at 10 sounds good. Looking forward to it.'

Joanna noticed Bonnie's smile as she read the message, and her curiosity got the best of her. "Bonnie, spill the beans. Who is this guy, and why does he have you smiling like that?"

Bonnie blushed but decided to share a bit about Jamie with her mum. She recounted the events from the night before, highlighting how Jamie had helped them when they were both in a state. Joanna listened with a mix of concern and amusement, realising that her daughter had found herself in a bit of an unconventional situation.

After hearing Bonnie's story, her expression softened. "Well, it sounds like this Jamie is a decent guy. Just be careful and remember to keep things responsible. And if you need a ride home tonight, just let us know."

Bonnie nodded, grateful for her mum's understanding. As she finished her coffee, she couldn't shake the excitement of the upcoming date with Jamie.

Despite the initial embarrassment and concerns, Bonnie felt a spark of something special, and she was eager to explore where it might lead.

Aurora then decided to lighten the mood with one of her infamous stories. She knew how to push Bonnie's buttons and couldn't resist the opportunity to embarrass her friend in front of her parents.

"So, Mr. and Mrs. Florence," Aurora began with a mischievous glint in her eye, "let me tell you about this one time Bonnie and I had the most hilarious adventure. It was during our vacation last summer, remember that, Bon?"

Bonnie's eyes widened in horror, knowing exactly where this was going. "Aurora, no…"

Bonnie's protest was ignored and Aurora continued. "We were at this beach resort, and Bonnie met this incredibly handsome lifeguard named Jake. Now, Jake was not only gorgeous but also very attentive. One evening, after a few too many cocktails, Bonnie and Jake decided to go for a midnight swim."

Joanna raised an eyebrow, intrigued. "A midnight swim, you say?"

"Yes." Aurora nodded, her smile growing wider. "It was all very romantic. They swam out to a secluded part of the beach where the moonlight was shimmering on the water. They ended up on a private little cove, and let's just say, things got quite steamy."

Bonnie's face turned beet red. "Aurora, please stop!"

But she was on a roll. "So, there they were, under the stars, the waves gently crashing around them, and things were heating up. They couldn't keep their hands off each other, and next thing you know, they were making passionate love right there on the beach."

Mick, who had been trying to maintain a neutral expression, choked on his coffee. Joanna's eyes widened in surprise, a mix of amusement and disbelief.

"Aurora, that's enough!" Bonnie's voice was a mix of embarrassment and frustration.

She finally relented, laughing. "All right, all right, I'm just messing with you all. It didn't go that far. They just kissed and maybe a little more, but nothing too scandalous."

Bonnie buried her face in her hands, groaning. "I can't believe you just told that story."

Joanna chuckled, giving Bonnie a reassuring pat on the back. "It's okay, Bonnie. We were young once too. And besides, it sounds like you had a memorable vacation."

Mick, still recovering from his shock, managed a weak smile. "Just... maybe keep the more detailed stories to yourselves next time, all right?"

Thoroughly enjoying herself, Aurora gave Bonnie a playful wink. "Don't worry, Mr. Florence. I'll make sure to keep it PG next time."

As they finished their coffee, the tension in the room

eased and conversation shifted to lighter topics. Despite the embarrassment, Bonnie couldn't help but smile at her friend's antics. It was just another unexpected twist in a day full of surprises, and she knew that with friends like Aurora, life would never be boring.

Later that evening, Bonnie, Aurora, and Joanna left the garage together. The day had taken unexpected turns, but Bonnie couldn't deny that it had been filled with laughter and the promise of new beginnings. As they drove home, Bonnie reflected on the strange twists of fate that had brought her to Jamie's flat and how, against all odds, it might just be the start of something wonderful.

CHAPTER 10

Can You Mend the Broken?

Jamie didn't sleep well Friday night. He was a little overtired from the events of Thursday evening at the club. Trying to keep himself busy all day Saturday, he had an early gym session followed by a sauna and steam. He even cleaned his flat from head to toe. Later that evening, he had a FaceTime call with his sister, Lauren, in the UK. She had a two-year-old, so he knew she would be up and about due to the time difference. Lauren was also really into her fitness, just like Jamie; she and her husband Andy had a big double garage where they trained.

Jamie's family was massively into rugby union. Their father, John, was a schoolteacher who also played and coached rugby. Lauren and Jamie often reminisced over some of the stories their dad told them about back in the day. John had coached Jamie's team from a young age. There were some awesome stories, but as Jamie joined the military at 18, he never really played much Colts rugby for his local team, which he kind of regretted, as he couldn't get that time back.

Today's story, which they didn't know how they got onto, was after an East Yorkshire schools match. Jamie's dad had borrowed the school minibus as 10 of the players from the same club were playing in the team. Lauren always went along to watch, and to be fair, she was probably better than most of the boys due to her speed. It was late, travelling back, and John had decided they were going to take some back roads renowned for wild camping, or travellers at the side of the road. John stopped just before turning down the back lane and said to the lads, "Right, just out and get some rocks. You're going to throw them at whoever is up ahead." The stupid thing was, the minibus had the school's name down the side.

"This was so silly, Lauren, wasn't it? We were only 15. What the hell was Dad thinking?"

"It was funny, though, wasn't it, seeing you lads hanging out the back door of the minibus throwing rocks?"

This is the sort of thing you would be locked up for now. Jamie had done many stupid things, but thinking back to it, a schoolteacher letting 15-year-olds hang out of a moving vehicle was ridiculous. And in the school bus! Lauren remembered the other coach saying, "Don't tell your mums about this," as everyone was getting way too excited about throwing rocks. These days, it would be all over Instagram just for likes. Jamie did think the world had gone a little mad – you couldn't get away with anything.

Reminiscing about their dad was part of the healing process for them both, as he had died a few years ago from prostate cancer.

"Do you ever think about how different things might have been if Dad were still here?" Jamie asked, a tinge of melancholy in his voice.

"All the time," Lauren replied softly. "I miss his crazy stories and the way he always knew how to make us laugh, no matter what."

"Yeah, he had a way of making everything seem like an adventure," Jamie said, a smile tugging at the corners of his mouth. "Even something as simple as a drive back from a rugby match."

They fell into a comfortable silence, each lost in their own memories. For Jamie, these conversations with Lauren were a lifeline, a way to stay connected to their past and to the man who had shaped so much of who they were.

"Jamie," Lauren broke the silence, "are you okay? You seem a bit... off."

"Just tired, I guess." He shrugged. "Thursday night was pretty intense. I had to take care of two very drunk girls, and it brought back a lot of memories. Made me think about how Dad would have handled it."

Lauren chuckled. "He probably would have turned it into some kind of adventure too. 'Right, Jamie, we're going to navigate these wild waters and rescue the damsels in distress!'"

Jamie laughed. "Yeah, he would have. I just hope I did okay. I want to be someone he would have been proud of."

"He would be proud of you, Jamie. You're a good man, just like he was."

He felt the weight of guilt as he remembered that he hadn't been around much for his family during the five years from his dad's first diagnosis to his passing. A military life didn't help with that. The first four years, his dad was doing okay; everything was kept under control with medication. But like everything, when those stopped working, they moved on to chemotherapy, then radiotherapy, and blood transfusions every few weeks.

Cancer is a horrible thing to see someone go through. Toward the end, Lauren was helping her mum every day due to their dad's deteriorating condition.

Anyone who has gone through this knows the struggles when cancer gets into the bones. Lauren recalls one morning describing her dad as looking like Gollum from *The Lord of the Rings* when seeing him just out of bed, trying to get to the bathroom. The stories kept him alive, and like any good memory, they brought Lauren and Jamie a little closer together.

Jamie felt he needed to tell his sister about Bonnie. He didn't really know her, but it felt right. It wasn't long before Lauren stopped Jamie and said, "Please don't just shag her. Remember, she may just have feelings, unlike most of the girls you have banged, shall we say."

Jamie didn't say anything for a moment. There was a long pause before he simply responded, "Yes, I've been a twat. Go on, say it – 'all you want to do is get your dick wet'."

Lauren wasn't a naïve girl. She knew all too well what rugby lads could be like and had fallen victim a few times in her younger days to lads talking total bull just to get her into bed.

"And on that note, Lauren, until next time. See you later." Jamie finished the call with a smile on his face.

As he put down his phone, Jamie reflected on Lauren's words. He knew she was right. He had to approach things with Bonnie differently. The memories of their dad's struggle and the bond it had strengthened between him and Lauren were a reminder that life was too short for meaningless encounters. He wanted more now, something real, and perhaps Bonnie was the beginning of that change.

Jamie had started reading more recently, driven by his passion for a good science-fiction novel, but also hoping it would help him fall asleep. One night, on a whim, he picked up a dark romance recommended by a friend. It was way out of his comfort zone, but he figured it was better than watching porn. The problem, though, was that these books often left him thinking about sex all night, waking up with the biggest erection and wishing he could have some naughty fun.

The chapter he had just finished was especially provocative. It described a strange ritual where men would take ownership of their partners, involving explicit acts that made Jamie's heart race. The passage read:

"Open your mouth." Her wide eyes gazed at the man's dick in terror. She gripped the base as it slid into the back of her throat. He wasn't gentle, and her gagging filled the room. Her head was controlled, bouncing up and down on his dick. When she tried to pull away, he gripped her hair harder, forcing more cock down her throat, making her gag again while his other hand explored her ass, sliding a finger deep inside her. His balls tightened as he forced her to

swallow, shoving her head down one last time.

Jamie did not expect this from the book, but for some reason, it excited him. It was a far cry from the stories of distant galaxies and futuristic technologies he was used to, yet it stirred something primal within him. The vivid imagery and raw intensity of the scene lingered in his mind long after he closed the book. It was a different kind of thrill, one that made him question his own desires and boundaries.

As he lay in bed, Jamie couldn't help but imagine Bonnie in such a scenario, feeling a mix of arousal and guilt. He needed to approach his feelings for her with respect, but these fantasies were hard to shake. He turned off the light and tried to focus on the sound of his breathing, hoping sleep would soon claim him. Yet, the words of the dark romance danced in his mind, intertwining with his own longing, making him eager for the next encounter both in the pages of his book and perhaps with Bonnie.

He found himself eagerly diving back into the dark romance, his curiosity piqued and his arousal undeniable. The next chapter began with the aftermath of the intense ritual. The narrative described how the woman, named Elena, was led to a secluded chamber adorned with dim, flickering candles and plush, velvet cushions. Her wrists were still bound, but the tension in her body had shifted from fear to a strange, intoxicating mix of submission and desire.

As she entered the room, the man, Dominic, untied her wrists and gently massaged the marks left by the bindings. His touch was surprisingly tender, a stark contrast to the brutal dominance he had displayed earlier. Elena's heart raced as she felt the dichotomy of his actions – the roughness that took her breath away and the gentleness that made her crave more.

Dominic whispered in her ear, his voice a low, commanding growl. "Tonight, you will learn the true meaning of surrender." He kissed the nape of her neck, his lips trailing down her spine, sending shivers through her entire body. He instructed her to kneel on one of the cushions, her back arched and her hands resting on her thighs.

"Eyes closed," he commanded, and Elena obeyed, her breaths coming in shallow gasps. She felt the soft brush of feathers against her skin as Dominic began to tease her with a flogger, each stroke more tantalising than the last. Her skin prickled with anticipation, the light touches igniting a fire within her.

Without warning, the flogger was replaced by the firm grip of Dominic's hand. He tilted her head back, capturing her mouth in a fierce, possessive kiss. Elena moaned into his mouth, her body responding instinctively to his touch. His hands roamed over her curves, squeezing and caressing, making her arch into him, desperate for more.

Dominic broke the kiss, leaving Elena breathless and wanting. "Stand," he ordered, and she complied, her legs trembling. He guided her to a large, four-poster bed draped in luxurious fabrics. With a swift motion, he pushed her onto it, spreading her legs wide. Elena's pulse quickened as he positioned himself between her thighs.

He began to kiss her inner thighs, slowly working his way up to her aching core. Each kiss was a promise, a tease that left her gasping for breath. When his tongue finally flicked against her clit, Elena cried out, her hips bucking involuntarily. Dominic held her steady, his tongue and fingers working in perfect harmony to bring her to the edge of ecstasy.

As the waves of pleasure crashed over her, Elena's hands gripped the sheets, her body quivering with the intensity of her release. Dominic didn't stop, continuing his relentless assault until she was a trembling mess beneath him.

Finally, he pulled back, his eyes dark with desire. "Now, it's my turn," he said, his voice dripping with promise. He flipped her onto her stomach, raising her hips and positioning himself at her entrance. With one powerful thrust, he filled her completely, both of them groaning in pleasure.

The pace was brutal, unrelenting, and exactly what Elena craved. Dominic's hands gripped her hips, guiding her back onto his cock with each thrust. She felt him everywhere, consuming her, owning her. The intensity of their connection, the raw passion, was like nothing she had ever experienced.

As they both approached their climax, Dominic leaned down, his breath hot against her ear. "You are mine," he growled, and with a final, deep thrust, they both shattered, their cries echoing through the room.

*

Jamie closed the book, his mind racing. The dark romance had captivated him in a way he hadn't expected, drawing him into a world of intense, forbidden desires. He couldn't help but wonder what it would be like to experience such a connection in real life, to surrender to passion so completely. As he drifted off to sleep, his dreams were filled with visions of dominance and submission, of a love that was both fierce and tender.

*

Bonnie hadn't been feeling great since Thursday night. The lingering hangover anxiety had settled in, leaving her uneasy even though it was now Saturday night. To distract herself, she had taken little Henry to a local toy store known for its impressive Lego collection. They both returned with new sets; Bonnie couldn't resist the Lord of the Rings Rivendell set, indulging in her inner geek. As she pieced together the intricate model, she suddenly realised she hadn't responded to Jamie's message, except for the one Aurora had sent on her behalf.

With a pang of guilt, Bonnie decided it was time to reach out. It was late, but she thought, *To hell with it.* What happened next was one of those moments where you intend to send a message but accidentally hit the call button. Panic set in as she quickly pressed end, knowing Jamie would see a missed call from her. Her heart dropped, and she felt a wave of anxiety wash over her. She needed to calm her racing pulse.

Bonnie put her phone down and went back to her Lego set, a bit more at ease. She fell into a rhythm, her hands working methodically on the model. She allowed herself to get lost in the task, the familiar comfort of Lego building soothing her nerves. This didn't last long so she rushed to the bathroom, where she splashed cold water on her face, trying to steady her nerves. She took a few deep breaths and decided she couldn't leave things as they were. She returned to her phone, contemplating what to say. Just as she was about to text, the phone rang. It was Jamie calling her back.

Jamie, on the other hand, had been in the middle of reading a particularly steamy scene from his book.

The scene began with the protagonist, Dominic, entering a dimly lit room where his partner, Isabella, was waiting. She was blindfolded, her hands bound behind her back, the soft light casting shadows that danced across her bare skin.

*

Dominic approached her, his presence commanding and intense. He whispered in her ear, his voice low and demanding. "You trust me, don't you?"

Isabella nodded, her breath hitching in anticipation.

Dominic's fingers traced the curve of her neck, sending shivers down her spine. He trailed them lower, skimming over her breasts before circling her nipples, eliciting a soft moan from her lips. He loved how responsive she was, how her body reacted to his touch.

He moved behind her, pressing his hard length against her back, his hands sliding down to her hips. "Spread your legs," he ordered. Isabella complied, feeling the heat between her thighs intensify.

Dominic's hand slipped between her legs, his fingers finding her slick and ready. He teased her, his touch light and maddeningly slow, until she was writhing with need. "Please," she begged, her voice trembling.

He chuckled, a dark, satisfied sound. "Not yet," he replied, his fingers withdrawing, leaving her aching and empty. He positioned her on her knees, her ass raised in the air, completely vulnerable to him.

Dominic unfastened his pants, his erection straining against the fabric. He positioned himself at her entrance, teasing her with the head of his cock. Isabella whimpered, her body tensing with desire.

"Tell me what you want," he commanded, his voice a rough whisper.

"I want you inside me," she replied breathlessly. "I need you."

With a powerful thrust, Dominic buried himself deep inside her, eliciting a sharp gasp from Isabella. He set a relentless pace, his hips slamming against her ass, the sound of their bodies coming together echoing in the room. She clenched around him, her moans growing louder with each thrust.

Dominic's hand found its way to her clit, rubbing it in time with his movements. The dual sensations pushed Isabella closer to the edge, her body trembling with the force of her impending climax.

"Come for me," Dominic growled, his voice filled with possessive lust.

Isabella's orgasm crashed over her, waves of pleasure rippling through her body. Her cries filled the room as she convulsed around him, her release triggering Dominic's own. With a final thrust, he spilled into her, their bodies locked in a primal, intimate connection.

*

Jamie felt his own arousal build as he read, his breath

coming faster. The intensity of the scene left him both satisfied and restless, his mind wandering to thoughts of Bonnie. Just then, his phone buzzed with Bonnie's accidental call, jolting him back to reality.

When he saw her name flash on his screen, his heart raced for a different reason. Before he could decide what to do, the call ended. He let out a sigh of relief but then thought, *Should I call her back?* The problem was, Jamie was super horny after reading his book. He literally wanted to have sex now but didn't want to have a conversation with Bonnie with a raging hard-on. He finished himself off instead and it was quick, 30 seconds or something. He laughed to himself, remembering a spinning instructor once saying you can do a lot in 30 seconds.

Jamie pressed call on Bonnie's number. Her phone went off and she jumped off the toilet seat. It must have rung five times. *Answer and say something funny*, she thought. She slid her phone to answer and said, "Make me a winner!" She frequently entered a competition on the radio where you had to say this. Bonnie was also taking a gamble that Jamie would see the funny side as thousands of locals entered this competition.

Jamie paused for just a second. "You're the lucky winner of 10 dollars. You can buy the coffee now," he said. They both let out a laugh. "Tomorrow then, 10:00. You know where I live," Jamie said jokingly.

Bonnie simply said, "You got it, I owe you one. Be ready, I'm a busy girl."

Bonnie and Jamie both ended the call a little confused as to what had happened. Were they going on a date? In any case, they were now going to meet in the morning.

Jamie thought to himself, *You really can do a lot in 30 seconds*, as that was how long the call lasted.

Bonnie didn't believe in 'love at first sight'. She thought you had to know a person to fall in love with them. How could you fall in love with someone you had just met? But that was before she met Jamie. They had collided in the doorway of Robbie's Coffee. After that first meeting, when he bought her that first cup of coffee, she looked up at him and felt her world shift.

What was she thinking, driving over to pick Jamie up? Her heart was racing, and her palms were sweaty. Luckily for Bonnie, he was waiting outside, so she didn't have time to overthink.

Jamie didn't believe in 'love at first sight'. He thought you had to know a person to fall in love with them. How could he fall in love with someone he had just met? This was before he met Bonnie.

Jamie knew a great little coffee shop called Jackdoors. Although he didn't know if it would be open as they randomly closed all the time. Besides this, they did the best flapjack and banoffee cheesecake. Luckily, Jackdoors was open. They had the best coffee and ended up treating themselves to dinner and a movie.

Afterwards, Jamie suggested a walk. They ended up on a play set in a park, talking about everything and anything. It was 3 a.m. when Bonnie needed to go home.

Outside Jamie's flat, there was a little silence that hadn't been there for hours. Bonnie wanted Jamie to kiss her. Jamie wanted to kiss Bonnie. Jamie wanted to kiss Bonnie once, twice. He realised he would never have enough.

Suddenly, he was kissing her. He was everywhere: up her back and over her arms, and kissing her harder, deeper, with a fervent, urgent need Bonnie had never known before. Jamie felt his lips come against Bonnie's, little shivers of panic and pleasure shooting through him. Both felt something. It was just a look. Jamie took Bonnie by the hand and made his way inside.

Once inside, Jamie pushed her hard against the wall, gripping her hair, yanking her head up. He kissed her neck and down towards her breasts. Then a calm settled over them. Touches became soft as they held each other, looking into one another's eyes. "Shall we make our way to your bed?" Bonnie whispered. Jamie didn't say a word.

*

Standing at the edge of the bed with Jamie close, Bonnie whispered, "You must be tired, Jamie."

"Yes, I'm tired but not anymore. Are you?" Jamie responded, his voice husky.

Bonnie felt Jamie's lips come against hers. His hands dropped to her shoulders, skimmed down her arms, and came to rest at the small of her back. Slowly undressing each other seemed to take a lifetime. For both Jamie and Bonnie there was a sense of something they had never felt before. The kisses from Jamie grew stronger once more as they lowered to the bed, staying as close as they could, never breaking eye contact.

Jamie could feel Bonnie's beating heart. Her legs wrapped around his body as they started to move as one. Jamie's breathing became more intense as he could feel himself climaxing and becoming harder inside Bonnie.

Bonnie flushed, as blood rushed to her chest and face. She had never come like this before; this didn't normally happen the first time.

As both began to doze off, they felt close. A warmth filled them as they held each other tight before relaxing as their breathing slowed.

*

Light shining through Jamie's window woke them. Still feeling close and warm, they shared a smile. "So, tell me. You have a girlfriend, Jamie?"

"No."

"Gay? How come a man so attractive, intelligent, well-spoken, and different in a seductive way, powerful, be all alone in this world?"

Jamie didn't say anything. He wasn't ready to go through the trauma of the things he had seen in the military or the passing of his father.

He did feel alone at times. Perhaps he should have stayed in the UK, closer to his sister and mum. If he had stayed, he would have felt lost. His life had brought him to this moment. "At times, I do feel alone. I'm lucky to have met you."

Bonnie didn't want to press any further and just replied, "I'm lucky to have met you too."

She needed to head home. School surf lessons started at 9:00, and she was due in at 11:00. She felt great; sleep didn't seem to matter in this moment. Jamie kissed Bonnie softly, holding her a little closer to him. Their warmth seemed to travel through their bodies. Bonnie wanted

Jamie inside her again. She could feel the sexual energy building, then Jamie pulled away.

"Come on, let's get you off. We can carry this on another time."

Bonnie was disappointed but also relieved. Jamie didn't just want sex from her; he seemed genuine with everything he said and did. She loved this.

As Jamie walked her out to her car, he stopped just before opening the door and turned her close to him, softly kissing her lips as if it was the first time again.

"Come meet me this afternoon at the surf club. I'll be finished around 4:00. We can do a little run, then go for that second date."

Bonnie couldn't believe she had just said this, knowing far too well that Madge Ward would be working on reception. Madge would drop Bonnie right in it, as she had no filter when it came to talking to people. She was a lovely lady but also had a screw loose.

"I would love to see you again today. Just don't make us run too far, as I will just end up looking at your bum." Jamie surprised himself with that, too.

"That's okay, you can look at it anytime. 4:00 then?"

"Love to see you later."

Jamie wondered what he had gotten himself into as he waved Bonnie off.

The morning light revealed a different Bonnie and Jamie, both feeling a connection that went beyond the physical. As Bonnie headed to her surf lessons and Jamie embraced the solitude of his flat, they carried the warmth of their shared moments with them.

Throughout the day, Bonnie couldn't help but replay the events in her mind. The undeniable chemistry between her and Jamie lingered in her mind, filling her with a sense of excitement and anticipation for their upcoming rendezvous.

Meanwhile, Jamie couldn't help but dwell on the unexpected turn of events. He had never been one to actively seek out romantic connections, but Bonnie had managed to awaken something within him. As he went about his day, preparing for their afternoon meeting, he couldn't shake the feeling of anticipation that coursed through him.

Despite the distance between them, they carried the spark of their connection with them, eagerly awaiting the chance to see each other again and explore where their newfound bond might lead.

CHAPTER 11

Worthy Love

One day, a husband brought home a bouquet of beautiful roses for his wife. The wife was pleasantly surprised and delighted, but before she could ask what they were for, their daughter piped up, "What are they for, Daddy?" Madge was telling anyone who would listen in the busy reception area of the surf school. Lucky for her, there were no under-18s around; this story was for adults only.

"Madge, we don't want to hear any more of your story, please." David, the owner of the surf school, had to step in sometimes. As funny as Madge was, she could get the school into trouble.

Luckily, most people around these parts knew her reputation. As someone who had stables, she had been into horseback riding in her younger years. She loved a young stallion back then, and no one to this day knew how old she really was. David had a running bet on who would get her to crack and let it slip first. The total was up to 500 dollars.

As the story went, she met her husband while he was on a painting job. Painting her back doors! Apparently, the future husband also 'painted her back doors in' after finishing the job, if you can imagine. When Madge first encountered her husband, he had 'sexy' nailed like a rock star. He possessed all the qualities mentioned and more: he spoke fluently in two foreign languages, cooked like a demon, and danced like Timberlake. He exuded sex appeal, and he knew it. He thought Madge was sexy, too. During those early months of their relationship, he would sometimes fix his stare on her, give a throaty rumble, and tell her that she was sexy. The comment always induced laughter followed by an unstoppable blush. Madge didn't always feel like a sexy woman, though she always saw the 'sexy' in her husband.

Madge had slept naked since the age of 16 and still talked about how she liked the feeling of a naked body next to her every night. So, the story goes.

David thought in some ways, *Good on you, Madge, but please don't tell everyone all the details. There are some things in life you just don't want to know.*

Bonnie hadn't been in long before Madge caught up with her, the shout travelling from one end of the building to the other. "Bonnie, girl, what's this I hear about you and some sexy-looking English bloke I hear from Aurora?"

Bonnie stopped. *What the hell has Aurora said?! Why on Earth would she tell Madge? Everyone will know now.*

"How you doing, Madge? Are you on a cigarette break already? Don't worry, I won't tell Dave," Bonnie said. Madge must be up to something. It was only last week she was found cooking bacon sandwiches for the reception team and then charging them after using ingredients from the surf café. Dave found out due to some stock issues and couldn't believe the downright cheekiness of it.

"Bonnie, let me tell you something, the only man who tells me what to do is my husband. Dave thinks he's in charge, but let's face it, Ronnie and I run things around here," Madge said, a little tongue-in-cheek.

"What's this I hear, Madge? You talking shit again?" Dave asked, coming up behind her.

Madge chuckled and replied, "Oh, Dave, you know I never talk shit. Just sharing some stories, keeping things interesting around here."

Dave rolled his eyes but couldn't hide a smirk. He knew Madge's antics well and appreciated the lively atmosphere she brought to the surf school.

Still puzzled about what Aurora might have said, Bonnie decided to play along. "Madge, you always have the juiciest stories. What's this about me and a sexy English bloke?"

Madge leaned in with a mischievous grin. "Well, my dear, Aurora mentioned something about sparks flying between you and an English charmer. Do tell!"

Bonnie laughed nervously, realising that Aurora had probably over-exaggerated a casual conversation. "Madge, you know how rumours spread like wildfire. There's nothing serious going on. Just a friendly chat, that's all."

Madge winked and said, "Oh, I see. But you know, around here, we love a good story. Keeps things interesting, just like those bacon sandwiches last week."

Dave, joining the conversation, added, "Madge, you're incorrigible. But I wouldn't have it any other way. Just keep it PG, all right? We don't need any scandal."

Madge saluted playfully. "Don't you worry, boss. PG it is. But a little spice never hurt anyone, right? Remember the story about our good friends Joanna and Mick? Bonnie, now is the time to put your hands over your ears. You don't want to hear this. To be honest, though, you know what your mum is like – we've all read her books and seen her on podcasts. There is nothing she doesn't know about sex and relationships."

Before Madge could say anything more, Bonnie cut in. "Don't you dare, Madge. And you, Aurora, don't need any more made-up stories. Got it?"

Aurora took one look at Madge and then Dave. "Fuck it, I want to hear the full wild shit Bonnie's mum and dad used to get up to. This is brilliant. I bet she loved sucking your dad's cock. I wonder if she was like you, Madge, loving getting her back doors smashed in," Aurora said, absolutely loving this.

The atmosphere in the reception area crackled with a mix of amusement and discomfort as Aurora's bold remarks hung in the air, causing a few awkward chuckles among the group.

Dave, always the peacemaker, tried to defuse the situation with a hearty laugh. "All right, Aurora, let's keep it PG, shall we? We don't need to delve into anyone's personal history," he said, shooting Madge a pointed look.

Madge, unfazed by the mild scolding, simply grinned mischievously. "Oh, come on, Dave, where's your sense of adventure? But you're right; Bonnie's family history is off-limits. We know it all anyway," she said, laughing and then steering the conversation back to safer waters.

Grateful for the intervention, Bonnie took a deep breath and mustered a weak smile. "Thanks, Madge. Let's stick to surfing tales for now, shall we?" she suggested, eager to change the subject. "So, I can't mention how your mum used to ride those long, hard boards all day long, and she loved going really hard even if only for 30 seconds?" Madge paused and lifted an eyebrow. "We are talking about surfing, though."

Aurora, though slightly disappointed, nodded in agreement. "Fair enough, Bonnie. But you can't blame a girl for trying to stir up some excitement," she said with a playful wink, already thinking of her next opportunity to inject some scandal into the conversation.

With the tension defused, the group settled back into their usual banter. The spicy exchange quickly became just another memorable moment in the colourful tapestry of life at the surf school. As laughter echoed through the reception area, Bonnie couldn't help but feel grateful for the eccentric cast of characters. As they shared more laughs, the school buzzed with energy, a testament to the camaraderie and humour that defined the close-knit community. And through it all, Madge continued to be the entertaining storyteller, weaving tales that kept everyone on their toes.

As Dave stepped away to take a call, Bonnie noticed

Henry looking a bit downcast. She approached him with a gentle smile, knowing how challenging it could be for him to navigate certain situations.

"Hey there, Henry," she said softly, crouching down to his eye level. "I heard you had a tough time in class today. How are you feeling?"

Henry sniffled and looked up at Bonnie, his eyes red from crying. "It was horrible, Bonnie. They made me read out loud, and I couldn't do it. Everyone laughed at me."

Bonnie's heart went out to Henry. She knew first-hand the struggles he faced with his learning difficulties, and she admired his resilience. "I'm sorry you had to go through that, Henry. But hey, it's okay to feel upset. You're brave for even trying."

Henry nodded, his expression still sombre. "Can you please take me home, Bonnie? I don't want to be here anymore."

"Of course, Henry. Let's get you home," she replied, offering him a comforting hug before guiding him out of the surf school.

As they walked together, Bonnie couldn't help but feel protective toward Henry. She vowed to speak to the school about the incident and ensure he received the support he needed to thrive in the classroom.

After arriving at Henry's home, Bonnie made sure he was settled in before heading off to meet Jamie at the surf club. Despite the unexpected detour, she felt grateful for the opportunity to support Henry and make a positive difference in his day.

Henry trudged into his house, still feeling the sting of

the day's events. The living room was a familiar sanctuary filled with his favourite things, including his extensive collection of Star Wars Lego sets. His mum was at work, so the house was quiet, just as he liked it when he needed to calm down.

He walked over to his latest Lego project, a nearly completed Millennium Falcon, and sat down on the floor. He picked up a small, intricate piece, turning it over in his hands. The repetitive, detailed work of building Lego models always helped him focus and relax.

As he clicked pieces into place, he let out a deep breath. The comforting act of constructing something from scratch was therapeutic. Henry imagined himself in the Star Wars universe, far away from the difficulties of school. In his mind, he was a brave pilot, soaring through space on daring missions, unbothered by the challenges of reading out loud or the snickers of classmates.

Piece by piece, the Millennium Falcon took shape. With each successful connection, Henry felt a little more in control, a little more confident. By the time Bonnie checked in on him via text, he was feeling much better.

'Hey Henry, how are you doing? Feeling any better?' Bonnie's message read.

Henry looked at his phone and then back at his Lego creation. He smiled slightly before typing a response.

'Hey Bonnie, I'm okay now. Just working on my Lego. Thanks for taking me home.'

Bonnie replied almost immediately, 'I'm glad to hear that. Remember, you're awesome. Keep building that spaceship, and I'll see you soon!'

Henry felt a warm glow from her words and returned his focus to the Lego pieces, his fingers moving with more purpose. Each small victory in his construction brought a sense of accomplishment, erasing the day's earlier humiliations bit by bit.

Later, when his mum returned home, she found him deeply engrossed in his Lego world. Seeing the calm and concentration on his face, she knew he was coping in his own way. She sat beside him, watching as he expertly added the final touches to the Millennium Falcon.

"Looks amazing, Henry," she said softly. "You did a great job."

Henry looked up at her, a shy smile spreading across his face. "Thanks, Mom. It helps me feel better."

She hugged him gently. "I'm glad you have something that makes you happy. And remember, no matter what happens at school, you're smart and creative. Never forget that."

Henry nodded, the reassurance from his mum and Bonnie fortifying his spirits. He felt a renewed determination to face the challenges ahead, knowing he had people who believed in him. For now, he was content in his Lego world, where he could be anything he wanted to be.

*

Bonnie arrived at the surf club just as lessons were wrapping up. The sun was beginning to set, casting a warm glow over the beach. She spotted Jamie near the shoreline, chatting with a couple of students. As soon as he saw her, he waved and started walking over.

"Hey, Bonnie," Jamie greeted her with a smile.

"Everything okay? You look a bit preoccupied."

Bonnie took a deep breath after seeing Jamie's heartwarming smile that made her heart skip a beat. The day's events still weighed on her. "Yeah, it's just been a bit of a tough day. One of the kids at the surf school, Henry, had a rough time in class. I took him home to make sure he was all right."

Jamie listened intently, his expression empathetic. "That's really kind of you, Bonnie. Henry's lucky to have someone like you looking out for him."

"Thanks, Jamie," she said, feeling a bit better. "I just hate seeing him so upset. Kids can be so cruel sometimes."

"They can be, but they can also be incredibly resilient," Jamie replied. "With someone like you in his corner, Henry's going to be just fine."

Bonnie smiled, appreciating his comforting words. "I hope so. Anyway, enough about my day. What do you have planned for our run?"

Jamie grinned, sensing the shift in her mood. "I thought we'd start with a light jog along the beach, then maybe head up to the cliffs for a better view of the sunset. Sound good?"

"Perfect," Bonnie agreed, feeling a sense of anticipation.

They set off at a steady pace, the rhythmic sound of their footsteps blending with the crashing waves. As they ran, Bonnie felt the stress of the day begin to dissipate. Jamie's presence was calming, and she found herself enjoying the moment, their feet sinking into the cool sand with each stride. The rhythm was soothing and the conversation flowed effortlessly. They talked about their favourite movies, shared childhood stories, and even delved into their dreams and aspirations. The connection between them grew stronger with every step, and the day's earlier tension melted away.

As they neared the end of their run, the sun hung low in the sky, casting a breathtaking array of colours across the horizon. They slowed to a walk, their breathing heavy but relaxed, and made their way to a secluded spot where they could watch the sunset in peace.

"This is beautiful," Bonnie said, her eyes fixed on the horizon.

"Yeah, it really is," Jamie agreed, but his eyes were on Bonnie.

Feeling his gaze, Bonnie turned to look at him. The warmth in his eyes mirrored the sunset and for a moment, the world seemed to stand still. Jamie took a step closer, his hand reaching out to gently cup Bonnie's cheek.

"Bonnie," he whispered, his voice filled with emotion. "I've never felt like this before."

Her heart raced, but it wasn't from the run. It was from the intense, undeniable connection she felt with Jamie. She placed her hand over his, her eyes locking with his.

"Me neither," she whispered back.

Slowly, Jamie leaned in, his lips brushing softly against hers. The kiss was gentle at first, a tentative exploration of newfound emotions. But as the sun dipped below the horizon, painting the sky in deep purples and reds, the kiss deepened.

It was as if the world around them had vanished, leaving only the two of them in a bubble of warmth and affection.

Bonnie felt a surge of electricity course through her, every nerve ending tingling with sensation. Jamie's arms wrapped around her, pulling her closer, and she melted into his embrace. The kiss was everything she had ever dreamed of and more – passionate, tender, and filled with a promise of something beautiful.

When they finally pulled apart, both were breathless, their foreheads resting against each other's. The last rays of the sun cast a golden glow around them, making the moment feel almost magical.

"Wow," Bonnie breathed, her eyes shining with unshed tears of happiness.

"Yeah," Jamie agreed, his voice equally breathless. "That was... incredible."

They stood there for a while, holding each other as the sky darkened and the first stars began to twinkle. It felt like the start of something extraordinary, a love story written in the stars and sealed with the perfect kiss.

As they made their way back to Jamie's place, hand in hand, the world sparkled with possibility. They both knew that whatever the future held, they were ready to face it together, their hearts intertwined like the colours of the sunset they had just witnessed.

CHAPTER 12

Fighting Back

It was early morning, and Shannon and Madge were sorting through the latest batch of bank cancellations. This recurring issue was particularly annoying for the surf school, as parents would frequently join, cancel, and then complain about not getting the lessons they wanted. Dave, the owner, was stuck between needing the business and dealing with the instability it brought.

Shannon sighed as she flipped through the stack of papers, frustration evident on her face. "Madge, I can't believe how many cancellations we're dealing with again. It's like a never-ending cycle with these parents."

Madge nodded, her brow furrowed in agreement. "I know, Shannon. It's so frustrating. They sign up their kids, cancel, and then complain about not getting the lessons. It's a real headache for Dave, and it's affecting the business."

Shannon recognised some familiar names on the list. "I swear, it's always the same parents. I don't get why they keep doing this. Don't they realise the impact it has on the surf school?"

Madge shook her head. "I don't think they care, Shannon. They just want what they want when they want it, without considering the consequences. Dave's been patient, but this can't go on."

Determined to find a solution, Shannon suggested, "Maybe we should have a meeting with Dave and discuss some changes. We need to come up with a strategy to handle these cancellations and ensure a more stable customer base."

Madge agreed. "That's a good idea. We could implement stricter cancellation policies or maybe require a deposit upfront. Something has to change. Dave can't keep bending over backwards for these unreliable customers."

After about four cups of tea, Shannon remarked, "I need another wee, Madge." She was at an age where tea and coffee made her go to the toilet all the time.

In typical Madge fashion, she replied, "Sod it, I'm off for a poo then." Shannon chuckled at Madge's blunt response, appreciating her friend's straightforward nature.

The surf school had recently been updated, boasting top-notch facilities, although there was still an old changing area with a communal toilet facility. Madge used this area all the time because it was closer to the admin office. It was also frequented by most of the male instructors, including Dave. The old ventilation system travelled all the way to the reception area, allowing anyone there to hear everything.

Madge had just settled in to quietly enjoy her rest time when Rod, followed by Dave, decided they needed a break too. There were five old-style cubicles, and both men walked in simultaneously.

"Madge, you in here?" they called out.

She rolled her eyes and didn't say a word, knowing what was coming. "Gentlemen, before you start, I am not partaking in your singing or seeing who can fart the longest and loudest," she said with intent. She didn't mind chatting, but the noises Dave and Rod could make were something to behold.

"Don't mind us, Madge," Dave said, starting to laugh. The pair of them let out the biggest farts around.

As the unconventional gathering unfolded in the old changing area, Madge couldn't help but shake her head in amusement at the sheer absurdity of the situation. The distinctive sounds of Dave and Rod's competition echoed through the aged cubicles, causing stifled laughter from the others who had joined the impromptu meeting.

Despite the unusual circumstances, Madge decided to steer the conversation towards the pressing issue at hand. "All right, enough with the noise, boys. We need to talk about these cancellations. Shannon and I were just discussing potential solutions."

Dave, still chuckling, replied, "You're right, Madge. We do need to address this. It's getting out of hand."

Rod, now more serious, added, "Maybe it's time we implement some stricter policies. Require deposits, or maybe a cancellation fee."

The others nodded in agreement, and for the next few

minutes, the communal restroom became an unlikely brainstorming session. Ideas were tossed around, jokes were made, and in the end, a plan started to take shape.

With a sense of accomplishment, Madge said, "All right, let's take these ideas to a proper meeting room and hash out the details. This is a good start."

Ronnie, Henry, Daniella, and the three feral ones entered the scene, probably drawn by the unexpected commotion. Ronnie raised an eyebrow, grinning. "What's going on in here? Did we stumble upon a secret club or something?"

Maintaining her no-nonsense attitude, Madge replied, "Oh, just the usual antics from these two. You might want to evacuate if you value your sense of smell."

The feral ones, always up for a bit of chaos, exchanged mischievous glances and giggles. Madge gave them a stern look. "Don't you dare encourage them. We're here for a serious discussion."

Dave and Rod emerged from the cubicles, still chuckling like schoolboys. Dave wiped away fake tears. "Ah, Madge, you're no fun. We were just trying to lighten the mood."

Madge crossed her arms, unimpressed. "We're dealing with cancellations, and you two are having a farting competition. Real mature."

Shannon, who had just returned from her bathroom break, raised an eyebrow at the scene. "What in the world is going on here?"

Madge rolled her eyes. "Just the usual madness. Now, can we get back to business and figure out how to stop these cancellations from wreaking havoc on the surf school?"

The group reluctantly shifted their focus back to the pressing issue at hand, determined to find a solution to the constant cancellations and ensure the stability of their beloved school.

Henry was due to meet Bonnie for a private lesson shortly. Ronnie, the director of the school, could teach her son Henry, but he adored Bonnie. There was no way Ronnie could get in the way of this. Daniella, Bella, and Toby were also having lessons. Little Jack was in the office with his grandma, Shannon.

Dave had retreated to his office. "Veronica, dear," Madge used Ronnie's full name from time to time if she was in one of those playful moods, "I think I have seen Bonnie waiting for Henry. She was with that Aurora girl down near the beach. All I could hear was the noise of that silly motorbike of hers. That girl needs to grow up a little." Madge wasn't Aurora's biggest fan.

Ronnie, engrossed in some paperwork as Henry sat quietly, now looked up and raised an eyebrow at Madge's comment. "Bonnie and Aurora, you say?" she asked, her interest piqued. "What are they up to? And what's wrong with Aurora's motorbike?"

Madge leaned against the doorframe, crossing her arms. "Oh, you know how I feel about those noisy things. They're like giant mosquitoes. As for what they're up to, I didn't stick around to find out. Just thought you should know they were down by the beach."

Ronnie sighed, putting down her pen. "All right, I'll go check on them."

As she made her way to the beach, she saw Bonnie and

Aurora in spirited conversation, Aurora's motorbike parked nearby. Bonnie noticed her approaching and waved.

"Hey, Ronnie! We were just talking about the lesson schedule," she called out, trying to mask any tension.

Ronnie nodded, glancing at Aurora, who was fiddling with her motorbike helmet. "Right. Aurora, can I have a word with you about something?"

Aurora looked up, a bit wary, but nodded. "Sure, Ronnie."

Ronnie gestured for her to follow a short distance from Bonnie. "Aurora, I know you mean well, but the noise from your motorbike is a bit disruptive. Could you try to keep it down, especially around the school?"

Aurora's face softened, understanding the concern. "I get it, Ronnie. I'll be more mindful. Sorry about that."

Ronnie smiled, appreciating the mature response. "Thank you. Now, let's make sure everything's set for the lessons. Bonnie, are you ready for Henry?"

Bonnie nodded enthusiastically. "Absolutely. Henry's looking forward to it."

Back in the office, Shannon was engaging Henry with some stories while he played with his Star Wars Lego set. Deeply engrossed in his play, he had built an epic battle scene, the earlier troubles forgotten for the moment.

As Ronnie made her way back towards the beach with Daniella now behind her, she wondered what Bonnie and Aurora had been doing before. The beach had always been a place of both work and leisure for the surf school crew, and any deviation from the norm was enough to stir curiosity.

Ronnie couldn't understand why Aurora always had to show off her body. She had now stripped off into a thong bikini and proceeded to find a spot to sunbathe. Ronnie was not impressed. "Aurora, this part of the beach isn't for you to flaunt your body like this."

Lying on her towel with her eyes closed, Aurora responded nonchalantly, "Come on, Ronnie. It's just a bit of sunbathing. What harm does it do?"

Ronnie glanced around and noticing a few raised eyebrows from other beachgoers, sighed in exasperation. "A bit of modesty wouldn't hurt, Aurora. We've got a surf school reputation to maintain here."

Aurora laughed. "Relax, Ronnie. It's just a beach. Everyone wears swimsuits."

Slightly annoyed, Ronnie motioned towards the water. "Well, not everyone decides to turn the surf school's section of the beach into their personal sunbathing area. And where's Bonnie? Henry is waiting for his lesson."

Aurora opened one eye and smirked. "Bonnie went for a quick swim. She'll be back soon."

Rolling her eyes, Ronnie walked over to Henry, who was now playing with some sand. "All right, Henry, let's get your surf lesson started. Daniella, make sure the other kids are ready too."

Ronnie found Bonnie just as she was emerging from the water, her hair dripping and a big smile on her face. "It's time to start Henry's lesson. We've got a schedule to keep," she said, trying to hide her frustration.

"Got it, Ronnie. I'll be right there," Bonnie replied, still catching her breath.

Aurora's carefree attitude and Bonnie's impromptu swim were causing more disruption than she'd anticipated. The sunbathing spectacle continued, and Ronnie couldn't help but think this school day was turning out to be more eventful than expected.

Aurora, meanwhile, had decided to cool off with a swim. She dove gracefully into the water, her toned body cutting through the waves with ease. As she swam back towards the shore, the sun glistened on her wet skin, and she emerged from the water like a scene out of a movie. Her hair clung to her back, and the droplets of water sparkled as they cascaded down her curves.

The young boys having lessons nearby were completely entranced. They stood frozen, surfboards in hand, their gazes fixed on Aurora as she walked slowly back to her towel. The sight of her had a magnetic effect, drawing the attention of everyone on the beach.

Ronnie noticed the distraction and sighed; she needed to redirect the focus back to the lesson. "All right, everyone, let's get back to it!" she called out, clapping her hands to get the kids' attention.

Bonnie, noticing the situation, decided to take charge. She paddled out on her surfboard, then expertly caught a wave, riding it with effortless grace and skill. She performed a series of impressive manoeuvres, carving through the water with precision and control.

The kids watched in awe as Bonnie made surfing look easy, her movements smooth and confident. She rode the wave all the way to shore, dismounting her board with a flourish. "Who's ready to catch some waves?" she called out, her enthusiasm infectious.

The young boys, snapping out of their trance, turned their attention back to Bonnie. They were inspired by her performance and eager to learn from such a talented surfer. Bonnie's display of skill and professionalism quickly shifted the focus back to the lessons, and the kids were soon back in the water, eager to practice their own surfing moves.

Ronnie felt a wave of relief wash over her. Despite the distractions, Bonnie had managed to captivate the kids' attention and get them excited about their lesson. Aurora, meanwhile, had settled back on her towel, sunbathing with a satisfied smile.

As the surf lessons continued, Ronnie couldn't help but feel grateful for Bonnie's ability to handle the situation with such grace. The day had certainly been eventful but with a team like hers, she knew they could handle anything that came their way.

*

Ronnie had forgotten Dave was waiting for her in his office. They didn't often get time to themselves away from Henry, so she wanted to surprise him with a treat he wouldn't be able to resist. Dave wasn't doing much in his office; he had actually thought about having a little sleep.

"Dave, are you on your own?" Ronnie opened the door slightly.

He replied in a bit of a shocked voice, "Of course I am. What do you think I'm doing?"

"Good. Sit back in your chair and close your eyes."

Ronnie closed the door behind her, making sure she locked it. Slipping off her oversized joggers and T-shirt revealed a very sexy lady. She quickly removed her bra and thong. Ronnie had the best bum and boobs you have ever seen; she was one of those ladies who was very modest and didn't like to flaunt her body for everyone to see.

Dave, still a bit confused, complied with Ronnie's request, sitting back in his chair and closing his eyes. The anticipation hung in the air as he wondered what surprise Ronnie had in store for him. The office, usually a place filled with paperwork and surf school logistics, was about to witness a different kind of activity.

Ronnie, now clad in nothing but a mischievous smile, approached Dave. The soft sound of her bare feet on the office floor betrayed her movements. She knew how to keep the spark alive in their relationship, especially with the challenges of parenting and running a surf school.

"Keep those eyes closed, Dave," Ronnie whispered with a playful tone. She moved closer, her hands gently caressing his shoulders. Dave sensed the change in atmosphere, and a grin formed on his face.

The warmth of Ronnie's breath tickled Dave's ear as she whispered, "Surprise," before placing a gentle kiss on his cheek.

Dave couldn't help but open his eyes, met with the sight of a completely unreserved Ronnie, her eyes gleaming with a mixture of playfulness and desire. The contrast between the usually business-oriented office and the unexpected intimacy created an electrifying atmosphere.

"Ronnie, what's going on?" Dave asked, a mix of curiosity and excitement in his voice.

Still embracing her bold side, she responded, "I thought

we could use a little break from the usual chaos. Just relax, Dave." Ronnie wanted to start slowly so Dave would be as turned on as possible, telling him how much she was looking forward to taking his big hard cock in her mouth, enthusiastically licking her lips in anticipation, as if it was the tastiest thing to ever enter her mouth. Ronnie roughly pulled Dave's pants down while she French kissed the head and played with the tip of his dick using her lips and tongue. Slow licks from top to bottom, then teasing the head with her tongue a little. She then started deepthroating Dave, licking the base of his cock with her tongue while constantly moaning and giving him lustful looks. She knew when Dave was approaching orgasm because of the way he moved and how hard he would feel in her mouth, so she backed off a few times to keep him on edge.

When she felt like it was time for Dave to cum, Ronnie deepthroated him nonstop and used her hand at his base. On this occasion the orgasm was so intense it spread through his whole body and went on for at least a minute. Dave felt like he was having multiple orgasms. He lost track of where he was and who he was and became lost in the pleasure. He couldn't even move for half an hour and every time Ronnie touched him he would shiver.

*

Jamie had pulled into the surf school car park. He could see lessons taking place in the distance and could just make out Bonnie at the water's edge. He thought it would be a nice surprise to bring some cheesecake, as Bonnie had said the way into every woman's heart is through food. She had also said she absolutely loved cheesecake. Jamie was a little anxious as he didn't really want to bump into that

Madge again. Not that he didn't think she was funny, he just didn't want to have to answer 300 questions about his life as soon as he entered the building.

Madge and Shannon were on another toilet break; this time they had walked to the newer part of the building as Madge really wanted to get her steps in. She was trying to increase her fitness after a knee replacement. This was some time ago, mind you, and she was still struggling.

As Jamie walked through the building, he hoped to navigate through without any encounters. Little did he know, the comical duo of Madge and Shannon might add an unexpected twist to his cheesecake delivery mission. There she was. Madge appeared from nowhere. "What have you got there for us? It's about snack time for me and Shannon."

Shannon simply replied, "Madge, you know I am on holiday in three weeks. I can't be eating cake or whatever he has."

Jamie didn't really know what to say. He stuttered a little and then thought, *I'm going to give this old girl a little back.* "By the look of you, you will never catch me. You can hardly move."

Madge just said to him, "I don't have to move. You will simply give it to me like the little boy that you are."

Jamie found Madge a little scary. *What the hell do I do?* He'd found himself in an unexpected exchange with her, unsure how to navigate the situation. He chuckled nervously, trying to keep the atmosphere light despite feeling a bit uneasy. "Well, I suppose you're right, Madge. But I can't resist bringing a treat for Bonnie. She's out there giving it her all in the surf, you know," he replied, attempting to shift the focus away from himself.

Madge raised an eyebrow, sizing him up with a scrutinising gaze. "Bonnie, huh? You're sweet on her, aren't you?" she remarked, a mischievous glint in her eye.

His cheeks flushed slightly at the unexpected directness of Madge's question. "Uh, well, I… uh…" he stammered, searching for the right words.

Before he could formulate a coherent response, Shannon interjected, saving him from further embarrassment. "Come on, Madge, let's not grill the poor guy. If he's got cheesecake, let's just take it and go," Shannon suggested, eyeing the dessert in Jamie's hands with a hint of longing.

Relieved by the diversion, Jamie eagerly handed over the cheesecake to Madge, who accepted it with a satisfied grin. "Thanks, kid. Tell Bonnie we said hi," she said, already beginning to walk away with Shannon in tow.

As Jamie watched them leave, he let out a breath he hadn't realised he was holding. "Well, that could've gone worse," he muttered to himself, shaking his head with a mixture of amusement and relief. With the cheesecake delivery complete, he made his way back outside to find Bonnie, hoping to avoid any further unexpected encounters along the way.

CHAPTER 13

Desire

Aurora's mind was consumed with thoughts of travel, particularly the Isle of Man TT. She couldn't shake the idea of experiencing the thrill of the race first-hand. However, she also realised Bonnie would soon be embarking on her own travels, thanks to her high-profile sponsor deal. With those increased commitments, Aurora knew their adventures together might become less frequent.

As she contemplated her own dreams of racing and travel, she reflected on her recent decision to part ways with Byron. Despite his good looks and athletic physique, she found herself drawn to someone new – Andy, an older rider with a wild spirit and a passion for the road.

Their connection had sparked over Instagram, where she discovered his adventurous and kinky side. It seemed that no matter where they were or what they were doing –

whether riding motorcycles or simply chatting – Andy always found a way to steer the conversation towards sex and his desires. This boldness and openness intrigued Aurora. She found herself drawn to his uninhibited nature, and the excitement of exploring new sexual experiences with him filled her with anticipation. With Andy, Aurora felt liberated to explore her own desires and indulge in the thrill of the unknown.

*

Bonnie was just about to finish a training session with Sally. CrossFit had been unbelievably hard today. She was a little frustrated; as always, Aurora had booked the session but turned up late. "I don't know why we bother inviting Aurora to the sessions, Sally. You can never rely on her to turn up. It's a good job it's not a partner WOD."

"Well I didn't want to say anything as I know you both are close, but she is so annoying thinking she is better than everyone. I know she has one of those bodies that looks and moves better than most without trying…"

Bonnie nodded in agreement with Sally's sentiments with a mix of frustration and understanding. "Yeah, she can be a handful sometimes. But you're right, she's got that natural athleticism that seems effortless. It's like she was born to excel in everything she does."

Sally sighed. "I wish she'd realise that not everyone can keep up with her pace. It's exhausting trying to match her energy and enthusiasm all the time."

Bonnie chuckled. "Tell me about it. But hey, at least we're getting a good workout in without her today. Let's make the most of it. There she is. Come on, dickhead." She was going to make Aurora pay for this.

"What! Don't give me shit, I'm absolutely hanging. I've never been fucked so hard in my life," Aurora said with a smile.

Bonnie couldn't help but laugh at Aurora's candid response, shaking her head in disbelief. "Well, that's one way to make an entrance, I suppose. Next time, try not to keep us waiting, especially when Sally's got the timer set."

Sally smirked, nodding in agreement. "Yeah, we were just saying how we can always count on you to liven things up."

Aurora grinned mischievously, unfazed by their playful scolding. "Hey, what can I say? I bring the entertainment factor. Now, let's crush this workout together, shall we? Deadlift? You know I'm good for them. If we're doing squats you know I will go deep." Laughing at her own joke, she continued, "Ladies, I will tell you what happened after. You're going to want to hear about it."

Bonnie's response was simple. "No, we don't, as I can imagine." She couldn't help but roll her eyes at Aurora's suggestive remarks. "Sometimes I wonder if you have any filter at all. But fine, let's hear your story after we finish this workout. Just try to keep it PG, okay?" She shot Aurora a teasing smile.

"Okay, I'll just say a few things. Andy practically wanted to fuck me like a doll. So, because of that kink, I had planned to let him essentially abduct me on one of my walks and do anything he pleases with me. He jumped out of the van and did whatever he wanted. He wasn't supposed to tell me when he was going to get me. He had pretty well constructed an entire sex torture chamber in the back of his van."

Bonnie's eyes widened in disbelief as Aurora recounted her encounter with Andy. "That sounds incredibly risky and dangerous. Are you sure you're okay with that kind of behaviour? It sounds like he's pushing some serious boundaries." She couldn't help but feel concerned for her friend's well-being, hoping that Aurora was fully aware of the risks involved. But this was Aurora; she liked to take risks no matter the cost.

"Girls, don't worry about me. When I tell you what he did to me, you'll want some. Come on, I need to get the last bit of this workout done."

It was especially hot; sweat everywhere. The girls finished with some strength work. Max deadlift for three reps. Aurora, as always, outlifted all the girls without even trying. "I'm done, ladies. Shower time."

Bonnie and Sally couldn't believe it. "She did it again."

They exchanged amused glances, shaking their heads at Aurora's consistent display of strength.

"She never fails to impress, does she?" Bonnie chuckled, wiping the sweat from her forehead. "But you know what? Let's use her competitiveness as motivation. Let's push ourselves even harder in the next session. We might not outlift her, but we can definitely make some gains."

Sally nodded in agreement, determination gleaming in her eyes. "Absolutely. Let's show her what we're made of."

With renewed energy, they headed towards the showers. Showering with Aurora was always an interesting experience and today didn't disappoint.

"What the hell is that on your bum?"

Aurora turned, showing her cheeks. "Yes, he's left a mark, hasn't he? I'm not going to lie, that was amazing, the way he spanked me."

Bonnie couldn't help but laugh at the candid response. "Well, I guess that's one way to leave your mark," she teased, shaking her head in amusement. "But seriously, girl, you always have the most adventurous stories. Sometimes I wonder if you're living in a movie."

As they continued showering and chatting, Bonnie couldn't shake off the thought of Aurora's wild escapades, always keeping life interesting with her daring experiences.

With the increased calls from her agent regarding tours, Bonnie was going to miss her friend while she was on her potential travels. It wouldn't surprise her, though, if Aurora randomly turned up in the UK or wherever she was. Bonnie was hoping she wouldn't, as she needed no distraction.

The girls decided to head to Robbie's Coffee, the perfect spot for Bonnie and Aurora to catch up over a cup of coffee. It was always nice to have a familiar place to relax and chat with friends. They exchanged knowing glances as they heard Byron's voice from a booth. It didn't take them long to figure out who he was with. "Addison," they said simultaneously, their expressions a mixture of amusement and exasperation. It seemed they couldn't escape the drama, even during a casual coffee outing.

Addison's head popped up over the booth. "Ladies, come join us."

Byron's heart dropped as he thought to himself, *Please,*

don't tell them about last night. They do not need to know what we did.

His mind drifted off to how he had fucked Addison in her ass. She had basically been begging for it all week, so finally, he gave her what she wanted and fucked her asshole all night. Hearing her scream, "My asshole is cumming!" was driving him crazy! It felt so good on his dick. When he told her he was about to cum to cum, she screamed, "Cum in my ass!"

I love fucking her asshole, he thought.

Addison shouted out, "You're going to want to hear about what we got up to last night! Sorry, Aurora, he's my toy now."

"Go on then, do tell, did he fuck you in the ass, did he?" Aurora laughed at Addison. "He's also had that dick in my ass."

The atmosphere at Robbie's Coffee was suddenly charged with tension as Addison's invitation drew Bonnie and Aurora closer to their booth. Byron's internal panic was palpable and he hoped the details of their escapades from the previous night wouldn't be divulged. Despite his apprehension, Addison seemed eager to share, prompting Aurora's playful inquiry about whether Byron had also engaged in anal sex with her.

The conversation took a provocative turn, highlighting the intimate dynamics between Byron, Addison, and Aurora. With emotions running high, it seemed that this coffee outing would be anything but casual.

Byron's sexual encounters with both Addison and Aurora involved anal sex, adding a layer of intensity and excitement to their interactions. Aurora's playful response suggested that she was not fazed by the intimate details and was perhaps even amused by the dynamic between Byron and Addison. Their conversation was characterised by openness and a lack of inhibition when it came to discussing sexual experiences. Their wild night together seemed to have intensified their connection, at least from Addison's perspective.

The conversation was filled with playful banter and perhaps a hint of competition for Byron's attention.

Luckily, Jamie walked in but straight in front of him was Rob Martin. Jamie didn't want to deal with this clown. Bonnie had been honest with him; he knew all about their history. Rob was definitely a little jealous. There was some tension brewing between them, especially with Rob's evident jealousy. Jamie's arrival might have provided a welcome distraction from the playful banter and competition for Byron's attention.

Bonnie's honesty with Jamie about their history helped him navigate the situation with confidence. Rob muttered under his breath, "Stupid pom," with a hint of playfulness as he wasn't really bothered. He could get the attention of many girls. "Hey, Bonnie, your friend has arrived," Rob said, with a smirk on his face. In a way, he wanted to antagonise Jamie. This was largely due to his arrogance, and it was his coffee shop after all.

Jamie felt a flicker of annoyance at Rob's comment, but refused to let it show. Instead, he greeted Bonnie with a warm smile and a quick hug before turning his attention to Rob.

"Hey, Rob," Jamie said evenly, ignoring the jab. "Thanks

for the heads-up."

Rob's smirk widened, clearly enjoying the discomfort he was causing. "No problem, mate. Always happy to help out a friend... or a competitor," he added, his tone dripping with sarcasm.

Jamie resisted the urge to roll his eyes. He knew Rob thrived on confrontation, but he refused to take the bait. Instead, he turned to Byron, who had been observing the exchange with amusement.

"Hey, Byron," Jamie said, shifting the focus away from Rob. "What's on the agenda for today?"

Byron grinned, eager to move past the tension. "Well, I was thinking we could start with that new indie film everyone's been buzzing about. Then maybe we can discuss some ideas for our next club event."

Jamie wondered to himself, *What is Byron on about?*

Bonnie quickly whispered in Jamie's ear, "You want to hear about Addison getting fucked in the ass last night?"

Jamie didn't really know what to say. He was busy thinking to himself, *This is going to be interesting.* And as for Rob? Well, he decided he would deal with him later.

Jamie's eyebrows shot up in surprise at Bonnie's unexpected revelation. He wasn't sure whether to be amused, shocked, or a combination of both. Byron, sensing the shift in the atmosphere, looked at Jamie with a quizzical expression.

"Everything okay, mate?" he asked, unaware of the bombshell Bonnie had just dropped.

Jamie cleared his throat, trying to regain his composure.

"Yeah, yeah, all good. Just didn't expect that on a morning."

Byron chuckled, completely oblivious to the private conversation happening between Jamie and Bonnie. "Well, you never know what to expect with this bunch."

Still revelling in the discomfort he had stirred up, Rob interjected with a smirk, "Oh, I'm sure Jamie's got plenty of unexpected stories to share too, don't you, mate?"

Jamie shot him a pointed look, irritation bubbling just beneath the surface.

Before he could respond, Bonnie cut in, her tone mischievous. "Oh, Rob, you have no idea. Jamie here is full of surprises," she said with a sly smile.

Sensing the tension escalating, Byron decided to steer the conversation back to safer ground. "I used lube on Addison's ass." Laughing, Byron then turned to Addison.

"All right, enough of the morning drama. If you want to fuck me again keep your mouth shut," she said very seriously.

Jamie's eyes widened at Byron's unexpected revelation, a mixture of surprise and amusement crossing his face. He couldn't help but laugh at the blunt and candid nature of Byron's comment, though he quickly composed himself when he caught Addison's reaction out of the corner of his eye.

Addison's cheeks were now flushed with embarrassment and she shot a playful glare at Byron, her lips curling into a smirk. "Oh, you're one to talk, Byron," she retorted, her tone teasing, yet tinged with a hint of defiance. "At least I don't announce my escapades to the whole coffee shop."

Byron chuckled, unfazed by her comeback. "Fair point," he conceded with a grin. "But hey, what's a little friendly banter among friends?"

Jamie couldn't help but shake his head in amusement at the exchange unfolding before him, despite the initial tension and discomfort caused by Rob's presence.

Rob, for his part, watched the interaction with a mixture of amusement and annoyance. Though he tried to maintain his air of nonchalance, it was clear he was not accustomed to being on the sidelines of the group dynamic.

"Cappuccino please, Rob," Jamie said, totally unfazed. They were going to have a coffee no matter what. Jamie wanted to talk about his friend Paul, whose dad had passed away recently. He really wanted to see Paul as FaceTime just wasn't the same when his friend needed some support.

Paul, like Jamie, shared a passion for sport. Unlike Jamie, Paul had been a competitive boxer at amateur level in the UK before relocating to Australia. They had boxed at the same club. Jamie did the training for more fitness, whereas Paul had really taken to boxing as a way of keeping himself out of trouble. As Jamie waited for his cappuccino, his mind wandered to memories of Paul and their shared love for sports. Boxing was Paul's passion, a way to channel his energy and stay focused. Jamie admired his dedication, even though he had never been as deeply involved.

Byron knew Paul from the surf school; he taught his two boys. It seemed a small world at times, that these two guys from the UK had both come to know Byron.

"Hey, Byron," Jamie began, turning to his friend with a thoughtful expression. "Do you remember when Paul used to talk about his boxing days back in the UK? It was like that ring was his sanctuary, you know?"

Byron nodded, a reminiscent smile playing on his lips. "Yeah, I remember. He always had this fire in his eyes whenever he talked about it. Boxing was more than just a sport for him – it was a way of life."

Jamie's thoughts drifted to the struggles Paul had faced, both in the ring and outside of it. He knew that losing his father had hit Paul hard, and he wanted nothing more than to be there for his friend in his time of need.

"I think seeing us today would mean a lot to him," Jamie continued, his voice tinged with determination. "Especially knowing that we've got his back, no matter what."

Byron nodded in agreement, his expression reflecting Jamie's resolve. "Absolutely, mate. Let's make sure we swing by after the coffee. I'm sure the girls won't mind. Paul's a fighter, but even the strongest of us need support sometimes."

Addison was trying to talk over everyone again. All she wanted was to talk about sex. She now wanted Byron to use more lube next time.

Rob, who was lingering close by, heard what she said. He couldn't help himself. "You are an absolute dirtbag. Why do you have to be so open? You do know this is a public place and I do not want to deal with complaints regarding your language."

Totally unfazed by this, Addison turned to Rob and simply said, "I've seen you take Bonnie upstairs before. Are you going to tell us what you used to get up to?"

Jamie sighed inwardly as she once again steered the conversation toward a topic he was not particularly keen on discussing in public. He exchanged a knowing glance with Byron, silently agreeing that they needed to redirect the conversation to more appropriate topics.

Before Jamie could interject, however, Rob jumped into the fray with a thinly veiled admonishment directed at Addison. His attempt to maintain order in the coffee shop was evident, though his frustration with her blatant disregard for decorum was palpable.

Addison, true to form, remained unfazed by the reprimand, instead turning the tables on him with a pointed retort about his own past indiscretions. Jamie couldn't help but chuckle at the unexpected turn of events, though he knew that Rob's discomfort was genuine.

Caught off guard by Addison's brazen response, Rob faltered for a moment before regaining composure. "That's none of your business, Addison," he replied, his tone laced with irritation. "And I suggest you keep your inappropriate comments to yourself."

Despite the tension, Jamie couldn't help but admire Addison's audacity in standing her ground. He knew that underneath her provocative façade, she was fiercely loyal to her friends and unapologetically herself.

With a resigned shake of his head, Jamie turned to Byron, silently repeating his desire to shift the conversation away from the brewing conflict. "So, Byron," he began, his voice deliberately casual, "what do you think of that new coffee blend they've got here? I've heard it's supposed to be pretty good."

Ever the peacemaker, Byron took the cue and ran with it, launching into a discussion about various coffee options available at the shop. As they veered away from controversy and back to more mundane topics, Jamie couldn't help but feel a sense of relief wash over him. Despite the occasional drama that seemed to follow them wherever they went, he knew that as long as they stuck together, they could handle anything that came their way.

"I think I need a beer after all that, maybe something hard that sends me wild between the legs as well." Aurora couldn't help herself; her suggestive remark hung in the air, prompting a mix of laughter and eye-rolling from the group.

Bonnie, clearly fed up with Aurora's antics, didn't hesitate to shut her down with a sharp retort. "Aurora, shut up," she snapped, her tone leaving no room for argument. "Why don't you go talk to Robbie or better still, why don't you and Addison exchange stories of Byron?"

Aurora's cheeks flushed with embarrassment at Bonnie's straightforward rebuke, realising she had pushed the boundaries a bit too far. She offered a sheepish grin and a muttered apology, acknowledging her mistake. "I'm sorry, guys," she mumbled, her tone contrite. "I'll behave, I promise."

Always the mediator, Byron decided to lighten the mood with a quick-witted response of his own. "I'm still here, ladies," he interjected with a grin. "Let's not fight over me now." His comment elicited a round of laughter.

Jamie couldn't help himself now. "So which one

takes...?" As Jamie's playful remark added to the banter, Bonnie swiftly intervened, putting an end to the teasing before it escalated further.

"Clearly Addison, by the sound of it. This is getting silly now," she interjected, her tone firm yet laced with amusement. With a quick excuse about her agent calling, she gracefully excused herself from the conversation, leaving the group to shift their focus elsewhere.

Jamie chuckled at Bonnie's swift intervention, grateful for her ability to defuse potentially awkward situations. With her departure, the conversation took a more relaxed turn, the tension of the moment dissipating into laughter and easy camaraderie.

As Bonnie walked away to take the call, Jamie's mind began to churn with ideas. He remembered his training kit in the car and the fact that Byron had shown interest in boxing. "Hey, Byron," he suggested, a thoughtful expression on his face. "How about a boxing session with Paul? Might be a good way to clear our heads."

Byron's eyes lit up with enthusiasm. "That sounds like a plan, mate. Let's do it."

CHAPTER 14

Healed Scars

Aurora was tired from training but didn't want to admit Addison was starting to annoy her, or that she'd had enough of her trying to get the last word. "Ladies, I'll see you later. Bonnie, I'm sorry but I need to go hard and fast."

"Will you just go already? Get on that bike and disappear." However, relieved that the situation seemed to be diffusing, Bonnie bid Aurora farewell with a nod of understanding. "No worries. Take care of yourself," she called after her friend, hoping that a bit of time alone would help her recharge and find some peace.

Bonnie hoped that would be it, now, and she could get to the surf school for a bit of training to focus her mind after talking to her agent. "Jamie, later gator, and you, get a room. Put it in her mouth to shut her up."

Byron simply said, "Yep, okay. Thanks."

As Aurora made her abrupt exit, her frustration with Addison's persistent need to have the last word was evident. She simply didn't have the energy to engage in more banter. After a quick farewell to the group, she made her way towards her bike, eager to escape the tension and clear her mind with a hard and fast ride.

With Aurora gone, Bonnie turned her attention to her own plans for the day. She needed to focus her mind, and what better way to do that than with some training? With a determined stride, she set off, ready to immerse herself in the rhythm of the waves and the physical exertion of surfing.

Sensing lingering tension in the air, Jamie offered a casual farewell to Bonnie before turning to Byron with a knowing smile, his tone light-hearted. "And you, my friend, should probably find a room if you want to shut Addison up."

Byron chuckled at Jamie's suggestion, appreciating the humour in his friend's comment. "Yep, okay. Thanks," he repeated, already thinking about how he could redirect the conversation once Addison inevitably returned to her playful banter.

As Jamie had brought up the idea of visiting Paul, Byron considered the suggestion. Before he could respond, Addison interjected with a possessive gesture, her hand resting on his leg. Her look conveyed a clear message: Byron was staying with her.

Byron glanced between Jamie and Addison, torn between loyalty to his friend and the desire to appease her.

He knew Paul could use their support, but he also didn't want to upset Addison or disrupt their plans.

"Um, actually, Jamie, I think I'll stick around with Addison for now," Byron replied, trying to navigate the delicate balance between his friendships. "But maybe we can catch up with Paul another time?"

Jamie nodded understandingly, though a hint of disappointment flickered in his eyes. "Sure, no worries. Just let me know when you're free, mate."

Jamie knew full well that Paul wouldn't be at work, and if he was, he could easily be persuaded to do a little training. He decided to WhatsApp video call Paul.

Jamie couldn't help but grin as Paul's face appeared on the call, his unique and lively personality evident from the start. He chuckled at the familiar greeting, the Yorkshire accent bringing a smile to his face. Despite the distance and the time that had passed since they last saw each other, Paul's warm and jovial demeanour remained unchanged.

"Hey up, mate! How you diddling, my old fruit cake?" Paul chimed, his enthusiasm contagious.

"Mate, I hope I'm the only person you say that to. You do know that means to have sex with, right?" Jamie teased, raising an eyebrow playfully and shaking his head at Paul's colourful language. "Good to see you too. I hope you're not calling everyone 'fruit cake'."

Paul laughed heartily, his voice booming through the phone. "Nah, just you, mate. You know you're my favourite fruit cake. I'm just saying hello. What can I do you for?"

Still sounding like he was straight out of Barnsley, England, Paul's proper Yorkshire accent added a touch of familiarity and warmth to the conversation. Despite the miles that separated them, the banter and camaraderie between Jamie and Paul remained as strong as ever.

"Well, I was thinking of swinging by your place for a bit of training. What do you say?" Jamie suggested, knowing that a bit of physical activity could be just what they both needed.

Paul's eyes lit up with excitement. "Training, eh? You must be bored if you want me to beat you up. But sure, why not? Come on over."

With plans set in motion, Jamie looked forward to spending time with his friend, even if it meant enduring Paul's unique sense of humour and a bit of friendly sparring.

Their friendship was built on a foundation of shared experiences and mutual understanding, even if it meant enduring Paul's habitual lateness. Their communication often took the form of video notes or voice messages, a modern twist to their traditional meetups.

Despite his tendency to keep Jamie waiting, he found solace in the warm company of Paul's family. Sadie, Josh, and Brodie welcomed him with open arms, their shared love for sports creating a bond that transcended borders.

Despite growing up outside the UK, the boys had developed a passion for football, much to Jamie's disappointment as he was such a rugby fan.

Sadie's past as a boxer added an intriguing dimension to their family dynamic, reflecting their shared love for physical activity and competition. Despite the occasional inconvenience, Jamie felt at home in their company, as if they had been friends for decades.

Their friendship was not just about the moments they shared but also the understanding and acceptance they had for each other's quirks and habits. In the end, Jamie cherished the warmth and camaraderie of their bond, knowing that no matter the distance or time, their friendship would endure.

He had become accustomed to Paul's perpetual tardiness, a quirk in their friendship that added a touch of humour to their meetups. Whenever they arranged to get together, Paul's familiar apologies would come through video notes or voice messages, explaining his delay with a casual, "Just got to pop out, mate."

Undeterred, Jamie would make himself at home in Paul's cozy abode, knowing Sadie and the boys would be there to keep him company. The lively atmosphere of their household, filled with the energy of Josh and Brodie's love for anything physical, made the wait more than bearable.

As Jamie sipped on a cup of proper Yorkshire tea while waiting for Paul, he couldn't help but appreciate the warmth that enveloped Paul's family. It was evident that the years had woven a tapestry of shared experiences and enduring connections among them. Even as Paul's tendency to be late remained a running joke, the familial atmosphere made every visit worthwhile.

Paul's sudden entrance was no surprise to Jamie, who greeted him with a knowing smile. "No worries, mate. Duty calls, huh?"

As Paul explained the reason for his delay, Jamie had to admire his friend's selflessness. Despite his own commitments and responsibilities, Paul always made time to lend a helping hand, whether it was fixing a neighbour's electrical issue or assisting a friend in need.

It was a testament to his character – compassionate, reliable, and always willing to go the extra mile for others. His generous spirit and big heart endeared him to everyone around him, making him not just a friend, but a pillar of support in their community.

Jamie nodded appreciatively, understanding that Paul's kind nature was simply a reflection of who he was – a person with an unwavering dedication to helping others, no matter the inconvenience.

"Hey, no worries, mate," Jamie replied, raising his cup of tea in a toast. "You're a good bloke, Paul. Wouldn't have you any other way."

"Get your stuff ready, 10K before the gym."

Jamie raised an eyebrow at Paul's sudden change of plans, but knew better than to protest. With a resigned chuckle, he quickly finished his tea and strapped on his rucksack, mentally preparing himself for the gruelling 10-kilometre run ahead.

As they set off towards the gym, Jamie couldn't shake his apprehension. Paul's relentless determination and endurance were legendary among their circle of friends. Whether it was ultramarathons or other extreme challenges, Paul always pushed himself to the limit, never backing down from a challenge. He knew today would be no different. With Paul leading the way, Jamie braced himself for a punishing workout, knowing his friend's indomitable spirit would drive them both to push past their limits.

Despite the physical strain, camaraderie forged through years of shared experiences and mutual support endured.

As they pounded the pavement, their conversation flowed effortlessly, a mix of banter and heartfelt discussions. Jamie found solace in their talks, knowing Paul was always there to lend an ear and offer support whenever needed.

And despite Paul's background as a boxer, there was an unspoken understanding between them. In the ring of friendship, Paul would always have Jamie's back, as long as he respected the boundaries.

As they approached the gym, Jamie was grateful for Paul's companionship and unwavering support. With him by his side, Jamie knew they could conquer any challenge.

*

Nearing the end of their gym session, Jamie's mind naturally wandered to the logistics of getting back to Paul's house. The thought had been nagging at him throughout their entire run, but now it loomed large as they finished up their boxing session.

Despite Jamie's focus on avoiding getting hit during their sparring, the impending transportation dilemma weighed heavily on his mind. However, luck seemed to be on their side as he remembered that Bonnie and Madge, who would be finishing their surf school session around the same time, could potentially give them a lift.

The prospect of spending time with Madge, though, brought a mix of anticipation and apprehension. Jamie couldn't forget the incident involving the cheesecake, a memory that still made him chuckle. Madge was undeniably a character, full of energy and unpredictability, making any interaction with her an adventure in itself.

As they wrapped up their training session and prepared to head out, Jamie wondered what escapades awaited them on the journey back home. With Paul by his side and the possibility of Bonnie and Madge's company, even the mundane task of transportation would be an adventure.

"You haven't met Madge before, have you, Paul?"

"Should I be concerned about this?"

"No, she's just this mental old lady who will rip into you at any opportunity if she can," Jamie replied, tongue-in-cheek.

Bonnie had warned Madge not to embarrass her with sex stories, or just about anything, really, especially since her mum had just done a new podcast on how to create the best sex ever.

Paul chuckled at Jamie's description of Madge, raising an eyebrow in amusement. "Sounds like quite the character. I reckon we'll survive the ride back, mate."

As they prepared to depart from the gym, Paul felt a twinge of curiosity about meeting Madge. Her reputation preceded her, and Jamie's warning only added to the intrigue. Bonnie's pre-emptive warning about Madge's potential for embarrassment only added to the anticipation. He made a mental note to tread carefully during the journey, fully aware of the potential for unexpected twists and turns.

With a shrug and a grin, Paul signalled his readiness to face whatever the ride back had in store, knowing that with Jamie by his side, they could handle anything – even the unpredictable company of Madge.

The mood was great between Bonnie and Madge.

"Please don't mention the podcast or talk about sex, Madge." One look was all it took.

"Bonnie, girl, don't you worry. We have far more embarrassing things to tell Jamie, don't we!"

Bonnie's face dropped as she had forgotten about the nose hair waxing with Shannon.

"Hey, Jamie," Bonnie said. Jamie turned to her, a curious expression on his face. He sensed a hint of trepidation in her tone, perhaps a lingering concern about what Madge might reveal.

"Yeah, Bonnie?" Jamie replied, his attention fully focused on her.

She took a deep breath before speaking, her voice tinged with apprehension and amusement. "Just a friendly reminder, Jamie. Let's keep the conversation light, yeah? No mentioning the podcast or, uh, certain personal experiences," she said, shooting a pointed glance at Madge.

Jamie couldn't help but chuckle at her caution, fully aware of the potential for embarrassment that lingered in the air. "Got it, Bonnie. Mum's the word," he replied, offering her a reassuring smile.

It didn't take Madge long. "Jamie, my sexy young man. Do you like pain?"

He took one look at Paul, then Bonnie. "Well, I've just been punched in the face multiple times and I've come back for more." Jamie awaited the next remark from Madge.

"No. Do you like kinky pain, my dear boy?"

Jamie's eyebrows shot up in surprise at Madge's bold question. He exchanged disbelieving glances with Paul and

Bonnie. Despite his best efforts to maintain composure, he couldn't suppress a twinge of discomfort at the unexpected turn in the conversation.

Clearing his throat, Jamie managed a nervous chuckle before replying, "Uh, well, that's, uh, quite the question, Madge. Let's just say I prefer to keep things, uh, traditional in that department." He tried to maintain his composure. "I think I'll stick to the pain that comes with a good boxing session. Keeps things simple, you know?"

He shifted uncomfortably in his seat, hoping to steer the conversation away from any further inquiries into his personal preferences. With a quick glance at Paul and Bonnie, he silently prayed for a change of topic.

"No, you miss my point. I'm not on about sex; we can leave that to Bonnie's mum on her podcast. Bonnie, it'll be a great episode; it'll make me feel like I could be a naughty young lady again."

Bonnie stood with her hands on her head. "Please, Madge, don't…"

"Bonnie, I am talking about our nose waxing today with Shannon."

Jamie let out a relieved sigh as Madge clarified her intentions, redirecting from potentially awkward territory. He chuckled nervously at the playful banter, grateful for the comedic relief.

"Ah. Got it, Madge. Nose waxing, huh? Sounds like quite the experience," Jamie replied, his tone lightening as the tension eased. He glanced at Bonnie, offering her a sympathetic smile as she braced herself for the inevitable embarrassment.

Bonnie's plea for Madge to change the subject only seemed to fuel her mischievous spirit. Jamie couldn't help but admire her quick wit and infectious energy, even if it sometimes veered into uncomfortable territory.

With amusement and relief, he settled into the newfound topic of nose waxing, a far cry from the potentially awkward inquiries about personal preferences. As the group continued their journey, Madge regaled them with tales of the afternoon's beauty adventures with Shannon.

"Shannon's a wizard with that wax, I tell you," she exclaimed, gesturing animatedly. "You haven't lived until you've experienced the wonders of a well-done nose waxing. Clears the sinuses like nothing else! Take a look at the photos we took. Look at the state of Bonnie. Anyway, podcast time, let's put it on. I want to hear about how to have the best sex ever with your mum."

Jamie's eyes widened in disbelief at Madge's unexpected request. He exchanged a bewildered glance with Paul, unsure of how to respond to such a bold statement.

Bonnie's cheeks flushed crimson with embarrassment as Madge pulled out her phone, seemingly oblivious to Bonnie's discomfort, and began scrolling through the photos they had taken earlier.

"Uh, Madge, maybe we should skip the podcast for now," Jamie suggested cautiously, attempting to avoid the potentially awkward topic. "How about we listen to some music instead?"

But Madge, with her mischievous grin firmly in place, was determined to proceed. "Oh, come on, Jamie, don't be such a prude," she teased, waving off his suggestion. "Let's give it a listen! I'm sure it'll be enlightening."

Jamie sighed inwardly, realising Madge was not going to let go of the idea easily. He exchanged a resigned look with Paul, knowing they were both in for an uncomfortable experience.

"All right, Madge," Jamie conceded reluctantly, "but let's keep an open mind, yeah?"

Madge's grin widened triumphantly as she tapped on her phone, cueing up the podcast episode. Bonnie shifted uncomfortably in her seat, clearly not thrilled about this.

As the podcast began, Jamie braced himself for whatever advice Bonnie's mum had to offer on the topic. He wondered how they'd ended up in such a surreal situation, but there was no turning back now. With a deep breath, he settled in, prepared for whatever awkwardness lay ahead.

He couldn't stop himself chuckling at Paul's reaction to the podcast and exchanged a bemused glance with him before replying, "Yeah, that's Bonnie's mum all right. Quite the traveller, it seems."

Bonnie's cheeks turned even redder with embarrassment as Paul's comment sunk in. She shifted uncomfortably in her seat, wishing she could disappear into the upholstery.

Meanwhile, Madge seemed to be thoroughly enjoying herself, eagerly interjecting with her own stories from back in the day. Her eyes sparkled with mischief as she regaled them with tales of her own adventures.

Joanna's podcast, 'Intimate Explorations with Joanna', had quickly gained popularity for its candid discussions about sex in relationships. With her warm and approachable demeanour, Joanna had a knack for making even the most taboo topics accessible and engaging. Each episode delved into different aspects of intimacy, aiming to help couples enhance their connection and explore their desires.

In the latest episode, which Madge was so keen to play, Joanna focused on the topic of kinks and how they could add excitement to a relationship. She began by explaining the importance of open communication between partners. "Before diving into any new experiences," Joanna said, "it's crucial to have an open and honest conversation with your partner. Discuss your boundaries, your interests, and any concerns you might have."

Joanna then outlined various types of kinks, from the more common ones like role-playing and BDSM, to the less discussed fetishes. She emphasised that there was no one-size-fits-all approach to intimacy. "What matters most," she explained, "is mutual consent and respect. Everyone has different comfort levels and fantasies, and it's important to honour those differences."

To illustrate her points, she shared anecdotes from listeners who had written in about their experiences. One couple, for instance, had discovered a shared interest in sensory play. "They started with something as simple as blindfolds and gradually incorporated other elements like feathers and ice," Joanna narrated. "It brought a new level of trust and excitement to their relationship."

Another story featured a woman who had always been curious about bondage but felt too shy to bring it up with her partner. "After listening to our episode on BDSM basics," Joanna said, "she finally broached the subject. To her surprise, her partner was not only open to the idea but also enthusiastic about exploring it together. They took a class on safe practices and now enjoy incorporating light bondage into their routine."

Throughout the episode, Joanna stressed the importance of safety and consent. "Always have a safe word," she advised. "This ensures that both partners feel secure and can stop the activity if it becomes too overwhelming."

Joanna also touched on the psychological benefits of exploring kinks. "For many people, engaging in these activities can be incredibly liberating," she explained. "It allows them to step outside their daily roles and experience a different aspect of themselves. This can be especially empowering and can strengthen the emotional bond between partners."

As the podcast continued, Joanna offered practical tips for those new to exploring kinks. She recommended starting slow and experimenting with different sensations to find what feels right. "It's all about discovery and play," she said. "There's no rush. Enjoy the journey and learn about each other along the way."

Joanna's soothing voice and empathetic approach made even the most hesitant listeners feel comfortable. By the end of the episode, it was clear why her podcast had resonated with so many people. She had a unique ability to demystify complex topics and encourage her audience to embrace their desires without shame.

Back in the car, Madge couldn't help but comment, "Your mum's a legend, Bonnie. She makes it all sound so easy and fun."

Though still embarrassed, Bonnie managed a smile. "Yeah, she does have a way with words."

Jamie, who had been listening intently, nodded in agreement. "It's really insightful. I can see why her podcast is so popular. It's important to talk about these things openly."

As they pulled up to Paul's home, Jamie felt a sense of warmth and familiarity wash over him. He smiled at Paul's invitation, appreciating the chance to catch up over a cuppa and some homemade carrot cake.

"Sounds perfect, Paul," he replied with a grin. "You know me too well."

Paul chuckled, glad to have Jamie's company. "Of course, mate. And the kids will be thrilled to see you too."

Jamie bid farewell to Bonnie and Madge, exchanging hugs and well-wishes. Madge, true to form, couldn't resist a cheeky request for cake, earning a playful rebuke from Bonnie.

Bonnie, on the other hand, wanted to give Jamie a proper goodbye. Jumping out of the car, she enveloped Jamie in a heartfelt hug, planting a little kiss on his cheek before bidding him farewell.

Jamie returned the hug warmly, feeling grateful for the friendship and camaraderie they shared. With a final wave to Bonnie and Madge, Jamie followed Paul into the warmth of his home, looking forward to a cozy chat.

Later that evening, as the sun dipped below the horizon, casting long shadows over Paul's cozy living room, Jamie found himself reluctantly roped into a marathon Monopoly session. Ever the enthusiast, Paul had insisted on playing, and Jamie, despite his initial hesitation, couldn't resist the infectious energy that Paul brought to the game.

"Come on, Jamie, it'll be fun," he urged, setting up the board with a gleam in his eye. "It's been ages since we had a proper game night."

Jamie sighed, settling into his chair. "All right, but no cheating this time. Remember, I know all your tricks."

Paul grinned, hands raised in mock surrender. "Scout's honour, mate. I'll play fair and square."

As the game progressed, laughter and good-natured banter filled the room. The intensity of their earlier workout was a distant memory, replaced by the comforting familiarity of friendship and the competitive spirit of Monopoly. Hours passed in a blur of property deals, strategic plays, and playful arguments over the rules.

But just when Jamie thought the night was winding down, Paul had another surprise in store. "You know, Jamie," he began, eyes twinkling with mischief, "I've been getting into ultramarathons lately. There's this documentary I've been dying to watch. Fancy joining me?"

Jamie groaned, feigning exasperation. "You're obsessed, mate. But all right, let's see what this is all about."

They settled onto the couch, the Monopoly board forgotten as Paul queued up the documentary. The screen flickered to life and soon they were immersed in the world of ultramarathons – gruelling races that tested the limits of human endurance and willpower. Jamie found himself captivated by the stories of the runners, their determination and resilience resonating deeply.

As the night stretched into the early hours, Jamie

admired Paul's relentless enthusiasm. Despite the exhaustion creeping in, he appreciated the passion his friend had for pushing boundaries and exploring new challenges. It was a reminder of the strength of their bond and the unwavering support they offered each other.

Eventually, as the documentary drew to a close, Jamie stifled a yawn. "All right, Paul, I think it's time to call it a night. But I have to admit, that was pretty inspiring."

Paul nodded, a satisfied smile on his face. "Glad you enjoyed it, mate. There's always something new to discover, isn't there?"

Jamie headed to bed with a deep sense of contentment. The day had been long and unpredictable, filled with moments of tension, laughter, and unexpected insights. But through it all, the bonds of friendship and the lessons from Joanna's podcast had made it all worthwhile, offering new perspectives and deeper connections.

CHAPTER 15

Brave New World

Bonnie received another call from her agent.

"Bonnie, pack your bags! You're going on a little trip. Nike wants you to do some promotions around Europe, and the first stop is in the UK," exclaimed Danny, her agent, with enthusiasm.

"Sorry, Danny, start again. I can't go around Europe," Bonnie responded, a bit confused. She wasn't sure about the sudden travel plans.

Danny chuckled. "This is a fantastic opportunity! Nike is launching a new campaign, and they want you to be one of the faces of it. You'll be doing events, interviews, and, of course, getting paid well for it. It's a big deal!"

Bonnie hesitated. Her mind raced with thoughts of her commitments at the surf school and her personal life. She loved the idea of being part of such a significant campaign, but the timing felt challenging.

"Bonnie, trust me on this. I've already confirmed your participation. You leave in two days. Everything is taken care of – flights, accommodation, schedule. It's a short tour, and you'll be back before you know it," Danny reassured her.

Reluctantly, she agreed. The opportunity was indeed a big one, and deep down, she was excited about it. As she began packing her bags for the European tour, she couldn't shake off the feeling that this trip might bring about changes she hadn't anticipated. Jamie was in total bemusement as to why Bonnie was packing already; she had two days to get her stuff together. He also thought to himself, *Isn't it getting cold over in the UK? It's nearly December.*

Jamie hadn't been back to the UK for some time now. He was feeling a little jealous as he would love to see his sister with her family and of course his mum again. FaceTime was starting to get a little tiresome.

As Bonnie continued to gather her things, she couldn't shake the mix of excitement and anxiety about the upcoming journey. Her mind buzzed with thoughts of the surf school, Henry, and the team. She knew her absence would create some challenges, but the opportunity with Nike was too significant to pass up.

While packing, she received a message from Ronnie.

'Heard you're off on a European tour with Nike! That's incredible news. I'm thrilled for you. We'll miss you at the surf school but go rock those promotions. Can't wait to hear all about it. Safe travels!'

Bonnie smiled at the message, appreciating the support from her friend. She replied, 'Thanks, Ronnie! It came out of the blue, but I couldn't say no. I'll make sure to bring some European vibes back to the surf school. Take care of everyone for me! I will try and have a chat to Henry before I go.'

She began to sort through her wardrobe, deciding what to bring for a European winter. This trip might not only be about professional growth but also a journey of self-discovery, and maybe a beer or two.

Jamie had been thinking to himself that this could be an opportunity for a visit home. He could surprise his sister and mum and his brother-in-law's garage gym was amazing. He could also do some winter hiking. He had the crazy idea of doing the winter Fan Dance event, run by the SF Experience company.

He'd done this before, as a soldier. A 24K route march in the Brecon Beacons, Wales, infamous within the ranks of all the UK Special Forces. Maybe Bonnie could do it with him, or maybe not as she would be way too competitive and want to beat him.

Jamie also thought it could be an opportunity to see his rugby mates and play in a local memorial game for ex-players who had passed away on Boxing Day. He was aware of another mate whose father had passed away from prostate cancer – that's who the game was being played for. This was very close to home. His thoughts turned to the rugby mates, the memorial game, drinking games, reminiscing about old times, and the poignant cause behind it all, triggering memories of his own father's battle with prostate cancer.

Even though Jamie and Bonnie had been dating for a few months, there were still secrets. Some of the things he had seen and been part of in the parachute regiment, he wasn't ready to talk about. Jamie hadn't mentioned anything about his past girlfriends. Three years ago he met someone that had a profound impact on him. His mind wandered as he thought back to one night in London.

*

While people-watching on a cold January evening, he met Terrier Tyndall. There was a feeling of companionship, that they were not on their own. Smiles shared with total strangers brought about a sense of peace. The odd couple having a conversation or laughing together was something special shared by onlookers. Walking the street, as so many other people were watching each other's faces, sharing moments before their eyes were closed. Jamie thought back to when he met Terrier Tyndall, with her eyes closed. Terrier's name was Marnie Tyndall (Mary) or Mee.

As the chilly wind swept through the crowded street, Terrier's mind drifted to that serendipitous encounter with Jamie. It was a moment frozen in time, much like the frost in the air that evening. They had found each other amid the hustle and bustle of the city, drawn together by the unspoken connection that seemed to transcend the ordinary.

Their conversation had started with a shared glance, a silent acknowledgement that there was something extraordinary about this chance meeting. Laughter had followed, echoing against the backdrop of the city lights. In that moment, they became an odd couple, a pair of kindred spirits weaving their own narrative into the tapestry of the bustling city.

As Jamie walked beside Terrier through the cold January evening, he marvelled at the interconnectedness of lives, the beauty found in fleeting moments shared with strangers. Memories of their first meeting lingered, and with her eyes closed, Terrier embraced the feeling of being part of something larger – a shared experience in the mosaic of human connections.

And so, on that chilly night, amidst the sea of faces and the shared glances of strangers, Terrier Tyndall and Jamie continued their journey, finding solace in the simple yet profound act of being present with one another in a world where everyone was, in some way, people watching.

Marnie had shared a few messages since Jamie had gone on his travels. For some reason she wondered if due to their rugby connection, from York and the small town of Bridlington on the east coast of the UK, Jamie might find his way to the memorial game (Waller Trophy) on Boxing Day.

Marnie thought back to the kiss she had shared with Jamie.

Without a word, Jamie cupped her face in his hands, his touch tender and reassuring. She could feel the warmth of his breath as he leaned in, their lips just a breath away from each other.

The kiss was soft and sweet, a perfect blend of passion and tenderness. It felt like a promise, an agreement between two souls who had found something rare and beautiful in each other. In that moment, they were not just kissing; they were expressing a depth of emotion that words could never capture.

As they pulled away, their eyes met once again and a shared smile passed between them. The perfect kiss lingered in the air, a fleeting moment of connection that left them both breathless and wanting more. In the quiet intensity of that exchange, Jamie and Marnie felt the weight of unspoken words and the promise of something profound stirring between them.

But as quickly as it had begun, reality intruded, pulling them back from the brink of that shared moment. Jamie's thoughts returned to his present life, his commitments, and the secrets he carried with him, while Marnie found herself wondering about the uncertainty of their connection and where it might lead.

For a moment, they stood in silence, each lost in their own thoughts, grappling with the implications of the kiss they had shared. It was a moment of clarity amidst the chaos of their lives, a glimpse of something more that left them both longing for answers.

But as the noise of the city enveloped them once again, Jamie and Marnie were left with nothing but the memory of that perfect kiss, a tantalising taste of what could be, and the uncertainty of what lay ahead. In that moment, they were two souls adrift in the vastness of the world, bound together by a single, fleeting kiss.

*

Bonnie decided she needed to see her mum and dad. She also wanted to spend some time with Henry before she left. Joanna hadn't seen much of her daughter since the introduction of Jamie; they were always out training together as well. She thought they must be at it like rabbits. At Bonnie's age, she and Mick enjoyed good sex two to three times a day. Joanna felt a pang of nostalgia as she reminisced about her own youth. As a therapist she knew all too well the difference between love stories and life stories. She pushed those thoughts aside, focusing instead on the excitement of seeing Bonnie. She knew how important this opportunity with Nike was for her daughter and wanted to offer her all the support she could.

As Bonnie arrived at her parents' house, she was greeted with warm hugs and smiles. Henry was already there, chatting with Mick in the living room. Bonnie's heart swelled with love as she looked at her family and friends gathered together. Over dinner, they laughed and shared stories, catching up on each other's lives. Bonnie cherished these moments, knowing that she would miss them dearly while she was away. She made a mental note to video call them as often as she could during her European tour.

After dinner, Bonnie pulled Henry aside for a private conversation. She held his hand tightly, her gaze earnest as she spoke. "Henry, I'm going away for a little while on this tour with Nike. I know it's sudden, but it's a big opportunity for me, and I couldn't turn it down."

Henry nodded understandingly, a small smile playing on his lips. "I'm happy for you, Bonnie. You deserve this chance to shine. Just promise me you'll come back to me in one piece," he said, his voice filled with affection.

Tears welled up in her eyes as she hugged Henry tightly. "I promise, Henry. I'll come back to you; I promise." As they held each other, Bonnie felt a mixture of emotions swirling inside her – excitement for the journey ahead, sadness at leaving Henry behind, but above all, a deep sense of gratitude for the love and support of her family.

The next two days passed in a blur of last-minute preparations and goodbyes. Ronnie and the team at the surf school threw her a farewell party, complete with laughter, music, and well-wishes for the adventure ahead. As Bonnie boarded the plane bound for the UK, she couldn't help but feel a sense of anticipation building inside her. She didn't know what the future held, but she was ready to embrace it with open arms. Meanwhile, Jamie was making plans of his own. Inspired by thoughts of home and the upcoming memorial game, he decided to book a ticket to the UK, surprising Bonnie and his family with an unexpected visit.

As the plane took off, carrying Bonnie across the ocean towards her new adventure, she closed her eyes and whispered a silent prayer for guidance and strength. Whatever lay ahead, she knew she was ready to face it head-on, with courage and determination in her heart.

CHAPTER 16

The Ties That Bind

The plane journey was no different to any other, apart from that she was in business class. Bonnie hadn't taken any notice of the brief regarding other athletes joining the tour. She did recognise a few familiar faces from the CrossFit and weightlifting community, though. Weightlifting was something she had always found fascinating and if she couldn't be a surfer, being a weightlifter in the Olympics would be something special.

It was going to be a long flight. One of Bonnie's special powers was that she could fall asleep anywhere, and this was no different. Within 15 minutes, she was fast asleep.

As Bonnie drifted into sleep, her mind wandered through a dreamscape of possibilities. Visions of podiums, medals, and the roar of the crowd filled her thoughts, fuelled by her passion for weightlifting. She could almost feel the cool metal of the barbell in her hands, the adrenaline coursing through her veins as she lifted with precision and strength.

In her dreams, she saw herself standing tall on the Olympic stage, representing her country with pride. Each lift was a testament to her years of dedication and hard work, a culmination of endless hours spent in the gym perfecting her technique. The cheers of the crowd echoed in her ears, pushing her to push herself further, to reach new heights of achievement.

But amidst the glory of her imagined victories, there lingered a sense of uncertainty. The path to Olympic greatness was fraught with challenges and obstacles, and Bonnie knew that the road ahead would not be easy. Yet, she was undeterred. With each passing moment, her resolve only grew stronger, her determination unwavering.

As the plane soared through the night sky, Bonnie slept on, her dreams carrying her closer to her goals and aspirations. And in that moment, she knew that no matter what the future held, she would face it with strength, and an unshakeable belief in herself. This was but a dream. Surfing was the dream she was living.

One thing Bonnie could do on a plane, was eat. As she indulged in the abundance of food offered, she found herself immersed in the captivating world of cinema. The documentaries she watched provided not only entertainment but also inspiration, each offering a glimpse into the lives of extraordinary individuals who had achieved greatness in their respective fields.

The CrossFit documentary resonated deeply, reminding her of the camaraderie and determination that defined her own journey as an athlete. It reignited her passion for fitness and competition, fuelling her desire to push herself to new limits.

But it was 'The Last Dance', chronicling the legendary career of Michael Jordan and the Chicago Bulls, that truly captured Bonnie's imagination. The story of perseverance, teamwork, and relentless pursuit of excellence struck a chord with her as she watched Jordan's unparalleled skill and unwavering dedication unfold on screen. Bonnie felt a renewed sense of determination wash over her. She was reminded that greatness was not achieved overnight, but through years of hard work, sacrifice, and unwavering belief in oneself.

As the credits rolled and the plane journey continued, Bonnie found herself filled with a newfound sense of purpose. Inspired by the stories she had witnessed, she knew that her own journey was just beginning, and she was more determined than ever to chase her dreams with everything she had.

As she had journeyed through her dreams, her mind danced between the realms of ambition and reality. While she slept, her subconscious stirred with visions of success and triumph, fuelled by her determination to conquer the challenges that lay ahead.

Yet, even in her dreams, Bonnie's connection to her true passion remained unbreakable. Surfing wasn't just a dream – it was her reality, her sanctuary amidst the chaos of life. The rush of the waves, the salty breeze against her skin, the thrill of riding the crest of a wave – all of it was ingrained in her very being, shaping her identity and fuelling her spirit.

But even as she lived out her dream on the waves, she

found inspiration in unexpected places. The words of Michael Jordan echoed in her mind. "I've failed over and over and that is why I succeed." A reminder that failure was not an endpoint, but a steppingstone on the path to success. With each wipeout, each missed wave, Bonnie knew she was one step closer to mastering her craft and reaching the pinnacle of her surfing career.

As the plane continued its journey through the night sky, Bonnie slept on, her dreams intertwining with her reality in a tapestry of hope and determination. And when she awoke, she would face the world with the same courage that had carried her this far. For Bonnie, the journey was just beginning, and she was ready to seize every opportunity that came her way, both on the waves and beyond.

*

Bonnie woke from her dream-filled slumber as the plane began its descent in the UK. The words of Michael Jordan echoed in her mind: "I've failed over and over and that is why I succeed." As she stretched in her seat, she reflected on the profound truth behind those words.

In surfing, as in life, failure was inevitable. There were days when the waves were relentless, tossing her about like a ragdoll. There were competitions where she fell short of her goals, despite giving it her all. But with each setback, Bonnie learned and grew stronger.

She decided that was enough screen time and decided to read one of her books to spice thing up a little, erotic fantasy was the choice of today.

As Bonnie delved into the pages of her chosen book, she allowed herself to be swept away by the tantalising world of erotic fantasy. With each word, she felt a surge of excitement and anticipation, her imagination ignited by the steamy scenes unfolding before her.

In the midst of her own adventures on the waves and in competitions, indulging in such literature offered Bonnie a welcome escape, a chance to explore desires and fantasies beyond the realm of surfing. The characters leapt off the pages, their passions and desires mirroring her own in some ways, yet transcending the boundaries of reality.

As the plane hummed steadily through the night sky, Bonnie lost herself in the sensuous prose, her heart racing with every turn of the page. For a brief moment, she was transported to a world where anything was possible, where pleasure knew no bounds.

And in that moment of blissful abandon, Bonnie found a sense of freedom and liberation, a reminder that life was meant to be lived to the fullest, both on and off the waves. As the words danced before her eyes, she savoured the thrill of exploration and discovery, knowing that adventure awaited her on every page.

As the plane touched down and Bonnie prepared to embark on her new adventure, she carried with her the wisdom of those who had come before her. Like Michael Jordan, she knew that true success was born from resilience, perseverance, and an unwavering belief in oneself.

With a smile on her face and a fire burning in her heart, she stepped off the plane, ready to face whatever challenges lay ahead. For she knew that no matter how many times she fell, she would always rise again, stronger and more determined than ever before.

As Bonnie stepped onto the wet tarmac, feeling the raindrops patter against her skin, she couldn't help but smile. This was familiar territory for her, the kind of weather that fuelled her passion for surfing. Despite the gloomy skies and blustery winds, exhilaration coursed through her veins.

"Florence, get that look off your face. You're working out with us later to get this journey out of our legs. I hear you love a little weightlifting!!" Tia Toom was one of the world's best female CrossFit athletes. She was also a fantastic weightlifter; she had represented at the Commonwealth Games.

Turning her attention to Tia Toom, Bonnie's smile widened at the prospect of a workout session. The invitation to join one of the world's best CrossFit athletes was an opportunity she couldn't pass up. And the mention of weightlifting only added to her excitement, knowing that they shared a common love for the sport.

As Bonnie and Tia made their way through the airport, their conversation flowed effortlessly, filled with laughter and camaraderie. Bantering with each other at customs, they were met by representatives from Nike, who greeted them warmly and ushered them towards a waiting cab.

The mention of a big schedule ahead reminded Bonnie of the whirlwind of activities that awaited them in the UK. Despite the jet lag that threatened to weigh them down, excitement surged at the thought of what lay ahead. The offer of rest from their representatives was met with a knowing glance between Bonnie and Tia. While the suggestion was well-intentioned, both women shared a passion for training that ran deep in their veins. Tia's defiant smirk spoke volumes, reaffirming Bonnie's own determination to seize every opportunity to push herself to new heights.

On entering the cab, Tia caught a glimpse of the book Bonnie had been reading. "What the hell is that? Let me take a look." Bonnie didn't have time to hand over the book or save anything, Tia had already popped it out of her rucksack. "You learn something new every day, don't you? I didn't take you for a reader of smutty novels and definitely not high fantasy. What the Hell? Is that like vampires having sex?" Tia clearly found this hilarious.

Bonnie couldn't help but chuckle at her reaction as she glanced at the book cover that had caught her attention. With a sheepish grin, Bonnie replied, "Well, you know, sometimes you need a little escape from reality. And yes, it's definitely on the steamy side, but there's more to it than just vampires having sex."

As Tia continued to laugh, Bonnie couldn't help but join in. The absurdity of the situation, coupled with Tia's infectious humour, lifted her spirits even further. "Hey, don't knock it till you try it," Bonnie teased, playfully nudging Tia's shoulder. "You might find yourself hooked on the romance and adventure."

With a shake of her head and a smile, Tia handed the book back to Bonnie, still chuckling at the unexpected discovery. "Well, I'll stick to my CrossFit and weightlifting for now, but I'll keep an open mind," she replied with a grin.

"Tell you what! Later on, I'll read some of the smutty stuff and let's see if you want to video call that husband of yours afterwards."

"Bonnie, I won't be video-calling him! I'll be taking myself to bed and sorting myself out, thank you. I'll keep that in mind as well, thanks. Looks like we're here. Let's get checked in – I've got the perfect CrossFit box we can go to. Beers later as well."

Bonnie was on for the ride. Something was telling her Tia was an absolute machine. This was going to be a good training session on tired legs.

Bonnie couldn't help but burst into laughter at Tia's bold suggestion, her cheeks flushing with amusement. "All right, Tia, you're on!" she exclaimed, still chuckling. "But no pressure, I won't judge if you decide to skip the video call and opt for some solo relaxation instead."

As the cab came to a stop, they gathered their belongings and made their way towards the check-in area. The prospect of a challenging CrossFit session followed by some well-deserved beers later in the day filled Bonnie with anticipation. She knew Tia was a force to be reckoned with, and was eager to see just how intense their training session would be.

As Bonnie stepped into the CrossFit box, a surge of excitement mingled with a hint of apprehension. The sight of some of the top British weightlifters training only added to her anticipation, their presence a testament to the calibre of the facility.

But it was the unexpected encounter with Sam Burton, the fittest woman on Earth a few years back, that caught Bonnie off guard. Despite her initial surprise, she had nothing but admiration for Sam's formidable reputation and undeniable talent.

As Sam greeted Tia with a playful insult and a hug, Bonnie stood aside, nervous but determined. She knew that training alongside athletes of this calibre would push her to her limits, but she was ready to rise to the challenge.

With a deep breath and resolve in her heart, Bonnie squared her shoulders and prepared to give it her all. She may have been a surfer by trade, but she was no stranger to hard work and dedication. And as she joined the others on the training floor, she vowed to show them what she was made of.

With Sam's savage workouts and dirty humour setting the tone for the session ahead, Bonnie knew she was in for a tough workout. But she was ready; it was moments like these that separated the ordinary from the extraordinary.

As the music blared and the weights clanged, Bonnie threw herself into the workout with everything she had. And as she pushed herself to new limits, with pride and satisfaction that she was holding her own among some of the best athletes in the world.

*

It was late. Jamie thought Bonnie would answer. If he video-called, it would be mid-day UK time. Bonnie answered, "Sorry, I can't talk now. Look where I am." She panned around the bustling CrossFit box to show him who she was working out with. His face lit up with surprise and excitement. He couldn't believe the scene unfolding before him – Bonnie surrounded by top athletes, immersed in a world of intense training and camaraderie.

"Wow, that's incredible!" he exclaimed, his voice filled with awe. "You're really living the dream, aren't you? I'm so proud of you, Bonnie."

Despite the distance between them, Jamie felt a sense of connection as he watched Bonnie in her element. He could see the determination in her eyes, the fire burning bright within her as she tackled each challenge with grit and determination.

With a wave and a smile, Bonnie ended the call, her heart swelling with love and gratitude for Jamie's unwavering support.

The ladies had smashed some big weights. The atmosphere was amazing, making Tia and Bonnie forget about how tired they were from all the travelling. Bonnie had been to some big commercial gyms and really loved the atmosphere of some. Mostly only encountered respectful, friendly people. The regulars would smile or wave, but were content to leave her alone while her headphones were in.

She had always made friends with people, wherever she was. One of them was teaching Bonnie how to do handstands! There were almost always other women in the free weights sections and she had never seen any of them take crap from the men in the gyms.

In a room full of mirrors, Bonnie sometimes noticed people looking at her. People were great about unracking and wiping down their benches and were always accommodating when anyone asked for help or a little extra space.

There had been a few bad eggs over the years who stuck out comically, and mostly got eyerolls from everyone around them. There was one guy who decided to catcall Bonnie one time when she walked past him. She told the girls she gave an enthusiastic bitch face and at least one other person gave him a dirty look. There was also the woman who was there primarily to make out with her gentleman companion. Bonnie went on to see them there fairly regularly, and she was pretty sure her lifting was entirely motivated by kisses as rewards for reps. Finally, the woman who totally disregarded the 'everyone must wear a shirt' rule and didn't ever seem to be working out. Bonnie would love to work out in just her sports bra! It was often more comfortable and had an 'IDGAF what I or anyone else looks like while at the gym' vibe.

Tia said, "I first saw this woman, I thought, "Oh, she must be new," because she wasn't wearing a shirt and she was just aimlessly wandering around. Months later, I still have no sense of what she does to work out and she still never wears a shirt! It's like she's literally just there to see and be seen. It's baffling and it made me a bit uncomfortable."

Knackered, Bonnie and Tia headed back to the hotel. Sam had invited them both out for drinks with some of the other ladies. There would be plenty of time for that later.

Both ladies had a quick beer in the hotel bar. The chatter veered back to Bonnie's reading choices. "You going to add to your highlight reel later after reading your x-rated book?" Tia was hinting as if to suggest she would have a personal call from Jamie later.

Bonnie chuckled at her teasing, taking a playful sip of her beer. "Well, you never know," she replied with a wink. "But for now, I think I'll stick to my current reading list. Who knows, maybe I'll find some inspiration for the highlight reel after all."

Tia laughed, shaking her head in amusement. "You

always know how to keep things interesting, Bonnie. But seriously, I'm curious to hear your thoughts on that book. It must be quite the page-turner."

"Okay, okay, Tia. I will read you a naughty bit just for you." Bonnie grinned as she knew just what to read.

As they made their way to their respective bedrooms, a mischievous twinkle lingered in Bonnie's eyes. She couldn't resist teasing Tia a bit more, knowing how much her friend enjoyed a bit of risqué reading.

"Just remember, Tia, I've got the perfect passage in mind," she teased, her grin widening as she glanced back at her friend.

Tia chuckled, her cheeks flushing slightly with anticipation. "I'm holding you to that, Bonnie," she replied with a playful wink.

Once alone in her room, Bonnie retrieved the book from her bedside table, flipping through the pages until she found the passage she had in mind. It was a steamy excerpt, filled with tantalising descriptions and sensual imagery. Settling into bed with the book, Bonnie couldn't help but feel a rush of excitement as she imagined Tia's reaction to the naughty bit she was about to read. She knew her friend would appreciate the playful gesture, and she couldn't wait to see the look on Tia's face when she heard the words.

Meanwhile, in her own room, Tia snuggled under the covers, her thoughts still lingering on Bonnie's promise of a naughty read. There was a flutter of anticipation, wondering just how spicy Bonnie's chosen passage would be. As she began to read aloud, her voice filled with dramatic flair, Tia listened intently from her room, her imagination running wild with the vivid descriptions and heated dialogue. With each word, she felt a growing sense of excitement, her pulse quickening as she surrendered to the allure of the forbidden narrative.

The passage described an intense encounter between the vampire lord and his human lover. They were in a secluded, candle-lit chamber, the air thick with anticipation and the scent of desire. The vampire's eyes glowed with a predatory hunger as he approached her, his movements slow and deliberate. He whispered dark promises into her ear, his cool breath sending shivers down her spine. She felt a mixture of fear and exhilaration as he trailed his fingers along her bare skin, igniting a fire within her. Their bodies moved together in a primal dance, each touch and caress pushing them closer to the edge of ecstasy. The scene was raw and unfiltered, capturing the intensity of their forbidden passion and the depth of their connection. As the vampire's fangs grazed her neck, the human lover's breath hitched, the pain and pleasure intertwining in a way that left her craving more. The darkness of their encounter was tempered by the undeniable bond they shared, a bond that transcended the boundaries of their worlds and drew them together in a desperate embrace.

By the time Bonnie finished reading, both women were left flushed and exhilarated, their hearts racing with the thrill of the moment. And as they drifted off to sleep, their minds filled with tantalising images and whispered fantasies, they knew their friendship was one that would always be filled with laughter, love, and a healthy dose of playful mischief.

"Yep, there's no wonder you can get turned on. I think I need to take myself to bed now," Tia said with a laugh. On that note, both ladies headed to bed, absolutely exhausted.

CHAPTER 17

A Tangled Web

Jamie thought about his plane ticket, which was now booked. *I'll tell Bonnie tomorrow that I'm heading to the UK*, he mused, deciding to keep it a secret from his sister for now. It would be a fun surprise.

A few days before his departure, he spoke with his friend Paul about the trip. With his obsession for the military, Paul immediately asked if Jamie was planning to participate in the Fan Dance event, a gruelling Special Forces selection march in Wales. Having done the march multiple times during his service, Jamie found the idea of doing it for fun less than appealing. Still, he considered it, knowing Paul would never let him live it down if he didn't.

Meanwhile, Aurora, aware of Jamie's plans to return to the UK, impulsively booked her own ticket. Jamie was caught off guard when she video-called him. "Hey, to what do I owe the pleasure of your call?" he asked.

THE LAST SURF

Aurora grinned with her typical bluntness. "Yes, you're blessed with my call. I've booked a ticket. You're welcome."

Jamie felt an immediate mix of surprise and concern. "You booked a ticket? Are you coming to the UK? Did you talk to Bonnie about this?"

"Of course not! Where's the fun in that? I wanted to surprise her. Plus, I've always wanted to see the Isle of Man."

Jamie sighed, worried about how this might affect their plans. "Bonnie might be a bit surprised by this."

Aurora's grin softened. "I hadn't thought about that. But come on, it'll be fun! We can all hang out together, explore the Isle of Man. Bonnie's surfing can take a back seat." Laughing, Aurora said, "I'll see you at the airport," and ended the call.

Jamie was frustrated by the casual dismissal of Bonnie's plans and her nonchalant attitude toward potentially disruptive behaviour worried him. He recalled the night at the club when he had to rescue them both from a dangerous situation, realising the potential for trouble if Aurora's visit turned into a series of wild nights out.

"Great, just great," Jamie muttered to himself, running a hand through his hair in exasperation. He knew that if Aurora crossed paths with some of his rowdier rugby mates, it could spell disaster for everyone involved.

Aurora thought hurriedly, *Better tell Bonnie's dad. Mick loves me anyway so I'm sure he wouldn't mind me having a month off work. I better reschedule my consultation for my boob job as well.* Looking in her full-length mirror, Aurora thought to herself, *I'm going to do some damage with some*

English boys.

Jamie couldn't shake off his concerns about her unexpected presence in the UK. He knew Bonnie might feel surprised and even annoyed once she found out her friend had seemingly followed her without prior notice. Despite understanding Aurora's passion for motorbikes and her desire to visit the Isle of Man, Jamie worried that her presence might strain their friendship.

Aurora's dream of attending the TT event and experiencing the thrill of riding around the Isle of Man had been a topic of conversation for some time. She was going; like it or not she was going to do what she wanted, when she wanted. She went for it with no regard to how anyone would feel.

Jamie pondered the situation, realising his assumptions about Bonnie's travel plans might have led to miscommunication. He thought Bonnie would likely visit Cornwall and a few other places. Jamie did know the East Yorkshire town of Scarborough, given its reputation for surfing, and hadn't considered Bridlington as a possibility. Bonnie had mentioned Bridlington, which sounded like a charming destination nestled on the East Yorkshire coast. Jamie was familiar with Bridlington, having visited many times and having connections with the local rugby club.

Despite his uncertainty, Jamie trusted that Bonnie had chosen Bridlington for a reason. He resolved to make the best of the situation, ensuring his surprise for Lauren went smoothly, while also staying mindful of Bonnie's whereabouts and making necessary adjustments to his plans. He hadn't told Bonnie that Aurora was also coming.

The flight was long, and Aurora spent most of it

drinking and chatting with other passengers. Jamie kept to himself, his thoughts preoccupied with how Bonnie would react to the surprise. When they finally landed, Jamie was tired and a bit on edge from Aurora's antics on the plane.

They went their separate ways at the airport. "Well thanks for nothing, Jamie. Just like when I first saw you outside Robbie's Coffee, I'm off. Don't tell Bonnie I'm here. I'll find her when I'm ready." She gave him a little wink, and she was off to her accommodation.

What the hell is going to happen with that one? Jamie wondered.

Brother-in-law Andy was waiting outside for Jamie. With arms open wide, he gave Jamie the biggest hug. "It's good to have you back. Your sister needs you sometimes, and your mum will definitely be pleased to see you. Please tell me you've told your mum."

Jamie gave a sheepish look. "Well, not yet. I thought we could do that now. We could all surprise Lauren." His face spoke volumes; he knew his mum would be mad at him. Ever since his dad passed away from cancer, he had been a little distant from his family.

Andy nodded, understanding. "All right, let's do it. She'll be thrilled to see you, even if she gives you a hard time at first."

They drove to Jamie's mum's house, which wasn't far from his sister's in York. The air was filled with anticipation. Jamie hadn't been home in a while, and he knew his absence had been felt. When they arrived, Andy rang the doorbell, and Jamie's mum answered.

Her eyes widened in shock, and then she pulled Jamie

into a tight hug. "Jamie! What a surprise! Why didn't you tell me you were coming?"

Jamie smiled sheepishly. "Wanted to surprise you, Mum. I'm here for a while."

They went inside, and Jamie spent the afternoon catching up with his mum and Andy. The atmosphere was warm and filled with laughter, and Jamie felt a sense of belonging he had missed for so long.

Andy's phone buzzed with a FaceTime call. "Shit, Lauren is expecting me back. I made up some story that I was doing a drop-off for my dad's business, which would take all day."

Jamie's mum, Julia, gave Andy a look that only a mother-in-law could. "You haven't told your sister, have you?" She turned her piercing gaze on Jamie. "And you better not be in on this. You'd better answer that, Andy, and we'll be on our way to your place."

Andy sighed and answered the call, trying to keep his cool. "Hey, Lauren! Yeah, just finishing up here. I'll be back soon."

Lauren's voice crackled through the phone. "All right, just hurry up. Dinner's almost ready."

Andy hung up, looking relieved but also a bit nervous. "Okay, let's get going before she gets suspicious."

They piled into the car and headed to Lauren's house. The drive was filled with excited chatter and nervous laughter as they anticipated her reaction. When they arrived, Jamie took a deep breath and knocked on the door.

Lauren answered, her eyes widening in shock. "Jamie! What are you doing here?"

Jamie grinned. Lauren could see her mum and husband Andy stood just behind. She didn't know if she wanted to cry or punch Jamie in the face. "Have you all been in on this? Mum, did you know Jamie was coming back?" She pulled Jamie into a tight hug. "You idiot! Why didn't you tell me you were coming?"

Jamie chuckled. "Wanted to surprise you. I'm here for a while. Don't blame Andy; I made him promise not to say anything."

Andy quickly pushed through and went straight into the house. "I will go sort the kids out," he said, trying to avoid eye contact with Lauren.

"Don't think you've gotten away with this that easily, Daddy. You should have told me," Lauren said, half-scolding, half-laughing.

Julia finally responded to her daughter. "No, I didn't know either. Come on then, let's all get inside and join you for dinner with the kids. I think Jamie has a lot to tell us, hasn't he?"

"Bonnie Florence!!" Julia added with a massive grin on her face.

They all walked into the house, the air filled with the warmth of family reunion and the scent of a delicious dinner. Inside, the kids were playing, their laughter adding to the lively atmosphere. Jamie was relieved and overjoyed to be surrounded by his family again.

Once everyone settled down, he began sharing stories about his time away. He talked about his adventures, the people he met, and his plans for the future.

His family listened intently, asking questions and filling in the gaps of the time they had missed together.

Julia, noticing the gleam in Jamie's eyes whenever he mentioned Bonnie, couldn't help but tease, "So, tell us more about this Bonnie Florence. You seem quite smitten. I would be too, looking at her on Instagram, and the fact that she's a top surfer. She's fit. I would."

Jamie blushed, scratching the back of his head. "Yeah, she's something special. We've been through a lot together."

Smiling warmly, Lauren added, "We can't wait to meet her, Jamie. She sounds wonderful."

As the evening went on, the family shared laughter, memories, and hopes for the future. The bond between them felt stronger than ever, and Jamie was grateful for the love and support that surrounded him.

Later that night, after the kids had been put to bed and the house had quieted down, Jamie and Lauren sat outside, looking up at the stars. "It's good to have you back, Jamie," Lauren said softly. "We've missed you."

Jamie nodded, feeling the weight of his absence lift. "I've missed you all too. I promise to make up for lost time."

Lauren smiled, her eyes reflecting the starlight. "We're just glad you're home."

As Jamie and Lauren sat under the stars, he began to open up about Bonnie and everything that had happened.

"Bonnie is amazing, Lauren," Jamie started, his eyes lighting up. "She's a pro surfer and teaches at this surf school run by this great guy and his wife, David and Ronnie. She's so passionate about surfing and loves teaching kids. You should see the way her face lights up when she talks about the ocean."

Lauren smiled. "She sounds incredible, Jamie. I can see why you're so taken with her."

Jamie nodded, then added with a laugh, "But you wouldn't believe it, Aurora followed me over here. She's Bonnie's mental friend who's really into motorbikes and works for Bonnie's dad, Mick, in his garage. She phoned me and just showed up at the airport, out of the blue. She's planning to surprise Bonnie, but I'm a bit worried about how that's going to go."

Lauren raised an eyebrow. "Aurora? The one who always has a knack for causing chaos? This should be interesting."

Jamie sighed. "Yeah, exactly. I'm just hoping it doesn't turn into a mess."

He went on to share more stories, "And then there's Madge and Shannon. Madge is this sweet old lady who works at the surf school. She's always looking out for Bonnie. There was this one time, I brought Bonnie a cheesecake, and Madge just took it off me, saying I needed to eat healthier! She's a character."

Lauren laughed. "Sounds like she cares about you."

"I wouldn't go that far," Jamie said, laughing. "And then there's Shannon. She's been a good family friend. Always there with advice and a helping hand."

Jamie hesitated for a moment, then continued, "And there's Paul. He's still obsessed with the military and the

Fan Dance event. He's been pushing me to do it again while I'm in the UK. I've done it before when I was in the Paras, and it's brutal. I'm not sure I want to put myself through that again, but I know he'd be thrilled if I did."

Lauren looked thoughtful. "It sounds like you have a lot of important people in your life now, Jamie. People who care about you and support you. And as for the Fan Dance, well, maybe it's worth considering. Are you going to do it on your own or get one of your old rugby mates to join you?"

Jamie nodded slowly. "Yeah, you're right. I'll try and get a few of us to do it. There's also the memorial rugby game for prostate cancer and the MND community. As luck would have it Bonnie will be in Bridlington at the same time as the game."

Lauren reached out and squeezed his hand. "Whatever you decide, we're here for you. And I can't wait to meet Bonnie but maybe not Aurora. It sounds like Bonnie has been a good influence on you."

Jamie smiled as a warmth spread through him. "Thanks, Lauren. It means a lot to me to hear you say that."

The reunion with his sister was heartwarming. They spent a few days catching up and enjoying each other's company. Lauren was thrilled to see Jamie and even more excited about the pending trip to Bridlington.

Meanwhile, Bonnie had a brief meeting with her agent in the UK regarding the itinerary of her tour. The destination of Bridlington was chosen due to a fascinating discovery just before the tour started. Her agent had come across an intriguing piece of history: a letter discovered deep in the archives of the Bishop Museum in Honolulu.

The letter described how two Hawaiian princes and their English guardian surfed in Britain in September 1890. Remarkably, this earliest record of UK surfing didn't occur in the surf meccas of Newquay or Croyde, but in the East Yorkshire resort of Bridlington, in the chilly, murky North Sea.

This new research was published as Europe's only dedicated surfing museum opened in Braunton, North Devon, putting British surfing history on a par with the likes of California. The letter, discovered by Hawaiian author and historian Sandra Kimberley Hall, detailed how the princes surfed daily, enjoying the rough sea. The Victorian locals must have been incredulous at the sight of the Hawaiian princes paddling out and riding back into shore on large wooden planks.

The Museum of British Surfing's researchers believed this story would make waves in the global surfing community, adding a new 'ground zero' to UK surf heritage. The north-east coast of England is home to world-class waves, but Bridlington had never been a popular beach for surfers. This historical discovery added a rich layer to the town's heritage.

Bonnie inevitably felt a surge of excitement as she delved deeper into the historical significance of Bridlington's surfing past. The idea that two Hawaiian princes had surfed in the chilly North Sea waters of Bridlington back in 1890 was nothing short of astonishing.

Sitting in the quaint café where she had arranged to meet her agent, she couldn't wait to share this newfound knowledge with him. When he arrived, she launched into an animated recounting of the historical discovery.

"Can you believe it?" Bonnie exclaimed, her eyes shining with enthusiasm. "Two Hawaiian princes surfing in Bridlington! It's absolutely fascinating."

Her agent listened intently, nodding along as Bonnie relayed the details of the discovery. "That's incredible," he agreed. "It's amazing how these little-known stories can completely change our perception of a place."

Bonnie nodded eagerly. "Exactly! I think it adds such a rich layer to Bridlington's heritage. It's not just a seaside town; it's a place with a deep connection to the global surfing community."

Her agent smiled, clearly intrigued by the historical significance. "This could be a great angle to incorporate into your tour," he suggested. "We could organise a special event or activity in Bridlington to highlight its surfing history. It could really set your tour apart."

Bonnie's eyes lit up at the idea. "I love it! Let's do it," she exclaimed. "I think it would be a fantastic way to pay homage to the town's surfing legacy and connect with the local community."

As they discussed the logistics of incorporating Bridlington into her tour itinerary, Bonnie couldn't shake the feeling of excitement. Not only was she thrilled to explore the town's surfing history, but she was also eager to share this newfound knowledge with her fans.

Leaving the café with a renewed sense of purpose, she couldn't wait to dive into the planning process. Bridlington may not have been on her radar initially, but now it held a special place in her heart as she embarked on this journey to uncover its hidden surfing past.

Days later, Bonnie found herself walking along the sandy shores of Bridlington, the wind whipping through her hair as she gazed out at the waves. The beach was quiet, with only a few locals walking their dogs or taking leisurely strolls. She imagined what it must have been like for the Hawaiian princes, paddling out into these cold waters over a century ago.

Bonnie took out her phone and began to record a video for her social media followers. She wanted to share her excitement and the incredible history she had learned.

"Hey, everyone," she began, her voice filled with enthusiasm, "I'm here in Bridlington, and I have some amazing history to share with you all. Did you know that the first recorded instance of surfing in the UK happened right here in 1890? And it wasn't just anyone surfing – it was two Hawaiian princes! How cool is that?"

She panned the camera around to capture the beach and the waves. "I'm so excited to be here and to explore more of Bridlington's surfing heritage. Stay tuned for some awesome events and activities we have planned to celebrate this incredible history. You won't want to miss it!"

As she finished recording, Bonnie embraced a deep connection to the place. She had always felt at home in the water, but knowing that Bridlington held such a unique and significant place in surfing history made it even more special.

The next day, Bonnie met with the local tourism board and community leaders to discuss the upcoming events. They were all thrilled about the historical angle and eager to support her tour. Plans quickly came together for a surfing exhibition, historical presentations, and a special surf session where Bonnie would demonstrate her skills and pay tribute to the Hawaiian princes.

Word about the events spread quickly, and soon, surfers from all over the UK were planning to visit Bridlington. The small town buzzed with excitement, anticipating the influx of visitors and the chance to celebrate its newfound place in surfing history.

Bonnie also took some time to explore by herself. She visited the old town, with its charming, cobbled streets and historic buildings, and met with local surfers who shared their own stories and experiences. She even found a quaint little surf shop run by an enthusiastic couple who had been surfing the North Sea waves for decades.

"Welcome to our little slice of surf heaven." the shop owner, Tom, greeted her with a warm smile. "We've heard all about your tour and the history you've uncovered. It's amazing to think about those Hawaiian princes surfing here all those years ago."

Bonnie smiled back, enjoying the genuine warmth and friendliness of the local surfing community. "It's incredible, isn't it? I feel so honoured to be here and to share this history with everyone."

Tom nodded, his eyes twinkling with excitement. "We're all looking forward to the events. It's going to put Bridlington on the surfing map, for sure."

Bonnie continued her preparations with a sense of fulfilment and anticipation. The upcoming events in Bridlington were shaping up to be more than just a tour stop; they were a celebration of history, community, and the enduring spirit of surfing.

Her journey to this point had been far from easy. The passion for surfing was born from a deep, almost primal connection to the ocean, but it was her grit and determination that had carried her through the toughest times. She often thought back to the words her father had told her when she was a young girl, struggling with the harsh realities of life.

"Some people are just born to fight," he had said, his voice steady and reassuring. "It's not that they are born brave, or born strong. It's just that the universe has decided they will have grit and fire and steel in their blood. You will be tested, Bonnie, but that cosmic metal of yours will keep you strong. You will face trial after trial, be broken and damaged in countless ways, but you were born to fight. Maybe you will not have chosen this life, maybe you will love to lay down your arms, but you were born to fight. That's what we know, that's what we do best."

Those words had stayed with her, echoing in her mind during the darkest moments. When she faced injuries that threatened to end her career, when she battled through gruelling training sessions, and when she confronted the relentless pressure of competition, it was her father's voice that gave her strength.

Bonnie's life was a testament to that cosmic determination. She had fought her way through the ranks, earning her place in the competitive surfing world through sheer willpower and relentless effort. Each wave she conquered was not just a victory over nature, but a triumph over every obstacle that had ever stood in her way.

On the morning of the main event in Bridlington, Bonnie felt that familiar fire burning within her. The beach was bustling with activity. Tents and stalls were set up along the promenade, offering everything from local food and crafts to surfing gear and memorabilia. The scent of freshly cooked seafood filled the air, and the sound of laughter and chatter created a lively atmosphere.

Bonnie stood on the beach, looking out at the crowd that had gathered. Surfers of all ages and skill levels were waxing their boards and chatting excitedly. Families with children explored the stalls, and local musicians provided a festive soundtrack to the day.

Taking a deep breath, she grabbed her board and headed toward the water, ready to make her mark in Bridlington not just as a professional surfer, but as someone who had brought the town's incredible surfing history to light.

As she paddled out, she felt a deep connection to the Hawaiian princes who surfed these very waters over a century ago. With each wave she caught, she honoured their legacy and celebrated the rich history that had brought her to this special place.

The crowd cheered as Bonnie rode wave after wave, showcasing her skills and passion for the sport with joy and fulfilment that went beyond any competition or accolade. This was about more than just surfing; it was about community, history, and the enduring love for the ocean that connected them all.

As the sun began to set, casting a golden glow over the beach, Bonnie paddled back to shore. She was greeted with applause and cheers from the crowd, and couldn't help but smile with deep gratitude for the experience.

That evening, as she sat around a bonfire with the locals, sharing stories and laughter, Bonnie realised that Bridlington had become more than just a stop on her tour. It had become a part of her own surfing journey, a place where history and community came together in a beautiful and unexpected way.

And as she looked out at the waves, she knew that this was just the beginning. Bridlington's surfing legacy would continue to inspire and connect people, just as it had connected her to this incredible community and its rich history. And through it all, Bonnie would carry her father's words with her, a reminder of the grit, fire, and steel that defined her spirit.

CHAPTER 18

The Fan Dance

Bonnie needed a break from the tour. She had been everywhere, from Northern Ireland to Perranporth, Sennen Cove in Cornwall, and Pease Bay in Berwickshire for surfing. Alongside surfing, she had also joined Tia for weightlifting and CrossFit seminars around London. The girls enjoyed everything the tour had to offer, including a few exciting nights out. Bonnie continued to update Tia on the high fantasy book she was reading, adding a touch of literary discussion to their dynamic.

As they debriefed over coffee, London buzzed with tourists and the air was filled with chatter and noise. This was fortunate, as the lively background noise masked their conversation, which could have easily been mistaken for a discussion between a couple of porn stars talking about their latest movie.

Bonnie reflected on how much she had enjoyed the tour despite its hectic pace. The surfing spots had been incredible, and sharing the experience with Tia made it even more memorable. The coffee shop provided a moment of respite amidst the bustling city, allowing the friends to relax and share a few laughs about their adventures.

Despite the busy surroundings, Bonnie found solace in these moments of connection with Tia. The tour had taken them to some amazing places, but it was the shared experiences and inside jokes that made the journey truly special.

The girls reminisced about a particularly wild night when they ended up in a strip club with some of the CrossFit participants from a seminar. Fortunately, Tia knew a few of them, which made the situation slightly less awkward. Bonnie recalled her initial reaction: "We really shouldn't be in this place." She remembered seeing a group that must have been out for someone's birthday. They looked like they had just taken lines of coke. "That one guy, Tia! Can you remember him saying, 'I have never kissed my girlfriend like that before,' and the other saying, 'Well, I thought you couldn't touch them. I just got a blowjob.'

"I'm so glad we bailed after that," Bonnie continued, burying her face in her hands. "That could have ended the tour for us, Tia."

Tia laughed, trying to lighten the mood. "Come on. We didn't get caught, and you have to admit it was funny. Some of the girls... I mean, they were fit. Not my thing, but you have to appreciate them. It was like something out of your book. Now tell me, if it was in your book, wouldn't fairies be dancing and seducing their human victims before eating their withered bodies after rampant sex? Tell me I'm correct! In fact, I want to hear some from the latest chapter."

Bonnie chuckled, shaking her head at Tia's enthusiasm. "You're not far off, actually," she admitted. "All right, let me set the scene. In the latest chapter, our protagonist stumbles upon a hidden glade where ethereal lights flicker in the moonlight. She senses an otherworldly presence and soon realises she's surrounded by fairies, their beauty both enchanting and terrifying. They dance around her, weaving spells with their movements, drawing her into their world. As she succumbs to their allure, she knows there's no turning back."

Tia listened intently, her eyes wide with fascination. "Wow. That sounds intense. You have such a way with words. I can almost see it happening."

Bonnie's voice was steady as she read another passage aloud, the words flowing with an almost hypnotic cadence. Tia listened in fascination, wide-eyed as the scene unfolded.

"And again, as before, Maria the fairy unzipped my fly, took out my penis, and put it in her mouth. The one thing different from before was that she did not take off her own clothing. She wore this strange glowing bodysuit the whole time. I tried to move, but it felt as if my body was tied down by invisible threads. I felt myself growing big and hard inside her mouth.

"I saw her fake eyelashes and curled hair tips moving. Her bracelets made a dry sound against each other. Her tongue was long and soft and seemed to wrap itself around me. Just as I was about to come, she suddenly moved away and began slowly to undress me. She took off my jacket, my tie, my pants, my shirt, my underwear, and made me lie down on the floor of the train carriage we were on. Her own clothes started to glow brighter with every minute. She sat on the bed, took my hand, and brought it under her dress. She was not wearing panties. Well, what I thought were panties anyway. My hand felt the warmth of her. It was deep, warm, and very wet. My fingers were all but sucked inside...

"Then Maria mounted me and used her hand to slip me inside her. Once she had me deep inside, she began a slow rotation of her hips. As she moved, the edges of the blue bodysuit changed to red. Her body caressed my naked stomach and thighs. With the skirts of the bodysuit spread out around her, Maria, riding atop me, looked like a soft, gigantic mushroom that had silently poked its face up through the dead leaves on the ground and opened under the sheltering wings of night.

"Her insides felt warm and at the same time cold. They tried to envelop me, to draw me in, and at the same time press me out. My erection grew larger and harder. I felt I was about to burst wide open. It was the strangest sensation, something that went beyond simple sexual pleasure. It felt as if something inside her, something special inside her, was slowly working its way through my organ into me. It was strange."

Bonnie paused, glancing up at Tia, whose expression was a mix of awe and curiosity. "This book," Tia said slowly, "is intense. The imagery is so vivid."

Bonnie continued reading, her voice taking on a more intimate, hushed tone as the story delved deeper into the surreal encounter between the protagonist and Maria, the fairy.

"As Maria moved, the glowing bodysuit seemed to pulse with a life of its own. Her eyes locked onto mine, a mischievous gleam in them that hinted at ancient secrets and forbidden pleasures. The train around faded away, leaving just the two of us in a timeless, ethereal space.

"I could feel every contour of her, the smoothness of her skin, the rhythm of her breath. Her movements were both graceful and urgent, a dance of seduction that drew me further into her spell. She leaned forward, her hair brushing against my chest, and whispered something in a language I couldn't understand, but the meaning was clear. She wanted all of me.

"Her hips began to move faster, a swirling, hypnotic motion that sent waves of pleasure through my body. It was as if she was weaving a web of ecstasy around us, each movement drawing us closer to a shared climax. The glowing edges of her bodysuit intensified, casting a warm, radiant light that enveloped us both.

"I reached up, my hands finding her waist, feeling the taut muscles beneath her soft skin. She responded with a soft moan, her body quivering with each touch. Her insides contracted and released around me, creating a sensation that was almost unbearable in its intensity. It was as if she was drawing the very essence of my being into her, merging our energies in a moment of transcendent pleasure.

"As we moved together, I felt a change within myself. It was subtle at first, a tingling sensation that started at the base of my spine and spread outward. Maria's eyes never left mine, and I could see she was aware of this transformation. She smiled, a knowing, almost predatory smile, and increased the pace of her movements.

"The sensations built to a crescendo, each thrust and grind pushing us closer to the edge. The light from her bodysuit now filled the entire carriage, creating a surreal, dreamlike atmosphere. I could feel my release approaching, a tidal wave of pleasure that threatened to overwhelm me.

"Just as I was about to climax, Maria leaned down and pressed her lips to mine. The kiss was electric, a jolt of energy that surged through my body and ignited every nerve. Our bodies tensed together, and in that instant, I felt something pass between us – a spark, a connection that was both physical and spiritual.

"I cried out, my release hitting me with the force of a storm. Maria's body shuddered atop mine, and I could feel her own climax, a powerful, pulsing wave that echoed through her entire being. For a moment, we were one, our bodies and souls intertwined in a perfect, blissful union.

"As the intensity subsided, Maria slowly lifted herself off me, her eyes still locked onto mine. She smiled, a soft, satisfied smile, and whispered, 'You are now a part of me, and I of you.' She then stood, her bodysuit returning to its original blue glow, and began to dress me with the same care and tenderness as before.

"When she was finished, she leaned down and kissed me once more – a gentle, lingering kiss that felt like a promise. 'Until we meet again,' she said, and with a final, enigmatic smile, she vanished, leaving me alone in the silent, frost-covered carriage, forever changed by our encounter."

Bonnie closed the book, a faint smile on her lips as she looked up at Tia. "It's an intense story," she said softly, "but it's the kind that stays with you, makes you think about the boundaries between reality and fantasy."

Tia nodded, her eyes shining with interest. "I can see why you like it. It's not just about the sex; it's about the connection, the transformation. It's... powerful."

Bonnie leaned back, sipping her coffee. "Exactly. It's those deep, transformative experiences that make the best stories. And maybe, just maybe, we find a bit of ourselves in them too." She nodded too, closing the book gently. "That's what draws me to it. The way it blends the supernatural with such raw, human experiences. It's almost... hypnotic."

Bonnie's phone buzzed as Jamie's name popped up. Tia put her hand on Bonnie's before she could answer. "Now, you better show him a good time, my sexy surf lady, just like your book, right?"

Bonnie laughed, a hint of mischief in her eyes. "You know I will." She picked up the phone, arranging a meet-up with Jamie before she headed to Wales, specifically Merthyr Tydfil in the Valleys, for a night in a cabin a few days before the Fan Dance event Jamie was doing. This would be a welcome break from her tour. They planned to spend some time visiting the Dan-yr-Ogof, the National Showcaves Centre for Wales, exploring the stunning underground scenery.

The days leading up to their rendezvous were a whirlwind for Bonnie. Things were going well, and she was about to make her way back up to the north-east coast.

Their night in the cabin was a serene escape. Nestled in the Welsh countryside, it offered a peaceful retreat away from the chaos of their busy lives. Jamie and Bonnie spent the evening enjoying each other's company, the warmth of the fireplace casting a soft glow over the room.

As they relaxed in the hot tub, their passion ignited and the night took on a steamy intensity. Just as they were lost in the moment, Bonnie's phone vibrated again. She groaned, ignoring it at first, but the persistent buzzing couldn't be ignored.

With a sigh, she reached for the phone, seeing Aurora's name on the screen. "It's Aurora," she said, rolling her eyes.

Jamie chuckled. "Answer it. Let's see what she wants this time."

Bonnie answered the call, trying to maintain her composure. "Aurora, this better be good."

Aurora's voice was bubbly and unapologetic. "Oh, Bonnie! Just wanted to let you know I've been having a blast here. The men in England are delightful! But enough about me, what are you two up to?"

Bonnie blushed, glancing at Jamie who was listening with a smirk. "We're just relaxing. Can this wait?"

Aurora's voice took on a teasing tone. "Relaxing, huh? Have you taken Jamie's cock deep into your mouth yet, letting him cum inside you?"

Bonnie's eyes widened in shock. "Aurora! That's a bit much, don't you think?"

Aurora laughed, not the least bit deterred. "Oh, come on. You know I'm just having fun. Anyway, I'm in the UK now. Maybe I should have told you sooner, but I promise not to get you into trouble."

Bonnie sighed, shaking her head. "Fine, just behave yourself, all right?"

Aurora's voice softened. "I will. Enjoy your night, lovebirds!"

Bonnie hung up, looking at Jamie with an exasperated smile. "She has the worst timing."

Pulling her close, Jamie chuckled. "Sounds like she's enjoying herself. But right now, I only care about us."

Bonnie smiled, kissing him deeply. "Me too."

The next morning, as they packed up to leave the cabin, they felt closer than ever. The night had been a perfect interlude, a reminder of the deep bond they shared. Bonnie was energised for her upcoming visit back in Bridlington, ready to uncover more of its hidden surfing heritage and continue her journey.

Jamie watched her with admiration as she talked about the historical surfing discovery, her passion and excitement evident. He knew that no matter where her travels took her, they would always find their way back to each other. And with the Fan Dance event looming, Jamie was eager to prove himself, knowing she would be there to support him every step of the way.

As they parted ways, Jamie whispered, "Be safe, and make the most of Bridlington. I can't wait to hear all about it."

Bonnie nodded, a determined glint in her eye. "I will. And you, focus on your event. I'll be cheering you on."

With a final kiss, they went their separate ways, both

filled with anticipation for what lay ahead.

Bonnie and Jamie parted with a lingering kiss and a promise to reunite soon. Bonnie set off for Bridlington once more, eager to explore the town's surfing heritage and a little more filming for her tour. As she drove, her thoughts were of the historical discovery and her recent escapades with Jamie and Aurora. The road ahead was a metaphor for her journey – filled with unexpected turns and new horizons.

Settling into her accommodation in Bridlington, Bonnie decided to unwind. Just as she was about to relax, her phone buzzed again. This time, it was a video call from Madge, Shannon, and Ronnie from the surf school in Australia. Bonnie smiled, swiping to answer the call.

The screen lit up with the faces of her three friends, all grinning widely. They were gathered in a cozy living room, each holding a waxing strip.

"Bonnie!" Madge exclaimed. "Look who's joining us for our little nose-waxing party!"

Bonnie laughed. "You three are crazy. Nose waxing, really?"

Shannon winked. "It's all in good fun. Keeps us young and smooth, right?"

Ronnie, always the practical one, chimed in. "Besides, it's a great bonding activity. And we get to catch up with you!"

Madge held up a waxing strip with a mischievous grin. "Ready, girls? On the count of three. One, two, three!"

The three women simultaneously pulled off their waxing strips, their faces contorting in humorous expressions of pain and relief. Bonnie burst into laughter, holding her stomach.

"You guys are nuts!" she managed between giggles.

Madge grinned, rubbing her nose. "Yeah, but you love us for it. How's Bridlington treating you?"

Bonnie nodded, her laughter subsiding. "It's fascinating. The historical discovery about the Hawaiian princes surfing here is incredible. I'm really looking forward to digging deeper into it."

Shannon's eyes sparkled with curiosity. "You always find the coolest places and stories. We miss you around here, though. The surf school isn't the same without you."

Ronnie nodded in agreement. "And the kids miss you too. Speaking of which, guess who else wants to say hi?"

Just then, little Henny's face popped onto the screen, his eyes wide with excitement. "Bonnie! Hi!"

Her heart melted at the sight of the enthusiastic youngster. "Henny! How are you, buddy?"

Henny grinned. "I'm good! I've been practising my surfing and wrote a story about you. When you come back, can you help me make it even better?"

Bonnie's eyes softened. "Of course, Henny. I'd love to read your story and help you with it. You're going to be an amazing writer."

Henny beamed. "Thanks, Bonnie! I can't wait to show you."

Madge, Shannon, and Ronnie shared a look of pride. "He's been working really hard," Madge said. "You've been such an inspiration to him."

Bonnie felt a warm glow inside. "That means the world to me. I can't wait to get back and see all of you."

The call continued with more laughter and updates, the bond between Bonnie and her friends unwavering despite the distance. As the conversation wound down, Madge gave a playful reminder. "Don't forget to show Jamie a good time."

Bonnie blushed, rolling her eyes. "You guys are incorrigible."

With promises to stay in touch, she ended the call and sat back, with a renewed sense of purpose and connection. The support from her friends and excitement from Henny gave her the strength to continue her journey with enthusiasm.

Bonnie spent the next few days in Bridlington and the surrounding area, exploring the rich history and surfing the surprisingly good waves. The story of the Hawaiian princes became a focal point of her visit again, adding depth to her experience.

As the date for Jamie's Fan Dance event approached, Bonnie's excitement and pride intensified. She knew he was prepared, and she couldn't wait to cheer him on. Their night in the Welsh cabin had strengthened their bond and Bonnie was eager to see what the future held for them.

Back in Bridlington, she took one last look at the ocean, grateful for the journey she was on. With a final deep breath, she packed up and set off to support Jamie.

Jamie had spent a few days in Wales, preparing for the gruelling event. It was one of the toughest challenges he had faced for a while, and he didn't really want to travel anywhere else. His training had been extremely intense and he knew it would be horrible if it was a hot day. He needed to stay focused. Unexpectedly, he received a call from one of his dad's old mates, Tony – affectionately known as Big Tony, though he stood only 5'5". Tony had been a significant figure in Jamie's life since he was a little boy, and he was always happy to catch up and train with him.

Tony, now 62, was a robust and energetic man. An electrician by trade who had also spent years running and lifting weights. He was a member of a local running club in York and had completed numerous ultramarathons. Jamie thought he'd even done one recently.

When Tony called, the conversation was typical of their friendly banter.

"Hay up, Jamie lad, it's Tony. Your sister tells me you're doing the Fan Dance. Well, you're in luck – I'm doing it too. Don't worry, I'll try not to beat you, unless I have to stop for a piss every mile. You know what I'm like."

Jamie laughed. "Tony, a simple 'how are you doing?' would have been fine. You could have come to the charity rugby game I'm heading to as well."

"I know, I know. I'm coming to that too. I'm not one to turn down a beer," Tony replied with a chuckle.

Later that day, Tony rolled up to Jamie's cabin in his camper van. They spent the evening reminiscing about old times and discussing their strategies for the Fan Dance. Tony's presence was comforting, a reminder of his dad and the supportive community he had grown up with.

*

The morning of the Fan Dance event was crisp and clear.

THE LAST SURF

Jamie's nerves and excitement mixed as he stood at the starting line with his 40-pound Bergen, which had just been weighed. The Fan Dance was a 24-kilometre route march in the Brecon Beacons, infamous within the ranks of all UK Special Forces. Jamie had been in the Paras, and he had done this before, but as a civilian now, it was different. He was going to test his strength of mind traversing Pen y Fan and the associated terrain before taking on the evil that is Jacob's Ladder on the return leg. With the Brecon Beacons towering above, Tony was there too, cracking jokes and lightening the mood.

"Ready to get your arse kicked by an old man?" Tony teased.

Jamie smirked. "Only if you can keep up, old-timer."

The DS gave a little speech, and they were off. The event began, and Jamie focused on the challenging terrain, each step bringing a new obstacle. The camaraderie among participants was palpable, everyone pushing each other to keep going. Tony was a constant presence, his years of experience evident in his steady pace. It was hot, and Jamie thought he needed to absolutely smash the first two miles to the top of the Fan. He figured he could do it in around 50 minutes and then just hang on to the end.

Two minutes from the red telephone box at the start line, Jamie was blowing out of his arse, with Tony just behind him. He didn't want to get ahead of himself and remembered the false summit was coming up. His legs were on fire and sweat was pouring. "Fuck me, why am I doing this? Better still, why do people pay for this shit?" Jamie said out loud. They were almost at Checkpoint 1 at the top of the Fan.

"Number?" a DS said to Jamie.

Jamie quickly replied, "Eight-nine," and headed down Jacob's Ladder. He had forgotten how steep this was but knew he had to make up time on the downhill before Windy Gap and the old Roman road. A fellow participant had fallen in front of him, blood coming from his bandaged hand. *Steady now, as the descent is so dangerous*, Jamie thought.

Checkpoint 2 at Windy Gap completed, and Jamie managed to jog all the way to the edge of the forest. It was a little further to the turnaround point, and Jamie thought, *I'm doing well here.*

As he pushed on, he heard Tony's steady footsteps behind him, a comforting reminder of their shared goal. Reaching the turnaround point, Jamie took a moment to catch his breath and rehydrate. Tony caught up and clapped him on the shoulder. "Not bad, lad. Keep this up, and you'll smash it."

Jamie grinned. "You too, Tony. Let's get this done."

The return leg was gruelling. Climbing back up Jacob's Ladder felt like endless torture, but Jamie kept his focus, one step at a time. The camaraderie among the participants was a vital boost, everyone encouraging each other to push through the pain.

Nearing the top again, Jamie's legs were screaming, but he pushed on, driven by sheer willpower. Tony was right there with him, matching his pace. They reached the summit, and Jamie felt a surge of triumph. Now, it was all about the descent to the finish line. This was possibly the hardest section, with both Jamie and Tony suffering cramps.

The final stretch was a blur of pain and determination.

Jamie's body was on autopilot, every muscle burning, but he kept going, Tony's presence a constant motivator. As they neared the finish line, the sight of cheering supporters gave him a final burst of energy.

Crossing the finish, Jamie felt a rush of relief and accomplishment. He turned to Tony, who was grinning from ear to ear. "We did it," Jamie panted, breathless but exhilarated.

"Damn right we did," Tony replied, pulling him into a bear hug.

Bonnie was there at the finish line with Tia, who had taken a break from the sponsorship tour. As a super-competitive person, Tia would have loved to participate in this event. She hadn't met Jamie before but was quick to give him some light-hearted abuse and gave Bonnie a knowing look.

"Well done, Jamie. How was it?" Bonnie asked with a touch of humour.

"Horrible, never doing it again," Jamie replied, still catching his breath.

Tony turned to Jamie. "I am. I want to get a better time. Four hours and eight minutes isn't bad, though, for an old man."

"I think I've lost a toenail," Jamie said, looking down at his feet.

At that moment, Jamie's phone started to ring. It was Paul calling all the way from Australia.

"Come on then, how was it?" Paul's voice crackled through the line.

"Brutal, mate. But we did it," Jamie said, grinning. "Wouldn't recommend it to anyone sane, though."

Paul laughed. "Sounds like you had a real adventure. Congrats, man." He paused for a moment, then added in his usual thoughtful manner. "Listen, Jamie, there's something I want you to remember. There are only two people you need to make happy in this world, and it's not your mum, your dad, or your wife. It's the eight-year-old you and the 80-year-old you. Think about it."

Jamie absorbed the words, feeling the weight of their meaning. "You're right, Paul. It's about living a life that both the child in you and the old man you'll become will be proud of."

"Exactly," Paul replied. "Keep that in mind, and you won't go wrong. Take care, mate."

As the call ended, Jamie had a renewed sense of clarity. He looked over at Bonnie, chatting animatedly with Tia. Their laughter and energy were infectious, and Jamie couldn't help but feel grateful for the people in his life who kept him grounded and inspired.

The next few days were filled with relaxation and exploration. Jamie and Bonnie took time to enjoy the serene beauty of the Welsh countryside again. The peaceful surroundings provided a welcome break from the intensity of the Fan Dance and the busy tour schedule.

On their first night in the cabin, as they relaxed in the hot tub Bonnie's phone buzzed with a call from Aurora. Once more, the timing couldn't have been worse, but Bonnie answered, laughing as she did.

"Aurora, you have the best timing once more," she said,

her voice dripping with sarcasm.

"What can I say? I have a gift," Aurora replied, clearly enjoying herself. "So, what are you two up to? Having fun, I hope?"

Bonnie rolled her eyes. "We were, until you called. What's up?"

Aurora didn't miss a beat. "Just wanted to know if you've taken Jamie's cock deep into your mouth and let him cum inside you yet? I know I asked before, but come on, have you?"

Bonnie sighed. "Aurora, seriously?"

"I'm just curious! You know how I am. Can I come and join you?" Aurora laughed.

Jamie chuckled, shaking his head. "Tell her she's always welcome, as long as she brings her own hot tub."

Bonnie laughed. "You heard him. Bring your own hot tub."

Aurora laughed again. "Deal. Enjoy your evening, you two. And Bonnie, don't forget to call me back with the juicy details!"

Bonnie ended the call, shaking her head with a smile. "She's something else."

Jamie wrapped his arms around her, pulling her close. "She certainly is. But right now, I'm more interested in us."

She leaned into him, the warmth of the hot tub and Jamie's embrace making her feel completely at ease. "Me too," she whispered, and they lost themselves in the moment, the world outside fading away.

CHAPTER 19

Home and Away

Since Bonnie left, Mick had been missing his daughter. He had even missed his surrogate daughter, Aurora. Although the conversation around the garage wasn't as smutty, and to be honest, the guys in the garage were happy with the welcome break from the endless talk about how good Aurora was on her motorbike. The endless sex talk and how she took it everywhere did get a little boring at times. Mick could retell the stories as if he were Aurora, as you had to hear daily about her masturbation. Self-pleasure was a special event for her; she had to pull out all the stops for it. Mick could hear her voice in his head and, more often than not, offloaded this to his wife, Joanna, who loved this as she had taken a few ideas for her books.

"Finishing work, I brush off the energy of the day dancing in the kitchen, blaring the dubstep version of 'Feeling Good', doing my S-Factor hip circles, pretending that it's the Divine Masculine Himself pouring me a glass of wine. I run a bath, use succulent oils and salts, have candles going, a waterproof vibrator, and bring the glass of wine." Aurora would still have the red Christmas icicle lights up because cellulite is undetectable in red light!

Mick chuckled as he recounted Aurora's vivid description. He could practically hear her voice as he mimicked her dramatic flair. Joanna listened intently, a twinkle in her eye as she took mental notes for her next book.

"Sometimes I read my Goal Achievement Script of my life a year from now, really feeling how gloriously delicious things are in my future. Sometimes I read sacred erotic material – love David Deida's *Blue Truth*. Sometimes I just sit in silence, visualising how my yet-to-meet lover will talk, touch, and be there for me."

Mick paused, shaking his head with a smile. "She's something else, that one." Joanna laughed, "I can see why you miss her. Her stories are... colourful."

"I get off imagining my lover is watching me rub glorious oil all over my body, honouring my skin, my hair, my curves. A piece of dark chocolate slowly savoured on the way to bed and perhaps one more slow, sensual dance by candlelight as I get into bed."

Joanna couldn't help but chuckle. "She really goes all out, doesn't she?"

Mick nodded. "Every detail. The guys at the garage can't handle it sometimes, but it's never dull when she's around."

Aurora would also candidly share with the guys:

"I'm definitely someone who really enjoys pornography.

I try to find a video that reminds me of my past boyfriends (ha-ha). Also, I love to masturbate and sext or sexy snap my boyfriends, too. I usually watch porn when I start – whatever seems most appealing from the front page of a site. I have a few toys that I use from time to time – generally just a vibrator. As a teenager, I'd do it daily, but now I do it two to three times a week. It's for a variety of reasons: when I can't sleep, when I'm stressed, or sometimes when I'm bored."

Joanna often found these stories both amusing and inspiring. As an author and therapist, she appreciated the colourful details and sometimes incorporated Aurora's creative descriptions into her own writing.

One evening, after recounting one of the latest escapades, Mick turned to Joanna and said, "You know, I miss their energy around here. It's quiet without them."

Joanna smiled, setting her book aside. "I know what you mean. But it's nice to have a bit of peace, too. And hey, it gives me plenty of material for my next book."

Mick chuckled. "You and your books. Just don't make me a character in one of those stories."

Joanna laughed. "Too late, dear. You're already in several."

As they sat together, the quiet of the evening was a stark contrast to the lively conversations they had grown used to. But they both knew it was only a matter of time before the house was once again filled with the spirited energy of Bonnie and Aurora.

That night, Mick didn't sleep well. He woke several times, short of breath and drenched in sweat. Joanna immediately thought it was his heart again; Mick had two stents fitted after an event some time ago following a run with Bonnie. His chest felt super tight, and he had an overwhelming sense of impending doom.

The next day, they phoned his doctor, fearing a heart attack. Both agreed they wouldn't tell Bonnie while she was on her tour as she would worry and want to come back from the UK. There was nothing she could do from so far away.

As Mick and Joanna sat in the doctor's office, the air was thick with anxiety. The doctor, a middle-aged man with a kind face, ran a series of tests. After what felt like an eternity, he returned with the results.

"Mick," the doctor began, "you did the right thing coming in. Your heart is under a lot of stress, and it appears there may be some complications with your stents. We need to admit you to the hospital for further observation and possibly more intervention."

Joanna's grip on Mick's hand tightened. "Will he be okay?" she asked, her voice trembling.

The doctor nodded reassuringly. "He's in good hands. We'll do everything we can."

Mick tried to put on a brave face, but the fear was evident in his eyes. "I guess I'm not as invincible as I thought," he joked weakly.

Joanna smiled though tears were brimming in her eyes. "You're strong, Mick. We'll get through this."

As Mick was wheeled away for further tests, Joanna sat in the waiting room, her mind racing. She thought about Bonnie and how much Mick meant to her.

Keeping this from her was the right decision, but it didn't make it any easier.

Hours passed before the doctor returned to update Joanna. "He's stable for now," he said. "We're going to keep him overnight for observation and run some additional tests in the morning. If all goes well, we can manage this with medication and lifestyle changes."

Joanna let out a sigh of relief. "Thank you, doctor."

The next few days were a blur of hospital visits and medical consultations. Mick was a trooper, cracking jokes with the nurses and reassuring Joanna that he was fine. But the seriousness of the situation was never far from their minds.

Back in the UK, Bonnie continued with her tour, blissfully unaware of the turmoil at home. She enjoyed the sights, met new people, and focused on her surfing discoveries. Mick and Joanna kept in touch through sporadic phone calls, careful to keep the conversations light and upbeat.

One evening, while sitting in the hospital room with Mick, Joanna received a video call from Bonnie. She quickly excused herself and stepped into the hallway to take the call.

"Hey, Mom!" Bonnie greeted cheerfully, her face glowing on the screen. "How's everything back home?"

Joanna forced a smile. "Everything's fine, sweetie. How about you? How's the tour going?"

Bonnie launched into an enthusiastic description of her latest adventures, and Joanna listened, her heart aching with the secret she was keeping.

THE LAST SURF

When the call ended, Joanna returned to Mick's bedside. He looked at her, understanding and gratitude in his eyes. "Thank you for not telling her," he said softly.

Joanna nodded, tears finally spilling over. "Just get better, Mick. That's all that matters."

As the days went by, Mick's condition slowly improved. The doctors were optimistic, and plans were made for his discharge. Mick promised to take it easy and follow all medical advice to the letter.

*

Fully recovered from the Fan Dance, Jamie turned his focus to the upcoming memorial game with his mates in Bridlington. Bonnie was scheduled to film a segment on the south side beach of Bridlington before moving on to Scarborough to join their surf community. Jamie was also aware that Marnie lived in the local area, and he wondered if he might have a chance encounter with her. Though he wasn't worried, he couldn't help but wonder if he would catch some feelings for her despite being with Bonnie. He had found her on Instagram and sent her a friendly, rugby-related message since he'd heard she was coaching for Bridlington.

The day of the memorial game arrived and Jamie felt a mix of excitement and nostalgia as he reunited with old friends. The camaraderie and shared memories of playing together brought a sense of joy and connection. The morning of the game, the lads decided, as they had been for a few beers, which quickly turned into a skinful, that they should all go for a sea swim. Jamie absolutely hated this; the North Sea was too cold but he did think it would wake him up. People loved this sort of thing.

"Jamie, get your stuff. It's not a far walk. Let's join the dry robe wanker for a sea swim."

*

Marnie stretched lazily, relishing the peace of the morning. With a contented sigh, she swung her legs out of bed and padded softly across the room to the window. Pulling back the curtains, she was greeted by a breathtaking view of the ocean, its azure waves dancing in the morning light.

As she made her way to the kitchen, the aroma of freshly brewed coffee enveloped her senses, promising warmth and comfort. With practised ease, she prepared a steaming cup, savouring the rich scent that filled the air.

Returning to her bedroom, she settled back against the pillows, cradling her coffee in her hands. Closing her eyes, she let herself drift, enjoying the precious moments of solitude before the day began in earnest. No ringing phones, no urgent emails – just the simple pleasure of being present in the moment.

Outside, the world stirred awake, sounds of life filtering through the open window. But in this cocoon of calm, Marnie allowed herself to linger a little longer, basking in the tranquillity of the morning.

She allowed herself this moment then took a deep breath. "Shit, was that Jamie who messaged me?" Marnie quickly remembered, after waking feeling very horny and adding to her highlight reel.

Marnie's mind raced as she recalled Jamie's message, her cheeks flushing with embarrassment at the realisation that her initial thoughts upon waking had strayed to something entirely different. She chuckled to herself, amused by the unexpected turn.

Quickly shaking off her momentary distraction, Marnie refocused her attention on the task at hand. With a deep breath, she pushed aside any lingering thoughts and focused on the present moment, determined to tackle the day ahead with renewed vigour and determination.

Her peaceful morning was abruptly interrupted by the incessant buzz of her phone, shattering the tranquillity she had been enjoying. With a sigh, she glanced at the screen, seeing a flurry of messages demanding her attention.

As she scrolled through the notifications, she noticed Jamie's message among the flood of texts. Despite her initial reluctance, curiosity gnawed at her, tempting her to open it. But before she could succumb to temptation, her attention was diverted by the rugby coaching group's messages.

Billy's voice boomed through the phone as he outlined plans for an impromptu training session on the beach. Marnie groaned inwardly, not quite ready to face the day's responsibilities. But duty called, and she knew she couldn't let the team down.

Resigned to the inevitable, she replied to Billy, acknowledging the change in plans. She quickly roused her son Adam from his slumber, urging him to get ready for practice.

"Mum, how long have we got? Charlotte is still in bed. Can I wake her to annoy her?"

"We have until 09:00, so about an hour. Leave your sister, I'll get her up and we can drop her off at Grandma's on the way."

Before Marnie could say another word, Adam had

pushed past his mum, gone straight into his sister's room and jumped on her, thinking he would annoy her. Little did he know, his sister was wide awake and expected nothing less from her brother. Like a lion, she pounced on him as he leapt onto her bed, putting him into a headlock and assuming side control. Adam should have known better, as Charlotte was a little judo expert. "You going to tap out, little brother, or do you need Mum to save you?"

Marnie chuckled as she watched the playful skirmish between her children unfold. She leaned against the doorway, arms crossed, enjoying the light-hearted banter that filled the room.

"All right, you two," she interjected with a grin, "let's save the wrestling matches for another time. Charlotte, get ready, we're heading to Grandma's soon."

Charlotte released her brother from her hold, a mischievous twinkle in her eye as she complied with her mother's instructions. Adam scrambled to his feet, rubbing his head where Charlotte's grip had been particularly firm.

"All right, all right," he conceded, flashing a sheepish grin at his sister. "But next time, you won't be so lucky!"

With laughter ringing in the air, Marnie ushered her children to get ready, grateful for these moments of playful chaos that brought warmth and joy to their home.

"No car today. Get your backpacks on – we're off on the scooters."

"Mum, are you for real? This is awesome!" Adam was loving this as he thought he could get his own back on his sister. She was crap at going fast on her scooter.

"If you get any ideas, Adam, boy, you're going to get it. I

will come down to the beach and beat you up in front of all the lads." Charlotte was trying her best to look menacing.

Marnie grabbed her dry robe and thought to herself, *How long will it be before someone shouts 'dry robe wanker' to her?*

She couldn't help but chuckle at Charlotte's playful threat, her daughter's feisty spirit adding to the excitement of their morning adventure. As she slipped into her dry robe, she couldn't shake the thought of the good-natured teasing she might encounter at the beach.

"All right, you two, let's not make any bets we can't keep," she said with a grin, trying to defuse the tension between her children. "We're here to have fun, remember?"

With their backpacks slung over their shoulders and the promise of an exhilarating scooter ride ahead, Marnie led the way out of the door, her children trailing behind with eager anticipation.

As they made their way to the beach a surge of excitement mingled with a hint of apprehension, but she pushed aside any lingering doubts, determined to embrace the spontaneity of the moment and create lasting memories with her family.

With the wind in their hair and the sun on their faces, Marnie and her children rode their scooters towards the beach, ready to seize the day and make the most of their time together. The lively banter and playful threats between Adam and Charlotte filled the air, adding to the excitement of the morning.

As they approached the beach, the sound of laughter and shouts grew louder. Marnie could see a group of men, some of whom she recognised as Jamie's old rugby friends, preparing for a sea swim. The sight brought a smile to her face, but her attention was quickly diverted as Adam, eager to get ahead, picked up speed on his scooter.

"Adam, slow down!" Marnie called out, but it was too late. In his enthusiasm, Adam swerved to avoid a bump, nearly colliding with Jamie and his rugby friends who were gathered at the edge of the beach.

"Watch out!" one of the lads shouted, as the group scattered to avoid the oncoming scooter.

Adam managed to regain control, but not before causing a small commotion. Charlotte, not far behind, tried to swerve to avoid the chaos but ended up losing her balance and veering towards the sand, narrowly avoiding Jamie.

"Hey, careful there!" Jamie called out, concerned yet amused.

Bringing up the rear, Marnie quickly assessed the situation and steered her scooter to a stop, laughing despite the near-accident. "Sorry about that! Overexcited kids," she said, trying to catch her breath.

One of Jamie's friends, still chuckling, shouted, "Watch out for the crazy lady with her kids on scooters!"

Jamie shook his head with a grin. "No harm done. Everyone all right?"

Adam, looking sheepish, nodded. "Yeah, I'm good. Sorry about that, guys."

Brushing sand off her knees, Charlotte added, "I'm fine too. Just a bit of a surprise, that's all."

Marnie looked at Jamie, "Oh, it's you!" and then his

friends, an apologetic smile on her face. "Sorry about the chaos. Guess we brought a bit more excitement than planned."

The rugby lads, already in high spirits, laughed it off. "No worries," one of them said. "We were just about to head into the water. You guys should join us!"

Marnie glanced at her kids, who looked eager despite the mishap. "Well, we did come prepared," she said, gesturing to her dry robe. "How's the water?"

"Freezing," Jamie said with a grin. "But it'll wake you up!"

With that, the group made their way to the water's edge. The North Sea was indeed cold, and Jamie shivered as he waded in, but he couldn't help but laugh as he watched his old friends and Marnie with her kids follow suit.

"Come on, it's not that bad once you're in!" one of Jamie's friends shouted, already chest-deep in the water.

Marnie hesitated for a moment, then took a deep breath and plunged in, the icy water sending a shock through her system. Adam and Charlotte followed, their initial gasps turning into laughter as they adjusted to the temperature.

"All right, dry robe wankers, let's see what you've got!" Jamie shouted, challenging his friends as they splashed around in the waves.

Despite the cold, the group enjoyed the camaraderie and fun of their impromptu sea swim. Now fully immersed in the moment, Marnie was grateful for the spontaneous adventure, the laughter of her children, and the chance encounter with Jamie and his friends.

As they eventually made their way back to shore,

dripping wet and exhilarated, Marnie looked at Jamie and smiled. "Thanks for letting us crash your swim."

He laughed, shaking water from his hair. "Any time. Just watch out for those scooters next time!"

The group gathered their things, the morning's excitement still buzzing in the air. With a renewed sense of energy and connection, they headed back towards the town ready to tackle the training session Marnie had planned for the kids.

As they were about to leave, Jamie walked over to her. "Hey, I thought I'd catch up with you. It's been a while since we met in London all that time ago. We should catch up properly at the memorial rugby game if you're going."

Marnie smiled warmly. "I'd like that. I'll be there."

Just then, two onlookers caught their attention as they prepared to enter the water. One was a short, older bloke with disproportionately large feet; he looked like a hobbit. The other was a tall blonde girl with a long bottom, resembling a character from Harry Potter. They seemed to be conversing in a different language, their accents thick and difficult to understand.

Jamie chuckled, remembering the local lingo of the north-east coast of England. "Looks like we've got some characters joining us."

The rugby lads watched the two newcomers with amusement as they entered the water. One of Jamie's friends, unable to resist, began doing a running commentary in a David-Attenborough-style voice. "And here we see the rare North Sea swimmers, braving the icy waters. Note the unique gait of the short one, reminiscent of a hobbit, and the elegant form of the blonde, gliding into the waves like a creature from the wizarding world."

The entire group burst into laughter, the playful commentary adding to the light-hearted atmosphere. The newcomers, oblivious to the humour, continued their swim, providing entertainment for everyone on the beach.

It was one of the funniest things anyone had seen in some time, the perfect ending to an unexpectedly delightful morning. Marnie and her kids headed back, grateful for these moments of spontaneous joy and connection, knowing that the day held even more promise with the upcoming memorial game.

*

As they warmed up on the field, the banter and laughter reminded Jamie of why he loved the game so much.

Meanwhile, Bonnie was busy with her filming segment on the beach. The scenic beauty of Bridlington provided the perfect backdrop for her project. She moved with ease, her natural charisma shining through as she interacted with the crew and the locals. Her passion for her work was evident.

During a break in the game, Jamie checked his phone and saw a response from Marnie. She had replied to his message, saying she would be at the game to support her team and would love to catch up afterward. She had enjoyed the sea swim and was looking forward to the antics after the game. Jamie felt a pang of anticipation but quickly reminded himself that he was with Bonnie and that his interest in Marnie was purely friendly.

The game was intense and competitive, but Jamie and his mates played with heart and determination. By the time the final whistle blew, they had secured a hard-fought victory. The celebration that followed was filled with high spirits and a sense of accomplishment.

After the game, Jamie spotted Marnie in the crowd. She waved and made her way over to him, a smile on her face. "Hey, Jamie! Great game out there."

Jamie returned her smile. "Thanks, Marnie. It's good to see you. How's coaching going?"

Marnie laughed. "It's going well. The kids are a handful, as you could see from this morning, but they're passionate about the game and that makes it all worth it."

The two chatted with ease and familiarity. It was clear their connection was rooted in a shared love of rugby. There was no lingering tension or unresolved feelings – just mutual respect and friendship.

Bonnie soon joined them, her filming for the day complete. Jamie introduced her to Marnie, and the three of them quickly fell into an easy conversation. Bonnie's warmth and openness made it clear she had nothing to worry about when it came to Jamie and Marnie.

The speeches after the game were definitely a little emotional, held in the spirit of remembering those who had recently passed and those lost over the years. The club captain's speech hit home for Jamie, reminding him of his own father's passing due to prostate cancer, and now a local star's death from MND. Diagnosed two years ago, the player had retired from his 17-year career with Bridlington.

"We will always remember those who have left us," the club captain began, his voice strong but filled with emotion. "They may not be here in body, but their spirit, their legacy, and the impact they had on this club and on our lives are still very much with us."

The crowd fell silent, each person reflecting on the memories of those they had lost. Jamie felt a lump in his throat as he thought of his father, a man who had been his hero both on and off the field.

"Today, we honour a local star who was more than just a player. He was a friend, a mentor, and an inspiration to all of us," the captain continued. "Diagnosed with MND two years ago, he showed incredible strength and courage. His 17-year career with Bridlington is a testament to his dedication and love for the game. We will always remember him."

Jamie glanced around at his teammates, many of whom had tears in their eyes. The shared grief and love for their fallen friend and teammate were palpable.

"We play this game today not just for ourselves, but for them," the captain said, his voice rising with passion. "For the ones who taught us what it means to be a team, to fight for each other, and to never give up. We carry their spirit with us every time we step onto this field."

As the captain finished his speech, the crowd erupted into applause, a heartfelt tribute to those they were honouring. Jamie felt a deep connection to his teammates and to the legacy of the club. The game they had just played was more than a match; it was a tribute to the memories and lives of those they had lost.

After the speeches, Jamie found himself surrounded by friends and fellow players, the atmosphere a mix of sombre reflection and celebratory camaraderie. He spotted Marnie nearby, speaking with some of the players and coaches, and made his way over to her with a small smile on his face. "Hey, Marnie. Thanks for coming today. It means a lot."

She returned his smile, her eyes warm and understanding. "Of course, Jamie. It was a beautiful game and a touching tribute. I'm glad I could be here."

They stood in comfortable silence for a moment, watching as the crowd began to disperse. Peace settled over him, knowing that he was surrounded by people who understood and shared his grief.

"How about that catch-up we talked about?" Jamie asked, breaking the silence. "Maybe over a drink?"

Marnie nodded, her smile widening. "I'd like that."

Aurora arrived in Bridlington with the characteristic roar of her motorbike, the sound echoing through the streets and announcing her presence long before she walked into the rugby club. Jamie and Bonnie spotted her immediately as she strode in, her leather jacket catching the light, and a confident grin on her face.

"Hey, you two!" she called out, weaving her way through the crowd to join Jamie and Bonnie. "Looks like I made it just in time for the fun."

The atmosphere at the rugby club was electric, the energy high after the emotional memorial game. The lads, buoyed by the camaraderie and a few too many pints, were in the midst of a rather rowdy celebration that included bar dives and impromptu performances.

Jamie had been a little apprehensive about how Aurora's presence might affect the night, but he needn't have worried. Her infectious energy and enthusiasm quickly endeared her to everyone. She joined right in, grabbing a drink and toasting with the lads, her laughter blending seamlessly into the already boisterous environment.

"There she is!" one of the rugby lads shouted, pointing at Aurora. "The legend herself!"

She raised her glass in acknowledgement, eyes gleaming with mischief. She leaned closer to Bonnie and Jamie, her gaze flickering to the rugby players who were now in various states of undress, their antics drawing cheers and laughter from the crowd.

"They play rugby, after all, so I'll have to give one of them some Hawk Tuah and Spit on That Thing," Aurora said with a wink, her voice filled with playful intent.

Bonnie laughed, shaking her head at her friend's audacity. Jamie just grinned, appreciative of the way Aurora could lighten the mood and bring carefree fun to any situation.

Her charm was undeniable and she soon found herself surrounded by admirers, all eager to share a drink or a dance. Shots were downed, toasts were made, and Aurora was in the thick of it all, her spirit lifting everyone around her.

As the night wore on, her antics became even more pronounced. She encouraged one of the lads to take her for a ride on the bar top, and the crowd roared in approval. Her uninhibited nature was magnetic, drawing everyone into her orbit.

By the end of the night, she was the life of the party and her infectious energy had made the evening unforgettable. One of the rugby lads, clearly taken with her, offered to take her home. Never one to turn down an adventure, Aurora accepted with a sly grin.

True to her word, she gave him a night to remember, complete with her signature Hawk Tuah. As the sun rose over Bridlington, she had left her mark, both at the rugby club and in the memories of everyone she'd met that night.

Jamie and Bonnie watched her go, shaking their heads in amusement.

"She's something else," Jamie said, his voice filled with admiration.

"She sure is," Bonnie agreed, her smile warm as she watched her friend disappear into the early morning light.

The night had been wild, filled with laughter and a sense of community, a fitting end to a day that had started with remembrance and ended with celebration.

CHAPTER 20

Tragedy

The morning after the rugby game and its subsequent craziness, Jamie and Bonnie decided to start their day with a refreshing sea dip. They headed down to the seafront, where they encountered a local character known as Sock Monkey Steph. Covered in tattoos, with a signature sock monkey inked on each arm, she was already in the water, having been there for 20 minutes.

Steph spotted Jamie and Bonnie as they entered. Recognising Bonnie from her surfing community days in Cornwall and as a top world-class athlete she followed on Instagram, Steph was thrilled and her excitement was palpable as she swam over to meet them. The tour's high publicity had given her hope that she might encounter Bonnie, and today was her lucky day.

After a lively chat in the water, they mentioned they

were planning to meet Aurora at a nearby coffee shop where they had encountered the lanky Scottish owner. He was singing to himself, punctuating his song with the occasional, "Fuck, fuck," as he organised the outside seating area.

"Want to join us for coffee?" Bonnie asked Steph.

"Absolutely!" she replied, her excitement not dimming. "I'd love to make you a sock monkey, Bonnie. It's kind of my thing. I have a store called Steph's Sock Monkey Store, and my monkeys are pretty popular around here."

The three of them made their way to the coffee shop. As they arrived, the Scottish owner was in the middle of a story, regaling anyone who would listen of how he once smuggled an ounce of cannabis from Cambodia to Thailand. "It wasn't even much, but it was something I had to do," he said, his accent thick and his expressions animated. "The plane flight was like, in slow motion the whole way. Needless to say, I'm still around to tell the story."

Inside, the two strangers who had garnered attention at the beach the previous day with their odd language and appearance, were also present. They were devouring a mountain of pancakes, conversing in a mumbling barrage that made little sense to anyone around them.

Jamie and Bonnie exchanged amused glances as they took in the scene. "This place is always this lively?" Jamie asked Steph.

Steph laughed. "Oh, you have no idea. This is pretty standard for here."

They found a table and settled in, ordering coffees and pastries. As expected, Aurora showed up looking a bit worse for wear, clearly hungover from the night before. She launched into a graphic recounting of her escapades with one of the rugby lads, leaving little to the imagination.

"So there I was," she began, "deep throating and gagging, taking it hard in my arse. You should have seen the look on his face!"

Used to the candidness, Bonnie rolled her eyes but smiled. "Honestly, one day, your stories will shock even you."

The Scottish owner came over, still muttering under his breath. "Coffee's ready. And if anyone wants to hear about the time I got lost in the Australian outback, I'm here all day." With a twinkle in his eye and a mischievous grin, he pulled up a chair and joined Bonnie, Jamie, and Steph at their table. "Ah, so you want to hear about my time in the outback, do you? Well, buckle up, because this one's a belter."

Bonnie and Jamie exchanged excited glances, eager to hear his tale.

"Right, it all started when I decided to take a wee holiday to Australia. I was young, wild, and full of the kind of confidence only a Scot with no knowledge of the outback could have. I decided to rent a camper van and drive across the country. How hard could it be, right?"

He paused for dramatic effect, and the girls leaned in closer.

"So, there I was, driving through the middle of nowhere, when my van decided it'd had enough and broke down. Not a soul in sight, just me and miles of red dirt. I thought, 'No worries, I'll just fix it.' But as it turns out, my mechanical skills were about as good as a kangaroo's knitting abilities. Absolutely hopeless."

Jamie snorted with laughter and Bonnie covered her mouth to stifle her giggles.

"Now, it was getting dark, and I figured I'd better find some shelter. I remembered reading something about digging a hole to stay warm, so that's what I did. But instead of staying put, I thought it would be a great idea to go looking for help. So, I started walking, leaving my perfectly good hole behind." The owner shook his head, as if still bewildered by his younger self's decisions. "As I was wandering, I came across this giant bird. Turns out, it was an emu. And let me tell you, those things are terrifying up close. It started chasing me and I ran like my life depended on it. Tripped over a rock and landed face-first in a prickly bush. By the time I got up, the emu was gone, but I was covered in scratches and my pride was in tatters."

Bonnie and Jamie were in stitches, barely able to contain their laughter.

"Then, just as I thought things couldn't get any worse, I stumbled upon a group of kangaroos. Now, I'd seen them on TV, hopping around all cute and whatnot. But these kangaroos were massive and looked like they were ready to box me. One of them, I swear, gave me a look that said, 'Go on, I dare you.' So, I did what any sensible person would do – I backed away slowly and tried to make myself look as non-threatening as possible."

He took a sip of his coffee, letting the suspense build.

"Finally, after hours of wandering, I saw headlights in the distance. A truck was coming my way. I flagged it down, and the driver, a burly Aussie with a thick accent, took one look at me and burst out laughing. 'Mate,' he said, 'you look like you've been through the wringer.' I nodded, too exhausted to argue. He gave me a lift back to civilization and even helped me fix my van the next day. Turns out, I had been just a few miles from a small town the whole time. So, there you have it, my ridiculous adventure in the Australian outback. Moral of the story? Never underestimate the outback, and always be prepared for a face-off with an emu."

Bonnie and Jamie had tears streaming down their faces. The Scottish owner grinned, clearly pleased with their reaction.

"Thanks for that," Bonnie managed to say between giggles. "That was just what we needed."

"Aye, anytime," he replied, standing up and giving them a mock salute. "Now, if you need any more coffee – or stories – you know where to find me."

The coffee shop was buzzing with a mix of locals and tourists, all adding to the eclectic atmosphere. Steph handed Bonnie a small, hand-sewn sock monkey, its bright colours and quirky design perfectly reflecting Steph's personality.

"Thank you, Steph," Bonnie said, touched by the gesture. "This is adorable."

"No problem at all," she replied with a grin. "Just a little something to remember Bridlington by."

As they sipped their coffees and listened to the various conversations swirling around them, Jamie, Bonnie, Aurora, and Steph enjoyed the vibrant, unpredictable charm of the seaside town.

Just across from the café stood a modern building that contrasted sharply with the old-style townhouses – a new leisure centre. Bonnie's ears perked up at the familiar sounds of a fitness instructor leading a class. "That's never Les Mills Body Pump, is it?" she said out loud, curiosity piqued. "Come on, let's go take a look."

Aurora groaned. "Really? We've come all this way, and you want to look at a fitness class? I remember the time you made me do a Pump class. The only good thing was the instructor's legs – it was horrible."

"Come on, you know how much I've always wanted to teach Body Combat and Body Pump," Bonnie replied, already heading across the road with Jamie following closely.

"Whatever, I'll catch up with you," Aurora said, rolling her eyes but smiling nonetheless.

For a small town, the leisure centre was impressive. The gym and café offered a panoramic view of the sea, highlighting why surfing was so popular in Bridlington. Surfing conditions were perfect, and the scenery was breathtaking. They could have been anywhere in the world.

Bonnie and Jamie entered the leisure centre, drawn by the energy of the ongoing class. Bonnie's face lit up as she watched the instructor lead the group through a series of moves, their synchronicity and enthusiasm palpable.

"Wow, this place is amazing," Jamie said, taking in the state-of-the-art facilities and the stunning view of the coastline. "I can see why you love this stuff."

Bonnie nodded, her eyes sparkling with excitement. "This is exactly what I dream of – combining fitness with this kind of environment. Imagine teaching a class with that view!"

Aurora caught up with them, a wry smile on her face. "Okay, okay, I admit it – this place is pretty cool. But I'm still not doing another Pump class, unless he takes it."

"Hard and fast, you know you like it. Don't you dare stop!" The male instructor was mid-squat, his voice booming with encouragement.

Aurora's eyes widened with admiration. "Yes, now that's what I like to see," she said, pressing up against the window of the class to get a better look. "Tight top on with legs on show. Look at his chest and arms – he can definitely throw me around."

Jamie chuckled and shook his head. "Aurora, you're incorrigible."

Bonnie laughed, pulling her away from the window. "Come on, let's not make a scene."

She reluctantly stepped back, her gaze still lingering on the instructor. "Fine, but only because I don't want to embarrass you guys."

As they made their way out of the leisure centre, Bonnie experienced a surge of excitement. This place, with its blend of fitness and stunning views, represented everything she loved. She glanced at Jamie who smiled back at her, sharing her enthusiasm.

"So, what's next?" Steph asked, her sock monkeys bobbing on her arms as she walked.

Bonnie grinned. "We need a better debrief with Aurora. Let's head to that café."

The group made their way back to the coffee shop, where the owner was now recounting another wild story. "So, there I was, in the middle of a Thai jungle, and all I had was a pack of smokes and a bottle of water..."

Jamie and Bonnie exchanged amused glances as they took their seats. The two strangers who had entered the water the day before were still there, conversing animatedly over a mountain of pancakes.

Aurora sat down, already starting to regale them with a wild story of her own. "You wouldn't believe the night I had. That rugby lad? Let's just say I gave him a night he won't forget."

Bonnie rolled her eyes, but couldn't stop herself from smiling. Aurora's energy was infectious, and despite her outrageous stories, she brought a unique spark to their group.

Bonnie's phone suddenly buzzed back to life, bombarded with messages. Her heart skipped a beat when she saw a series of missed calls from her agent. The urgency in the messages made her anxious. She dialled back immediately.

"Bonnie, you need to call your mum. It's urgent. It's about your dad."

Her heart stopped. She quickly dialled her mum's number, hands trembling.

Joanna's voice was shaky on the other end. "Bonnie, it's your dad. He's had a massive stroke. It's bad. You need to come home."

Bonnie felt a wave of nausea. She turned to Jamie, her face ashen. "I need to go home. My dad... he's had a stroke."

Overhearing the conversation, Aurora looked devastated. Without a word, she stormed out, emotions overwhelming her. She mounted her motorbike and roared off, leaving her friends behind in a cloud of dust.

Jamie embraced Bonnie tightly. "I'll stay here and handle things. You need to be with your family."

Bonnie nodded, tears streaming down her face. She reached out to her fellow athlete and friend, Tia, for support. 'I have to leave the tour. My dad... I need to be with him.'

'Go, Bonnie. We'll be thinking of you,' she replied.

The journey back to Australia was torturous. Bonnie endured the longest flight of her life, her thoughts consumed by fear and sadness. She managed a video call with her mum during a layover. Joanna's face was a mask of worry and exhaustion.

"He's in a really bad way, Bonnie. The doctors don't know how long he has."

When Bonnie finally arrived in Australia, she rushed to the hospital, only to find that it was too late. Her dad, Mick, passed away just days after her return. The grief was unbearable. Her friends from the surf school reached out, offering their condolences and support.

Back in the UK, Jamie felt helpless but knew Bonnie needed time with her family. He reached out to Aurora, worried about her sudden departure, but she was nowhere to be found.

The loss of her dad was a heavy blow for Bonnie. She found solace in the company of her mum and the close-knit surf community that had always been like a second family to her. The pain of her father's passing would take time to heal, but surrounded by love and support, Bonnie knew she would eventually find her way through the darkness.

The months following her father's passing were some of the darkest Bonnie had ever experienced. The grief was all-consuming, a heavy weight that followed her every step. For her mum, it was no different. The loss of her husband left a gaping hole in her life, one that no amount of comforting words or condolences could fill.

Bonnie and Joanna spent countless hours together, often in silence, just being there for each other. They took long walks on the beach, a place that had always brought them peace. The rhythmic crashing of the waves provided a soothing backdrop to their shared grief. They reminisced about Mick, sharing stories and memories that made them laugh and cry in equal measure.

Despite the supportive environment, Bonnie's dyslexia began to resurface with a vengeance. The stress and emotional turmoil exacerbated her condition, making it harder for her to focus and process information. Reading, something she had come to enjoy in recent years, became a struggle again. She felt overwhelmed, her mind fogged by the dual burdens of grief and dyslexia.

It was during one of these difficult days that little Henry, Ronnie's son, came to visit. His innocent joy and boundless energy were a welcome distraction. Henry adored Bonnie, and his presence brought a flicker of light into her dark days.

One afternoon, Henry brought over a box of his favourite Lego bricks. "Bonnie, can we build something together?" he asked, his eyes shining with excitement.

Bonnie smiled, grateful for the diversion. "Of course, Henry. What should we build?"

Henry thought for a moment, then declared, "Let's build a castle with a dragon!"

They spent hours on the floor, surrounded by colourful pieces. Henry's imagination was infectious and Bonnie found herself getting lost in the creative process. They built an elaborate castle, complete with turrets and a fierce dragon. Henry made up stories about brave knights and magical adventures, his voice animated and full of wonder.

These building sessions became a regular part of Bonnie's routine. They gave her something to look forward to, a way to escape the weight of her grief and the frustrations of her dyslexia. Henry's enthusiasm was contagious, and his love for storytelling reignited Bonnie's own passion for creating narratives.

In the evenings, Bonnie and Henry would sit together with a stack of picture books. Reading aloud to him became a source of comfort and joy. They made up their own stories, with Henry providing the ideas and Bonnie bringing them to life. The process was therapeutic, allowing her to reconnect with her love for storytelling and to feel a sense of accomplishment despite her struggles.

Joanna watched these interactions with a mix of relief and gratitude. She saw the light returning to Bonnie's eyes, the way Henry's presence helped her daughter cope with the pain. Joanna herself found solace in her own way, returning to her hobby of gardening. She spent hours tending to her flowers, finding peace in the simple, nurturing act of caring for something beautiful.

Bonnie and Joanna leaned on each other, their bond growing stronger through their shared sorrow. They talked about Mick often, keeping his memory alive through stories and laughter. They allowed themselves to grieve but also sought out moments of joy and connection.

One evening, as they sat on the porch watching the sunset, Joanna turned to Bonnie and said, "Your dad would be so proud of you, Bonnie. You're stronger than you realise."

Bonnie felt a lump in her throat. "I miss him so much, Mum."

"I know, sweetheart," Joanna replied, her voice gentle. "But he's still with us, in our hearts and in everything we do. And we have each other. We'll get through this together."

Bonnie nodded, feeling a sense of hope for the first time in a long while. She looked at Henry, playing contentedly with his Lego bricks, and felt a surge of gratitude. The road ahead would still be challenging, but with her mum and Henry by her side, she knew she would find the strength to keep moving forward.

The grief would never fully disappear, but with time it became more bearable. Bonnie and Joanna learned to carry the memory of Mick with them, allowing it to enrich their lives rather than weigh them down. They found joy in the little things, the everyday moments that reminded them of the love and happiness Mick had brought into their lives.

Through the darkness, they discovered a new kind of light – a light born from love, resilience, and the unbreakable bond of family.

While they found solace in each other and in little Henry, Aurora took a different path. The loss of Mick, her surrogate dad, hit her harder than she let on. To the outside world she was the same vibrant, carefree Aurora, but inside, she was a storm of unresolved emotions and pain.

After Bonnie left for Australia, Aurora stayed in the UK. She filled her days with a relentless schedule of drinking, partying, and riding her motorbike at reckless speeds. The adrenaline and alcohol were temporary escapes from the gnawing grief she refused to confront.

Her nights became increasingly wild and dangerous. She frequented bars and clubs, often ending up in trouble. Her charming demeanour and good looks masked the turmoil she was feeling, but those closest to her could see the cracks starting to show.

One particularly reckless night, Aurora found herself in a high-speed chase with the police. She had been drinking heavily and decided to take her motorbike for a spin, pushing it to its limits. The thrill of the speed was a momentary distraction from her pain, but it nearly cost her everything.

The chase was chaotic, with Aurora weaving through traffic and narrowly avoiding crashes. Her heart pounded with a mix of fear and exhilaration. Eventually, she lost control and skidded off the road, coming to a halt just inches away from a steep drop. The police caught up with her and she was arrested, her night ending in a cold, sobering cell.

The incident was a wake-up call, but not the kind that led to immediate change. Aurora returned to Australia but was a shadow of her former self. She avoided reconnecting with Bonnie and the surf community, isolating herself instead. The familiar surroundings only served to remind her of Mick and the loss she couldn't face.

She continued to drink heavily, numbing the pain that refused to go away. She rode her motorbike aimlessly, the roar of the engine drowning out her thoughts.

She felt adrift, untethered from the people and activities that once brought her joy.

Despite her self-destructive behaviour, Aurora managed to avoid any further legal trouble. She was careful not to push too far, always pulling back just before things got too dangerous. But the emotional toll was evident. She was a shell of the vibrant woman she once was, her spark dimmed by the weight of her grief.

One evening, after another aimless ride, Aurora found herself at the edge of a cliff overlooking the ocean. The sun was setting, casting a golden glow over the water. She sat down, staring out at the horizon, and finally allowed herself to cry. The tears came in a torrent, years of pain and loss pouring out.

In that moment of vulnerability, Aurora realised she couldn't keep running from her emotions. She needed to confront her grief, to allow herself to feel the pain she had been avoiding for so long. It was the first step towards healing, a small but significant shift in her journey.

She didn't have all the answers, but knew she couldn't continue down this path. She needed to reconnect with the people she loved and rediscover the parts of herself she had lost. It wouldn't be easy, but for the first time in a long while, there was a glimmer of hope.

She stood up, the cool breeze brushing against her tear-streaked face, and took a deep breath. The road ahead was uncertain, but Aurora was ready to face it, one step at a time.

CHAPTER 21

One Year Later

A year had passed, and life had continued to weave its unpredictable path. Aurora had drifted away, her presence marked only by occasional, brief messages. Her absence was felt keenly by those she had left behind, but everyone respected her need for space.

Jamie had been supporting his sister through difficult times. Her husband had fallen seriously ill, and Jamie's role as the supportive brother was more crucial than ever. He had been a pillar of strength for her, juggling his responsibilities and personal life with grace. Bonnie and her mum, Joanna, were still navigating the choppy waters of grief. They found solace in their own ways – Bonnie by diving into fitness, and Joanna by spending time with her friends, particularly little Henry, Ronnie's son.

Bonnie had found a new passion that helped her cope with her father's loss. She became a certified Body Combat and Body Pump instructor, pouring her energy into something that challenged her both physically and mentally. This new focus had been a lifeline, helping her navigate the dark days and giving her a renewed sense of purpose. Her mother had found comfort in helping their neighbour's daughter Daniella with her energetic grandchildren, keeping busy and finding joy in the chaos they brought.

Bonnie also spent countless hours with Henry. Together, they built elaborate Lego structures and spun fantastic stories. Henry's vivid imagination and endless curiosity provided Bonnie with a much-needed distraction and a connection to simpler, happier times.

Surfing, once Bonnie's greatest love, had taken a backseat. The ocean's call was still strong, but her grief and new commitments had kept her away. However, her sponsors were beginning to pressure her to return to competition, threatening to pull their support if she didn't compete again soon. She knew she needed to get back on the board, but the thought of it was daunting.

The distance between Bonnie and Jamie had grown. Despite their efforts to stay connected, the physical miles and emotional burdens had taken a toll. They both felt like they had found the right person but at the wrong time. It was one of the hardest feelings to navigate – loving someone deeply but knowing that circumstances made a relationship impossible. They rarely spoke about it, clinging to a thread of hope that someday, things might change.

Jamie found himself lying awake at night, his thoughts consumed by Bonnie. He trusted in the universe, hoping that one day, fate would bring them back together. But for now, he focused on being there for his sister and her family, finding fulfilment in supporting them.

One crisp autumn afternoon, Bonnie stood at the edge of the beach, her surfboard in hand. The waves crashed rhythmically against the shore, a soothing yet powerful reminder of the life she once knew. She closed her eyes, took a deep breath, and let the salty air fill her lungs.

"Bonnie?" A familiar voice broke through her thoughts.

She turned to see Jamie walking towards her, his expression a mix of surprise and relief. They hadn't planned to meet, but somehow, the universe had brought them together at that moment.

"Jamie," she said, her voice tinged with emotion. "I didn't expect to see you here."

"I needed to clear my head," he admitted, running a hand through his hair. "It's been a tough year."

Bonnie nodded, understanding. "For me, too."

They stood in silence for a moment, the weight of their unspoken feelings hanging in the air.

"I've missed you," Jamie finally said, his voice barely above a whisper.

"I've missed you too," she replied, tears welling up in her eyes.

He took a step closer, his gaze locking onto hers. "Do you think... Do you think we could ever find a way to make this work?"

Bonnie sighed, her heart aching with the same question. "I don't know, Jamie. But I hope so. I really do."

Jamie reached out, taking her hand in his. "Then let's

not give up. Let's keep trusting that the universe will bring us back together when the time is right."

Bonnie squeezed his hand, a small smile forming on her lips. "Okay. Let's do that."

She opened her eyes, watching the waves roll in. The familiar rhythm of the ocean brought a sense of peace she hadn't felt in a long time. She didn't have all the answers, but for now, she had hope – and sometimes, that was enough.

Even Addison and Byron, now engaged, had tried to encourage Bonnie to get back into competition. Addison's explicit sex stories still made Bonnie roll her eyes, but they also made her laugh, a reminder of simpler times. Madge, as ever, was a pillar of support for all. She even invited Bonnie and Joanna to her home for nose-waxing sessions from time to time, and, if all else failed, she made cheesecake for everyone.

Little Henry was having his regular surf lessons with Bonnie. As he paddled beside her, he looked up with his wide, innocent eyes. "Aunt Bonnie, you're great. If you compete one last time, I promise to write a story about you one day."

Bonnie smiled, touched by his earnestness. "You will?"

He nodded vigorously. "Yes! You'll be the hero."

That look – Henry's sincere, hopeful gaze – was the push she needed. She had to do it.

*

The day of the big surf competition arrived. Bonnie was back, ready to face the waves with the spirit of her father guiding her. The event was broadcast live around the world, and she could feel the energy of the global audience rooting for her. She was alive once more, her father's love and memory a driving force within her.

Jamie had made his way from the UK, spurred on by his friend Paul's encouragement. He knew he had to support Bonnie, even though she didn't know he would be there. As he stood among the crowd, he felt a rush of pride and anticipation.

Everyone was watching her:

Her mum, Joanna, tears of pride in her eyes.

Her friends Shannon and Sally, cheering loudly.

Old Madge, who had even brought one of her famous cheesecakes to share with the other spectators.

Ronnie with her son, little Henry, who waved excitedly from the shoreline.

Byron and Addison, engaged and more in love than ever, their support unwavering.

Daniella and her three feral children, a lively bunch that added to the energy of the crowd.

Aurora, finally arriving on her motorbike, her own adventure to be continued after supporting Bonnie. Having returned to Australia, she was determined to reconnect with her roots and find herself again. She took up competitive motorbike racing, channelling her energy into something constructive. Her natural talent and newfound focus quickly propelled her to the top, earning her accolades and respect. But despite her success, she still felt something was missing.

Hearing about Bonnie's return to the surf competition

reignited something in Aurora. She felt the pull of her old life, the community she had drifted away from. Arriving just in time for Bonnie's big day, she felt a sense of belonging she hadn't experienced in a long time. She knew she was ready to support her friend and find closure for herself.

As Bonnie paddled out, the familiar feeling of the board beneath her feet, the salty spray of the sea, and the roar of the crowd filled her with determination. She glanced back at the shore and saw all the familiar faces. Her heart swelled with emotion, and she knew this was her moment and maybe her last surf.

The waves were perfect, each one an opportunity. Bonnie felt the rush of adrenaline as she rode the first wave, carving through the water with skill and grace. The crowd erupted in cheers, the sound echoing over the beach.

Her focus was unbreakable. She rode wave after wave, each one better than the last. The judges took notice, her performance impeccable. As her final wave approached, she could see her dad among the crowd. She hesitated, then went for it. Everything was in slow motion; it didn't feel right, but there was a sense of fulfilment and joy she hadn't felt in a long time.

Back on the shore, Jamie pushed through the crowd, his heart pounding. He had to see her, had to tell her how proud he was.

It felt like something pushed Bonnie from her board. That was it – she was under the water. The crowd was silent, and the millions around the world watching gasped.

As Bonnie emerged the crowd surrounded her, cheering and clapping. Jamie reached her, and their eyes met. No words were needed; the connection was palpable. He wrapped his arms around her, and she hugged him back tightly, both of them overwhelmed with emotion.

"You did it," Jamie whispered.

Bonnie nodded, tears in her eyes. "We did it."

As the sun set over the ocean, Bonnie looked around at her family and friends, feeling their love and support. It had been a long, hard journey, but she had made it through. With the spirit of her father guiding her, she knew she could face anything.

Standing nearby with her motorbike, Aurora caught Bonnie's eye and gave her a thumbs-up. "Your adventure isn't over yet. There's more to come."

Bonnie smiled, feeling the truth of those words. The future was still unwritten, but with the people she loved by her side, she was ready for whatever came next.

Aurora revved her bike's engine, feeling the familiar thrill of the road ahead. She had come full circle, from running away from her emotions to confronting them head-on. Now, she was ready to embrace the future, whatever it held. With a final wave to her friends, she rode off into the sunset, the open road a symbol of the endless possibilities before her.

Henry, sitting watching from a distance, thought to himself, *This would make a great story one day.* He took some photos, pulled out his pen and paper, and started to write.

The words began with:

The Last Surf

CHAPTER 22

Over the Hills and Far Away

Henry stood by his father's bed; Dave had only been in the care home for three days. His condition had worsened over the last six months after moving into a bungalow, and Ronnie couldn't look after him anymore. Dave had been battling prostate cancer for five years, and though the treatment had extended his life, it had not been a cure. If not for that treatment, he would have passed away within six months of his diagnosis. Henry felt gratitude for the five years they had gained, years in which Dave had been able to be part of his grandchildren's lives, even if only for a short time. Sasha and Andrew, aged four and two, adored their grandad, and their innocence and joy had been a light in his darkest times.

The doctor had just left, saying Dave had only 24 to 42 hours left. Henry didn't want his dad to go. Two days earlier, he had told Henry that this moment would come.

Despite his frustrations with his dad, Henry still needed his advice. Now, he lay asleep, his breathing laboured and his body dehydrated.

Henry spoke to his father, hoping he could hear his words. "I hope you are proud of the man and father I have become. Who would have thought that the boy with the 'broken brain' due to dyslexia would make something of himself? I still struggle to read or write coherently, and the ridicule from others was tough. But you always believed in me. You pushed me to do my best and showed me that my worth wasn't determined by my challenges."

As Henry spoke, he gazed at his father's peaceful face, trying to convey the depth of his emotions. The room was silent, except for the occasional distant murmur from the care home.

He continued, "Sasha and Andrew love you so much, Dad. They won't fully understand why you have to go, but I'll make sure they remember you and the joy you brought into their lives. You were the best grandad they could ever have."

Henry's voice wavered with a mix of sadness and gratitude. He remembered the times his father had spent with Sasha and Andrew – laughter echoing through the house, playful moments in the garden, and the simple joy of being together. The innocence of childhood had brightened even the darkest days of Dave's battle with prostate cancer.

With a heavy heart, Henry acknowledged, "I don't know how I'm going to navigate life without you, Dad. Your advice, even when it drove me crazy, your obsession with the weather and how you would have been a geography teacher in a different life. I'll miss hearing your stories, your laughter, and even your occasional grumpiness. But I'll carry your lessons with me, and I promise to keep making you proud."

As the room remained still, Henry sat by his father's bedside, playing his favourite song, 'Over the Hills and Far Away' performed by John Tams, with its haunting beauty, followed by the uplifting anthem 'World in Union' performed by Katherine Jenkins. A bittersweet atmosphere, capturing the essence of both loss and enduring love. In these final moments, he cherished their shared history, the love that had woven their lives together, and the undeniable impact Dave had on shaping the man Henry had become. The impending loss was heartbreaking, but the legacy of a father's love and guidance would endure.

Henry's voice, though filled with sorrow, resonated with a deep sense of love and gratitude. As he continued to talk to his father, he found solace in expressing his feelings, sharing memories, and acknowledging the profound impact Dave had on his life.

With a gentle smile, Henry whispered, "Dad, I've been thinking about the book I told you I wanted to write. The one that captures the essence of our journey, the highs and lows, the laughter and tears. I've found the perfect title – 'Over the Hills and Far Away'. Or should it be 'The Last Surf', which I came up with years ago? It reflects our adventures with friends and family, especially Bonnie and Jamie, the distances we've travelled together, and the love that spans beyond any physical boundaries."

The room seemed to hold its breath as Henry continued, "It's a tribute to you, Dad. A way to immortalise the beautiful story of navigating through life, overcoming challenges, and embracing the joyous moments. It's a story of love that extends beyond the hills and far away, a love that will continue to resonate in the hearts of those who read it."

As Henry concluded his words, he pressed play on more of his father's favourite songs, letting the familiar melodies fill the room.

In those final moments, Henry sat by his father's side, holding his hand, sharing the music that had been a part of their journey. The room was filled with the shared history, the laughter, and the unspoken bond that transcended the limitations of mortality.

A tribute to anyone who has ever lost someone, a wise dad once said, "Sometimes we lack the bravery because we fear the end. Someday we will see the victory we need. We rush to grow up, long to be children again, lose our health to make money then lose our money to restore our health. Thinking anxiously about the future, we forget the present. As such, we live in neither the present nor the future; we live as if we are never going to die and die as though we never lived."

As the songs played on and the final chapter of Dave's life unfolded, Henry found comfort in knowing that their story would live on in the pages of *The Last Surf*. It was a tribute to a father who had shaped his life, a legacy of love that would continue to echo through the hills and far away.

*

Henry met his wife and two kids at the local food festival. His mum Ronnie walked towards them, and he thought as he looked onwards, this was everything he ever wanted, right in front of him.

Suddenly, his friend Tom came from nowhere with his three little girls. "Mate, my best mate. How are you?" He was stuffing his face with a burger, food all around his mouth.

"I'm good, Tom. I was just thinking about what's next for me."

"Mate, you are a world-famous writer, and your last sci-fi book has been turned into that TV show," Tom said, wiping his mouth. A few onlookers, recognising Henry, now came over for autographs.

With open arms, Tom exclaimed, "This is the life we chose. Who would have thought the boy who could barely read or write would become as famous as you have, for the thing he couldn't do?"

Henry smiled and replied, "Tom, it's these words that have helped me all these years: Some people are just born to fight. It's not that they are born brave or born strong. It's just that the universe has decided they will have grit and fire and steel in their blood. You will be tested, but that cosmic metal of yours will keep you strong. You will face trial after trial, be broken and damaged in countless ways, but you were born to fight. Maybe you will not have chosen this life, maybe you will love to lay down your arms, but you were born to fight. That's what you will know, that's what you will do best."

ABOUT THE AUTHOR

From a young age, I was enchanted by stories. My name is Robert Waller, and today, as a fitness manager, I channel my passion for storytelling into helping others achieve their health and wellness goals. My journey is a tapestry of challenges and triumphs, each thread shaping who I am.

Raised by school teachers who cherished education, I grew up immersed in narratives that sparked my imagination and nurtured my love for storytelling. However, despite this early love, I faced significant hurdles with reading and writing. At 19, I was diagnosed with dyslexia, an explanation that shed light on my academic struggles but also introduced new challenges. Throughout these difficulties, I found solace and confidence in sports, especially rugby – a passion inherited from my father, a dedicated player himself. Rugby not only helped me manage my frustrations but also instilled a profound sense of teamwork and belonging.

This affinity for physical activity steered me towards a career in fitness. Starting as a fitness professional, I rose to become a manager, specialising along the way in cardiac and cancer rehabilitation and earning credentials as a mental health specialist. These qualifications have enabled me to support individuals with specific health challenges, deepening my commitment to making a meaningful difference.

For over 17 years, I've led diverse group fitness classes – from aqua fit and chair aerobics to Body Combat and Body Pump – cherishing every moment spent guiding others toward their fitness milestones. The fulfilment derived from helping improve others' well-being is truly immeasurable.

My experiences with dyslexia, my love for rugby, and my career in fitness all fuel my enduring desire to positively impact lives. Whether through targeted rehabilitation or dynamic group classes, my aim is to leave a lasting, positive mark on everyone I encounter.

Printed in Great Britain
by Amazon